The Case of the Sleeping Beauty

(A challenge for Commissario Beppe Stancato)

Richard Walmsley

Other novels by the same author in
the "Puglia" series
Dancing to the Pizzica *(2012)*
The Demise of Judge Grassi *(2013)*
Leonardo's Trouble with Molecules *(2014)*

"Long Shorts"
A collection of unusual and humorous short stories *(Updated 2015)*

Novels in the Commissario Beppe Stancato series

The Case of the Sleeping Beauty *(2015)*
A Close Encounter with Mushrooms *(2016)*
The Vanishing Physicist *(2017)*
Death Is Buried *(2020)*
The Vendetta Tree *(2022)*

Puglia with the Gloves Off – Book One – Salento
(A travelogue – 2020)

The Curse of Collemaga *(A novel – 2019)*

Also available in Italian translation:
Nella morsa della Pizzica – Dancing to the Pizzica
La metamorfosi del giudice Grassi – The Demise of Judge Grassi

Cover design by Esther Kezia Harding
esther@kezcreative.com

Published by nonno-riccardo publications
Email: author@richardwalmsley.com
Web: www.richardwalmsley.com

Copyright: Richard Walmsley 2015

All rights reserved

This book is copyright. Subject to statutory exception and to provisions of relevant collective licensing agreements, no part of this publication may be reproduced, stored in a retrieval system, or transmitted in any form or by any means, without the prior consent of the author.

In this work of fiction, the characters, places and events are either the product of the author's imagination or they are used entirely fictitiously. The moral rights of the author have been asserted. Any resemblance to actual persons, living or dead, is purely coincidental.

Author's Preface

Welcome to my fourth novel. For a change, the story is set in Abruzzo instead of Puglia. Abruzzo is just over half way down the Italian Peninsula on the Adriatic side, facing Croatia across the waters. Abruzzo's capital city is called L'Aquila – perched high up in the Apennine Mountain range. Its name means "The Eagle". The story is set in 2009 at the time of the catastrophic earthquake which struck L'Aquila at 3 o'clock one morning in April, claiming the lives of 309 people.

The main protagonist is a chief inspector named Beppe Stancato, who has been transferred from his native Calabria to escape from his local mafia.

The events surrounding the disappearance of a twenty-two-year-old girl – nicknamed The Sleeping Beauty by the team of police officers – test Commissario Stancato's investigative and leadership skills to the full.

Although essentially a novel of suspense and intrigue, the story is full of humour and local colour – not least in praise of Abruzzo's scenery, food and wine.

I would like to thank my friend Beppe Tristano – who corresponds exactly to my image of the main protagonist in the story – for allowing me to purloin aspects of his appearance and character. My thanks also go to Rina Culora, Karina Graham and Rod Davies – a musician from the famous musical group, The Quarrymen. They all made encouraging noises as they read the draft version of the novel – whilst pointing out inconsistencies and slips of the 'pen' along the way.

The Prologue should be read first since it forms an integral part of the plot – and sets the scene for the whole story.

I have included a glossary of Italian words used in the story – also included in the Kindle version. This section, at the end of the book, also includes notes on cultural references.

Prologue

I'm telling you now, they'll be baying for our blood over the next few weeks - you mark my words.

I think you have become obsessed, amico mio! There is no earthly reason why anyone should blame us for the earthquake – tragic though it was. It was just an act of God, as the insurance companies like to say. We knew that a seismic event might occur, but it is, as you are well aware, almost impossible to predict the exact moment when...

But we *did* suspect that it would be imminent. We just opted not to spread panic, if you care to recall the meeting which we held just days before it happened. All the signs of an impending disaster were there.

You must not allow your natural feelings of anguish and guilt to cloud your judgement, Romano. Keep calm, my friend. And above all, do not fall for the facile mistake of talking to the press – as if you were going to tell a priest in the confessional - just to make you feel better. We must stick together and remain detached from that tragic event. It took us all by surprise.

But that is so far from the truth...

Your reaction is beginning to alarm me. I implore you not to anticipate the worst-case scenario before it happens. If the occasion arises, I shall be able to handle everything. Stop worrying, Romano. We have science and cold logic on our side. We cannot possibly be blamed for the magnitude of that disaster.

And apart from all that, they are now saying that the mafia has managed to infiltrate the rebuilding programme – despite all the precautions. The media will be busy looking for a scapegoat as usual. That may well turn out to be *us*...

Basta, Romano! Go and have a glass of your favourite red wine and set your fears aside. You will achieve nothing by becoming paranoid about our role in this tragic event...

And then there's the matter of your precious niece, who seems to be a singularly well-informed young lady...

Enough, Romano! That is not a subject to be discussed over the phone. I bid you a final 'goodnight'.

(Telephone conversation, May 2009)

1: *A seismic event*

"Where were *you* when the earthquake[1] struck?" was the predictable question on the lips of the shocked and shaken – all too literally in many cases – population of Abruzzo after that fateful night. Most people had been in bed asleep, since the quake had occurred at round about three o'clock on the morning of April 6th 2009 high up in the Apennine mountain range in Abruzzo's capital city of L'Aquila. The city sits just to the south of that region of the Apennines known as the Gran Sasso d'Italia. After the event, it was claimed that this solid wall of rock might have cushioned those townships on the north-eastern side of the mountain range from the worst effects of the violent tremors. But it could not save the 309 inhabitants of L'Aquila who lost their lives on that horrendous night of fear and terror. The shock waves were felt as far away as Rome and many of L'Aquila's neighbouring villages suffered severe damage too.

Beppe Stancato would never forget that night. Barely a month had elapsed since he had arrived in Abruzzo from his native Calabria in order to take up his post as *sostituto commissario*[2] of police in the town of Pescara. *He* could honestly reply that he had not been in bed at the time of the earthquake.

"I was on my boat floating around in the harbour gazing up at the stars," he told anyone who ventured to ask where he was. His answer usually managed to side-track those who had posed the question from going into the gruelling details of this devastating natural disaster.

---

[1] The earthquake which struck the capital city of L'Aquila in 2009 is a real event.
[2] One grade beneath a fully-fledged Commissario

Allowing people to pursue such a line of conversation usually led to unanswerable philosophical conjectures being raised as to why God had allowed the earthquake to happen at all, especially at such a dangerous time of night when escape from the violent tremors was rendered so much more problematic. Beppe had to admit that this aspect of the tragedy threw some doubt on the notion that God is merciful - one of the most tragic aspects of that night's quake had been the damage to the university students' dormitory building in which several young people had lost their lives. The collapsing building's main entrance door had jammed, trapping the young people inside. If God had wanted to save the innocent, he could at least have spared that building from the worst effects of the disaster, surely.

However, Beppe preferred to come to terms with such catastrophic events at his own pace, after digesting the initial emotional shock to his system. The truth of the matter was that the huge loss of life had in many cases been due to the poor quality of the building materials rather than any lack of mercy on God's part, he had reasoned.

It had seemed weirdly odd that it should have been that night of all nights when he had been totally unable to sleep. The recently appointed *sostituto commissario* had decided that the gentle motion of the sea would be more likely to soothe him than lying tossing and turning in conflict with a tangled, sweaty duvet. Despite the surname Stancato – meaning the 'weary one' – Beppe was one of the least sleep deprived people he knew. But on that particular night, sleep just seemed to elude him. He had got dressed at two o'clock and driven down to the harbour where his little boat was moored. He envied the fact that his colleagues were undoubtedly asleep with their families, spouses or partners whilst he was driving through a deserted Pescara.

Up until now, it had been his tireless persistence in getting to the core of any crime that he and his team were involved in which left his colleagues wondering when they would next have a chance to grab a few hours slumber. His supplies of energy seemed to discharge with imperceptible slowness. To his family and colleagues, he appeared to have endless reserves of mental and physical stamina – fed entirely by a regular intake of pasta, fresh tomatoes, mozzarella and basil leaves, as far as his colleagues could ascertain.

"Beppe, why are you always so restless?" his doting Calabrian mother would constantly chide him. "Why can't you be more like your sister, Valentina? She is so much more *tranquilla*[3] than you are." Beppe would shrug his shoulders, patiently repeating: "How should I know, *mamma?* You were the one who made me, after all."

"Leave him be, *mamma*," Valentina would say soothingly. His sister had not even tried to deter him from making the journey by sea from Calabria, up the Adriatic coast to Pescara. He had refused to leave his precious boat behind in the harbour of Catanzaro Marina, when his transfer to Abruzzo had been settled. From the hysterical reaction of his mother, one would have assumed he was intending to cross the Atlantic in a hurricane in mid-winter.

"I'll be fine, *mamma*," he had reassured her hourly. "I'll phone you every day to let you know where I am."

"Every day!" she had muttered darkly: "Me who brought you into this world! Every day, indeed! Why don't

---

[3] Easy-going : relaxed

you just phone me whenever the Blessed Virgin manifests herself to you?" she added with what was intended to be heavy sarcasm.

Beppe had set off at the crack of dawn. Only his quietly adoring father had been there to hug him and wave a resigned hand in farewell as the boat set off eastwards across the grey waters.

His mini voyage, single-handed across the Gulf of Taranto towards Puglia, was entirely uneventful. The only rough patch of sea had been going round the heel of Italy at Santa Maria di Leuca where the deep waters of the Adriatic meet the Ionian Sea. He had weathered it out for a few days in the harbour at Leuca, where he had refuelled and restocked the tiny refrigerator on board. After that, it had taken him fifteen serene days to reach Pescara. He had had plenty of time for nostalgia. Leaving behind his family and *fidanzata*[4] of ten years' standing, Laura, had not been easy and many a tear had been shed. Laura had promised to join him 'one day soon' when she no longer needed to look after her sick father. Beppe Stancato had had ample time to meditate upon his 'escape' from Calabria. He had been too close on the heels of members of the Spanò clan for comfort – *their* comfort, that is. They had reacted with unequivocal menaces, threatening him personally with mutilation of various clearly specified types. On one occasion, the clan had even threatened to feed his body live to the wild boar on a farm up in the mountains. When that had proved to be an ineffective ploy, the clan had promised to 'take care' of his family members too.

---

[4] Fiancée / girlfriend. The two words are almost synonymous in Italian!

"You can't argue with an organisation that represents 3.5% of Italy's GNP," Beppe's chief had reasoned with him, referring to the whole Calabrian mafia, the violent and ruthless *'ndrangheta*.[5] "You're too good a policeman to waste your life combatting that level of power single-handed," his *capo* had told him. He had helped Beppe out of his dilemma by arranging his transfer to Abruzzo for a period of five years.

"We hope to see you back here well before you reach fifty!" his chief had declared with bitter humour as they embraced warmly before taking leave of each other. Neither had had dry eyes – an expression of the frustration they both felt at having to combat the darker side of life in their beautiful land with insufficient manpower at their disposal.

Beppe Stancato had settled in quickly at Pescara's main police headquarters in Via Pesaro. The smell of the sea and of fish was in the air – even if this air was not quite as intoxicating as in his beloved Calabria. He had been greeted guardedly but respectfully by his new team – the 'respect' stemming from the fact that news of his solo voyage by sea had preceded his arrival. It was several days later that he learnt he had been nicknamed 'Colombo' – but whether this was a reference to Columbus the voyager or the detective with the shabby raincoat, he did not bother to ask.

His team had been instantly put at ease by the appearance of their new *capo*.[6] He didn't look as if he needed to throw his weight around to get attention. His face looked reassuring - even if it seldom smiled and always looked as if it needed a shave by midday. There was something slightly

---

[5] The Calabrian mafia. The word is derived from the Greek and means 'virtue and honour'. No comment!
[6] Chief – lit. head

wild about the look in his restless brown eyes – as if they were casting around to spot some elusive meaning to life that his brain had not yet identified.

Being *Abruzzesi* almost to a man, his new colleagues had an easy-going tolerance towards the world in general. This relaxed attitude towards life, Beppe Stancato quickly realised, was quite natural for a people who shared the sea and the mountains in equal measure, enjoyed excellent food and wine and lived in one of the most unspoilt regions of Europe. The infiltration of the mafia was reckoned to be 'not a serious threat as yet'.

The newly appointed *sostituto commissario* soon struck up a close working relationship with two uniformed members of his team in particular; a young officer called Pippo, who, like Beppe, was an escapee from the mafia. Pippo was from Foggia and, he explained, he had had a brush with the local *SCU*[7] clan. They joked about having the same first name – Giuseppe – even though they had ended up with two entirely different diminutive forms of the same name.

The second member whom he identified as a special colleague was a policewoman in her early thirties called Sonia. She was quite short in stature. She had short cropped hair and a pair of sparkling blue eyes like the sea in Calabria. She knew and was known by everyone in Pescara, being a *Pescarese* born and bred. She could settle disputes as if by magic between warring neighbours or irate motorists without ever raising her voice or losing her smile.

* * *

---

[7] Sacra Corona Unita – the name of the Pugliese mafia. 'Sacred United Crown'

Beppe Stancato was gazing at the stars above and being rocked gently by the swell of the sea on that sleepless night. He was mesmerised by the spectacular silhouette of the mountain range called *Il Gran Sasso d'Italia,* which rose up to meet the skies beyond the city of Pescara. It was uncanny how the shape of this mountain range resembled the figure of a woman lying down with her long hair stretched out behind her. No wonder the *Gran Sasso* was nicknamed *La Bella Addormentata*[8] by the locals, he thought. She was indeed the Sleeping Beauty. Her breasts rose up to meet the heavens and her long legs stretched out to the southern-most reaches of this section of the Apennines.

He was mulling over everything that had happened in the first few weeks of his life in Pescara. They had only had to deal with relatively minor incidents; a few burglaries, a drugs raid, a case of a teenage girl disappearing into thin air. It transpired that the teenager had merely taken refuge in a school friend's house in the neighbouring village of Pianella to avoid the unwanted attentions of her music teacher. But she had not thought to tell her parents where she was. Discovery of her whereabouts, however, had involved a painstakingly anxious investigation that had lasted nearly twenty-four hours and involved the whole of Beppe's team. His colleague, Sonia, had quietly reduced the hapless girl, Luciana, to tears of shame, before she had tactfully and gently coaxed the real reasons for her flight out of a very reluctant Luciana. Beppe had thanked Sonia afterwards and complimented her on her expert handling of the teenage girl.

---

[8] The Sleeping Beauty. Also the nickname of the mountain range because of its resemblance to a supine young woman.

"I was a teenager once too, you know, *capo*," she said her eyes full of irony yet smiling gratefully for his appreciation.

He was lying back on the padded seats of his boat, thinking how good it would be to rent an apartment on the sea front. He should talk to Sonia. She was bound to know the right estate agent. Yes, an apartment with a balcony overlooking the harbour would suit him perfectly...

That was as far as his musings reached before he heard something resembling a clap of muted thunder. He felt the tremors and saw the surface of the water changing into agitated little ripples. The seagulls floating on the surface of the sea rose startled into the air, squawking in instinctive alarm. All the dogs in Pescara began barking simultaneously.

Beppe Stancato knew it was an earthquake, of course. He could not have known that the nine-kilometre-deep shift in the complex tectonic plate system upon which Italy sits had wrought such destruction and human tragedy in the mountain-top city of L'Aquila. By dawn, everybody was aware of the scale of the tragedy. For Beppe Stancato, April 6th marked a transformation in his life in Abruzzo. His tranquil existence, which he had assumed would continue indefinitely, was shattered. In retrospect, he had the distinct impression that the strangest and most complex case that he had ever dealt with began from that moment in time.

The earthquake seemed to create a rift in human affairs. An underlying sense of insecurity and a loss of reason pervaded the people of Abruzzo as if in mimicry of the fissure in life's fabric that had taken place deep in the bowels of the earth. The churches were suddenly full of people attending mass. The priests in their sermons tried to explain the inexplicable workings of God's mind and hand out small doses of consolation as best they could. Some of the families had lost loved ones in the earthquake. Only the archbishop of Pescara had stood in the pulpit and shed tears which he was unable to control. The text for his sermon had been simply the words of Saint Paul in his epistle to the Romans: *Weep with them that weep...*

Pippo Cafarelli was the first of his team to put this sensation of a deep unease into words. They had spent days shepherding the refugees from the mountains into the many hotels in Pescara, whose owners, with scant hope of adequate remuneration, had of their own free will offered to host the families who had fled from L'Aquila. Late in the evening, the weary team of policemen was reunited in a local bar at their new chief's suggestion.

"Does anyone else here have the impression that the world has gone mad?' Pippo enquired of any or all of his colleagues. 'It feels quite literally as if the earthquake has left us without a hold on reality. As if..."

"...we don't have a leg to stand on?" another officer called Giacomo D'Amico finished off his sentence for him almost facetiously.

There were sage nods of agreement all round. Pippo looked at his chief for approval but his eyes seemed to be roving round the bar as if looking for confirmation of what his sergeant had been saying. *"Capo...?"* he enquired.

"Mi dispiace,[9] *Pippo,"* replied their chief apologetically. "I was just looking to see if there were any beautiful women in the bar that I could chat up. I am sorry. I am such a shallow man, you must understand."

---

[9] I'm sorry. *'di-spi-a-chay'*

Most of Beppe's team grinned politely at his words. Only the beguiling Sonia looked at him seriously, imperceptibly shaking her head as if in denial of his facile and unconvincing auto-analysis. Her gesture was noted and Beppe flashed a brief appreciative smile in her direction. In reality, he had not felt ready to face up to the hidden truth behind his younger colleague's words - not quite so soon at least.

The next few days were taken up coping with the now routine influx of people arriving from the mountains. It was heart-warming to witness how many people in Pescara and the towns along the coast were willing to open their doors to these shell-shocked immigrants. Their open-armed generosity was marred only by a very ill-chosen public statement from the Prime Minister, Sergio Balducci, who wished upon the fleeing mountain population 'a very relaxing and happy holiday by the seaside'. The Prime Minister's team of spin-doctors justified his words by saying it was just an example of his particular sense of humour; no insult had been intended. But most of the citizens of Italy found the words totally lacking in respect for the plight of the earthquake victims, despite their leader's promises to repair the city of L'Aquila by releasing all the necessary funds to achieve this goal immediately. Beppe Stancato, being a staunch socialist, poured private scorn on the sentiments expressed by their Prime Minister.

But life went on as it always does, filling the vacuum left by any disaster.

Until, one morning, sometime after that fateful night, a diminutive, ascetic-looking lady in her late sixties presented herself at the reception desk of the police headquarters in Via Pesaro.

"How can we help you, *signora?*" said the police officer on duty that day. He was, naturally, being excruciatingly polite, although he was certain that she had come to report that her cat or dog had been spirited away by a hungry family of Chinese immigrants.

"I'm here to report a murder," stated the lady unexpectedly. "I'd like to speak to *Agente*[10] Sonia Leardi, please."

The desk sergeant did not demur. "May I ask your name, please *signora?*"

"My name?" asked the lady, taken by surprise at such a personal question. "Di Agostini Brunella," she admitted as if under duress. Behind her back, the team would soon take to referring to her as *'La Piccola Suora'* – The Little Nun.

"How can I help you, *Signora* Brunella?" Sonia asked her in a kindly voice when she arrived at the desk. Sonia vaguely recalled seeing her in connection with some relatively trivial incident at a block of apartments along the seafront.

"I have to report a murder," she repeated, "a young woman who lives in the apartment opposite me."

"Why didn't you phone us first, *signora* Brunella?" asked Sonia, curious that this lady had gone to the trouble of coming to the police station in person.

"I never use the telephone unless it is something trivial," was the terse reply. "Besides which, I needed the exercise."

There was something illogical about this reply. If one wants to report a murder, one chooses the most immediate method available, surely, thought Sonia Leardi. It did not

---

[10] Agent - officer

augur well. The police woman suspected that they were about to become embroiled in the fanciful imaginings of a lonely spinster. But, in these strange times, when *everyone* seemed to be acting weirdly, I suppose one shouldn't prejudge, Sonia noted mentally.

"So what makes you think that this young woman has been murdered, *signora?*"

"Well, I saw her, of course!" Brunella Di Agostini replied tartly. "She was standing in her hallway."

The desk sergeant had to take himself off before he began to splutter with laughter.

"Excuse me being a little unclear, *Signora* Brunella," said Sonia Leardi patiently. "You say this dead woman was *standing* in the hallway?"

"Precisely, officer!"

"*Bene*," continued Sonia cautiously. "If she was standing up, what makes you think she was dead?"

"Because the man was holding her upright," replied the diminutive lady as if she was stating the obvious. "The woman's face was as white as a sheet and her eyes were staring without blinking."

"So you saw her looking dead being held up by this man?" asked Sonia.

"That's just what I told you, *agente.*"

"Would you recognise this man again?"

"Well, maybe. I'm sorry I can't be more helpful, *signorina*. It was only for a split second before the man shut the door in a hurry when he noticed me standing there on the landing."

"But if they are your neighbours, *Signora* Brunella, surely you must know them well?"

"Listen to me, *Signorina* Leardi – *agente*. That apartment has been empty for at least six months, don't you see?" answered the woman. "That's why I came to see *you* in person," she continued. "I remember you from the time you came round to our building when that man rang on all our doorbells, pretending he was from *ENEL*[11], claiming he wanted to change all our electricity meters."

That was where she had seen this lady before. There was nothing for it. Sonia Leardi was convinced the elderly lady was not being delusional. She went off to speak to her chief, telling Brunella Di Agostini to wait where she was.

"The desk sergeant will need to make a note of your name and address and take down your statement," said *Agente* Leardi, looking at her colleague and nodding as if to say that they should take this elderly lady seriously.

"I think we might have a problem, *capo*," she explained to Beppe.

"Take Pippo with you, Sonia," said Beppe. "If you find that something is really wrong, give me a call and I'll join you at once."

"*Sì, capo. D'accordo!*" said Sonia and went off in search of her colleague. "Come on Pippo," she said. "We have to check up on a suspected dead woman last seen standing upright in her hallway," she added enigmatically.

---

[11] Ente Nazionale per l'Energia Elettrica. The body supplying Italy's electricity. State controlled!

2: *'La Bella Addormentata'*

The trickiest moment for the two police officers, Sonia Leardi and Pippo Cafarelli, was to persuade the Little Nun to go back inside her own apartment and stay there. She was overcome with curiosity and a desire to prove to them that she was not just an over-imaginative spinster. It had taken all Sonia's tact and powers of persuasion to convince the lady that this was now a matter for the police.

"Why don't you go and prepare us a nice cup of coffee for when we've finished, *Signora* Brunella?" Sonia had said in desperation. "I'm sure we are going to need one in a short while."

While the *Piccola Suora* was still on the landing, they had been ringing the doorbell and knocking increasingly loudly, calling out "Is there anyone at home?" But all to no avail. Other residents had begun to poke their greying heads nervously out of their front doors.

Pippo made a wry face at his colleague, clearly meaning they should stop drawing attention to what they were doing.

"We'd better put your other skill to the test, Pippo," suggested Sonia.

Pippo often jokingly pretended that he had been a burglar back in Foggia and had learned to open any normal door within minutes. The two officers would only have the door broken down as a last resort, which would have required a door ram.

They were inside within five minutes. Sonia carefully reclosed the door behind them to prevent any incursion from an over-inquisitive Brunella. A strange smell struck their noses immediately. It was difficult to define, but at least it was not the smell of death, they decided.

"I know what it reminds me of," whispered Pippo. "It's a hospital smell."

Sonia nodded in agreement.

The two officers called out softly: *"C'è nessuno?"*[12] But there was no reply. So they took a deep breath and began to look into each room of the spacious apartment. It did not take them long. A young woman was lying stretched out on a double bed. She was dressed in a pretty, full length nightie. Her dark hair flowed back on the pillow. She was young - probably no more than twenty-two years old at a guess. She had a beautiful face that was a ghostly white in colour, in sharp contrast to the pink sheets upon which she was lying. She was alarmingly motionless. Nevertheless, by peering at the swell of her breasts, Sonia thought she detected the slightest rise and fall of her breathing. She instinctively placed two fingers on the girl's neck. She let out a sigh of relief. There was a slow, almost undetectable pulse.

"She's alive, Pippo," she said quietly.

The two decided that the circumstances were sufficiently unusual to justify calling their *capo*. Sonia went into the kitchen to make her call, as if she was afraid of waking their 'sleeping beauty'. The way she was lying on the bed with her hair stretched out behind her was so similar to the shape of the mountain range behind them that it was uncanny.

Beppe Stancato was there within ten minutes. His first words were: *"Ah, la Bella Addormentata!"* He felt for the pulse in the girl's neck just as Sonia had done and said

---

[12] Is anybody there?

immediately: "She's been heavily sedated with some concoction of drugs. We must get her to hospital immediately before she goes beyond our reach."

"Shall I call for an ambulance, *capo?*" asked Pippo. Beppe did not reply immediately.

"Just let me think for a second," he said finally. "What floor are we on?"

"Third floor, chief," replied Pippo, waiting patiently for Beppe to complete his thought processes.

"Right, Pippo," said Beppe finally. "Phone the hospital, but ask for *Dottore* Esposito, if he's available. Tell him from me that it's important... that we've got a very unusual situation and can he possibly come with the ambulance. Ask him to make sure that the ambulance has its siren turned off as it approaches this address. We really can't afford to attract a lot of attention over this one."

The *commissario* fell silent again, obviously working out the ramifications of the situation. Sonia was keeping pace with his thoughts.

"I'll go with the ambulance, *capo,* and stay with the girl. I guess we shall have to insist on an isolated room for her. Pippo can stay here in the apartment until..."

"Would you like to take over the case for me, Sonia?" said her chief smiling ruefully.

"No thanks, *capo,*" she said seriously. "You're doing fine. I'm just trying to keep up with you."

"She is right, of course, Pippo. I'll stay in the apartment until we can get a couple of the others to come over here. The same for you, Sonia – I'll send somebody over to relieve you as soon as possible."

Pippo had just caught up with their line of reasoning.

"*Ho capito,*[13] *capo.* Somebody, possibly the man whom the Little Nun saw, is bound to turn up sooner or later to finish off what they've started – whatever that might be!"

"We have to get to the bottom of this," added Beppe nodding in acknowledgement of his young colleague's grasp of the situation. "I have an intuitive feeling that there is something sinister going on."

Pippo, who had gone into the kitchen to phone the hospital, came back smiling.

"We are in luck, *capo.* Doctor Esposito was there and will come with the ambulance. He said he can sort out an isolation room for...our Sleeping Beauty."

Sonia looked quizzically at her chief.

"Esposito? Isn't he the specialist in toxicology?" she asked.
"He helped us after the drug raid to identify the various substances that were found. He's really immensely knowledgeable – far beyond the normal call of duty," explained Beppe. "He even knows how to prepare curare, he told me," added the commissioner, whose eyes were travelling round the room as he was talking, looking for the hidden meaning behind this drama.
His eyes alighted finally on Pippo, who was staring at the motionless figure lying on the bed.

"Yes, Pippo, she really is very beautiful, isn't she!" he said mischievously.

Pippo was young enough to blush slightly but not naïve enough to be caught out so easily.

---

[13] I get it Lit: 'I have understood'

"Yes, *capo,* I know she is. But I am sure I've seen her face before somehow, somewhere, in a totally different context. It'll come to me in the end."

"Well, that could turn out to be important," said Beppe regretting his puerile comment of a few seconds previously. He apologised yet again for being so 'shallow' – as he was wont to describe himself. It was a kind of unconscious psychological test, he considered, to winkle out how perceptive others were at understanding him. Always assuming he understood himself, of course!

They were all startled by the sound of the doorbell. It was too soon for the ambulance to have arrived.

"I can guess who *that* is," said Sonia. *"La Signora* Brunella to tell me my cup of coffee is getting cold – and to see if she can satisfy her curiosity."

"You had better forestall her then," said Beppe. "We don't want her outside on the landing when we take our protégée out on a stretcher. It'll be common knowledge inside five minutes otherwise." He was about to warn Sonia not to tell the spinster lady anything, but realised that this would sound as if he did not trust her judgement. "We'll let you know the minute the ambulance is here," he added instead.

The coffee was cold but it didn't matter. Sonia barely had time to reassure the Little Nun that there was nothing to worry about. "The young lady has just gone out shopping," invented Sonia on the spur of the moment. Beppe Stancato rang on the doorbell ten minutes later and deftly stepped into Brunella's apartment to prevent her coming out on to the landing as Sonia slipped out. The Sleeping Beauty was being carried to the lift on a stretcher by two of the ambulance crew, with the doctor, Bruno Esposito, walking by the girl's side. He was nodding sagely to himself.

In Brunella's apartment, Beppe Stancato said the first thing that came into his head to distract her attention. "I was wondering, *Signora* Di Agostini, if you could give me a description of the man you saw holding up the young lady - who is feeling a lot better now, by the way."

"But she shouldn't have gone out shopping so soon afterwards!" stated the lady in total disapproval. Beppe realised just in time that this explanation must have come from Sonia.

"Oh, she'll be fine now," he assured the lady. "She just needs a lot of sleep tonight to make sure she's really better. She fainted you know. That's why the man was propping her up."

According to the Little Nun's description, the mystery man was about two metres tall, wore purple-tinted sunglasses and had one leg shorter than the other. It didn't really matter too much how she had answered, since *anyone* who turned up at the flat opposite was likely to be involved in this odd affair. Beppe took his leave as quickly as he politely could.

* * *

The two uniformed officers who took over in the vacated apartment, Danilo Simone and Gino Martelli, settled in for the first watch. They had been thoroughly briefed by their chief and warned to be very much on their guard against any individual who arrived at the flat.

"There's nothing innocent about what is going on here. Apparently, the man whom *la Signora* Brunella saw is two metres tall and has a limp! But we only have her word for that. You should definitely have surprise on your side, *ragazzi* - just make sure you confiscate his mobile phone before he can raise the alarm..."

"Excuse me, *capo*," interrupted Pippo Cafarelli, who then made a discreet suggestion in Beppe Stancato's ear, which earned him an admiring look from his *capo*.

"*Bravo*,[14] Pippo! You'll be a *commissario* in no time! *You* explain your tactic to Danilo and Gino, please. I must go straight to the hospital now."

* * *

Agente Sonia Leardi was standing guard outside a room on the top floor of the *Ospedale dello Spirito Santo*[15] in Pescara's city centre as Beppe Stancato stepped out of the lift and walked up a deserted corridor towards the private room where they had taken the sleeping girl. He grinned briefly at Sonia whilst raising an inquiring eyebrow.

"The doctor is in there with her; and a nurse," she said.

There was a little rectangle of reinforced glass in the door through which Beppe peered to see what was going on. All he could make out was the green-robed figures of *Dottore* Bruno Esposito and the nurse bending motionless over their patient as if performing some mystical rite. Beppe then made out that they were carefully taking a blood sample from the girl's left arm. The doctor handed the phial to the nurse who headed for the door. The phial was inside a little plastic bag marked with a yellow skull-and-crossbones

---
[14] Well done!
[15] The Hospital of the Holy Spirit

symbol. It had the word *URGENTISSIMO*[16] printed on it. The nurse nodded at the two police officers as she passed. "The doctor will come out and see you in a moment," she said, removing the white face mask.

Il Dottore Esposito emerged a few minutes later with many a backward glance towards his 'patient' as if loath to leave her side. He looked like a typical doctor, clinically detached from his patient and without apparent emotion on his impassive face. The two police officers looked at him expectantly.

"This is a most unusual case, *commissario – agente*," he added, thereby including Sonia within the framework of his comments. "She's been sedated by some concoction that I can't quite identify. I know I'm obsessed by narcotics," he said, with the first sign of a twinkle in the eye. "But I would swear that part of the compound includes some mild form of…"

"Curare?" Beppe slipped in during the slight pause. The doctor smiled but shook his head.

"I see I've spoken to you on the matter of unusual narcotics on a previous occasion. But if she had been given curare, she would be well past the breathing stage by now. No, I was going to say that it looks like a small dose of rohypnol - the so-called date-rape drug, *commissario*."

"I'm only a substitute commissioner, *dottore*."

"Life's too short to call you by your proper title," said the doctor with an impudent grin.

"Call me Beppe, then."

"Call me Bruno, then," he echoed. "And for heaven's sake let's *darci del tu*." [17]

---

[16] Very urgent. -issimo on the end of an adjective turns it into a superlative.
[17] Impossible to translate. The doctor wishes to use the informal form of

"Agreed, Bruno," said Beppe with some relief that they were able to dispense with the inevitable social convention of using the formal manner of addressing a stranger.

"And you, *signorina,* if you so wish," added the doctor kindly, seeing Sonia shifting uncomfortably on her feet at all these signs of male bonding.

Sonia looked at him straight in the eye and said simply: *"Grazie,"* with a warm smile of appreciation that the medic had not wished her to be excluded. Her heart was warming to this outwardly conventional doctor.

"And what should we conclude, Bruno, from the use of this drug?" asked Beppe.

"Oh come now, Beppe. I'm still a medical man," he replied with genuine warmth and humour. "You don't expect me to commit myself until I've had the results of the blood test, do you? But whatever drugs have been used on her, I would say that someone is very keen to keep her as nearly unconscious as possible."

"Couldn't you just give us your ill-considered opinion, *dottore?"* asked Sonia looking appealingly in his direction.

"Alright, just this once, and only because it's you two," smiled Bruno Esposito.

Beppe and Sonia were looking in anticipation at the *medico* while he assembled his thoughts.

"This girl matters to you, doesn't she?" he began. Beppe shrugged his shoulders and nodded in a single gesture. Sonia continued to look expectantly in the speaker's direction.

'you' to his new friend.

"Well, our *Bella Addormentata* ..." he began, but stopped when they both laughed.

"You call her that too!" explained Sonia. Bruno Esposito looked enlightened and continued:

"So... I would conclude that whoever is administering this sleep-inducing concoction must be a doctor, a biologist – or maybe just a scientist of some sort. It has to be a very precise dosage indeed. Too much would send her into a permanent coma; too little and she would not remain unconscious. It's a fine balance. Let's just say you're not dealing with amateurs."

"Why on earth would anyone go to these lengths to...?" began Sonia, thinking out loud.

"Ah, that's a policeman's domain!" said the doctor with something akin to relief in his voice. "Now, I really must be off. I'll phone you, Beppe, as soon as I have the results."

"When might that be?" asked Beppe.

"By this evening, I hope. If not, tomorrow morning – no later than that, I promise, or they'll have me breathing down their necks. You two make a very good team," concluded Bruno Esposito unexpectedly, with a positive gleam in his eye, as he shook both of them by the hand.

"How long before she regains consciousness, in your opinion, Bruno?" asked Beppe.

"Hard to say; you should see signs of recovery by this evening. But she may be disorientated for a little longer after that," replied the doctor. "Make sure she drinks a lot of water. She really *is* very beautiful," he added ambiguously over his shoulder as he walked away down the corridor leaving Beppe and Sonia not quite knowing where to look after the unexpected compliment of a few seconds earlier.

"There are hidden levels to that man," thought Beppe Stancato, whose eyes had been darting round in an attempt not to catch the eye of his companion.

Sonia recovered as quickly as she could from her mild blush of embarrassment.

"I'll stay here if you like, *capo,* until you send another of the team along to keep me company."

"Thank you, Sonia. I won't forget you're here. If she wakes up, phone me whatever the time. And thank you…" he added again, intending to mean for just being Sonia.

"*Capo,*" she said, since Beppe had shown no immediate signs of departing. "What do you think this is all about?"

"It's a mystery at the moment. Obviously, they want to keep her quiet for some reason. So we must conclude that she knows something important that they want to keep a secret."

"But why don't they just *farla fuori?*[18] They are obviously ruthless enough."

Beppe Stancato looked at his colleague with secret relief that he could share his suspicions with someone else.

"That is exactly what I have been asking myself, Sonia…"

---

[18] Bump her off

3: Now you see her...

Back in the vacated apartment, the two police officers, Danilo and Gino had whiled away the time checking out the spacious flat thoroughly. They declared that it would be a highly desirable place to live – on a chief inspector's salary.

There was the barest minimum of food and drink in the kitchen; a few tins of soup, milk and water and some basic fruit in a bowl. In the *en suite* bathroom, they found a bar of soap and a bottle of shampoo along with a lady's hairbrush.

"They obviously didn't intend to go overboard looking after her," observed Danilo.

"They would have to come once a day though to keep her alive and keep her clean one assumes," added Gino.

"Well, I hope we don't have too long to wait."

In truth, they were looking forward to a bit of action. In relatively law-abiding Pescara, there was not much call for the use of force. Keeping a beautiful woman imprisoned and sedated seemed to be a wholly justified occasion to exact a bit of 'real justice'. They were somewhat inexperienced in face- to-face conflict with the undesirable elements of Italian society. If the two young officers were guilty of anything, it was no more than a tendency to underestimate the nature of the opposition. But they were armed with a pair of handcuffs and pistols, which had only ever seen action on the police firing range, so they felt quite able to cope with whoever turned up at the apartment.

It was almost midnight before they were alerted to somebody's arrival by the surreptitious sound of a key being turned in the lock. They had almost fallen asleep around the kitchen table in the darkened flat. They were alert in an instant, their hearts beating faster. They stood up and moved towards the corridor. Both of them had instinctively drawn their pistols from their leather holsters and were pointing them in the direction of the open doorway waiting for the intruder to draw level in the darkened flat. What they had not expected was for the intruder to switch on the lights in the kitchen. Neither had they expected the man, who was indeed not far off two metres tall but certainly did not limp, to look at them in only mild surprise and say: *"Buonasera, signori. Dov'è la señorita, por favor?"* It was a disconcerting experience for Danilo and Gino, who instinctively lowered their weapons as a reaction to the man's unruffled demeanour.

"Please don't shoot me, officers," he was saying calmly. "I'm only a doctor." Danilo put his pistol back in its holster. Gino held his weapon loosely, pointing it at the floor.

In that instant of time, the 'doctor', with a degree of athleticism that was remarkable for his height, was out of the kitchen in a flash and heading up the hallway towards the front door. He had even managed to flick the light switch into its 'off' position so that the kitchen was plunged into darkness once more.

Gino first and then Danilo were galvanised into action in an attempt to remedy their catastrophic underestimation of the nature of their prey. Like a scene from a Buster Keaton film, they both tried to get through the kitchen doorway at the same time and lost a precious second untangling themselves. Danilo, unhampered by the gun in his hand, was the first to escape the human knot and run blindly up the hallway in the unaccustomed darkness. The 'doctor' had his hand on the door latch. Its stiffness gave Danilo time to perform a painful rugby tackle round the escapee's left leg.

The gesture gave Gino, by now in hot pursuit, the opportunity of jabbing his raised pistol roughly into the man's left flank. "Stop or I shoot," he yelled with a note of hysteria in his voice just as the 'doctor' managed to open the door of the apartment.

The doctor, if indeed he was what he claimed to be, went suddenly limp and allowed himself to be escorted back to the kitchen at gunpoint. He slumped, apparently defeated, onto a kitchen chair. Gino and Danilo were both breathing heavily, whereas their captive looked as if he had been for a stroll along the beach.

At this point of proceedings, it would have been a sensible precaution to handcuff the man to a kitchen chair without delay. But both officers were mindful of their colleague's wily subterfuge of giving any captive the opportunity to make one phone call on their mobile before confiscating the device prior to the conversation getting underway. The logic behind Pippo's suggestion was theoretically sound; this manoeuvre just might give them a lead as to who was behind the kidnap and sedation of their Sleeping Beauty. It did not occur to them that this two-metre-tall man might simply *be* the one responsible. Gino's most complicated thought was that the Little Nun's impression that 'he had one leg shorter than the other' must simply have been because of the way he had been standing when he was supporting the girl against the wall.

They were beginning to feel as if they had the situation under control. Thus, when the 'doctor', in a heavy accent, asked if he could go to the toilet, the two officers looked at each other and smiled obligingly at their insecurely restrained captive. They accompanied the man to the toilet door at pistol point making it quite clear that he must not lock himself in.

"If you *do* lock the door, I shall shoot your *coglioni*[19] off," proclaimed an emboldened Gino with suitable menace in his voice. Danilo and Gino were beginning to think they had the upper hand.

Pippo's plan to allow their prisoner time to extract his mobile and alert someone on the outside as to the presence of the police in the apartment looked as if it was going to work a treat. The two young *agenti* had their ears pressed to the door. Sure enough, after a brief pause, they heard their captive whispering urgently: *"Signore, c'è un problema..."* as he went through the motion of flushing the toilet.

The speed with which they burst through the door and snatched the phone out of his left hand did them credit, taking the 'doctor' by complete surprise. Unfortunately, they had to confess to Beppe later on, they had assumed the battle was won at this stage. Their lofty adversary had been sitting on the closed toilet seat with his trousers fully in the upright position. Using both his arms and hands simultaneously, the man aimed his cupped palms under the chins of each police officer with jaw-cracking strength. Then he shot out of the toilet and headed for the corridor, leaving the two young *agenti* staggering to keep their balance.

Danilo was still clutching the mobile phone in his right hand but had taken the blow to the chin more painfully than his colleague. Gino, standing on the doctor's right flank was only momentarily disabled. He was out of the toilet and running in pursuit of the departing giant within seconds.

---

[19] Balls!

Nevertheless, the 'doctor' had already reached the landing on the second floor, taking the descent two steps at a time when he could. It was a waste of time for Gino to summon the lift. He had no alternative but to race down the stairway in pursuit of their prey. The noise had alerted the Little Nun whose door opened cautiously as she peered out on to the landing. She heard a stampede of buffalo charging down towards the lower reaches of her domain. This was another emergency, she decided, and went back indoors to phone 112 to call out the *Carabinieri.* A telephone call was the only recourse on this occasion, she reckoned.

Gino reached the main entrance to the flats just in time to see the escaping doctor leaping into his car which roared off into the night.

"*Merda!*" he exclaimed as he went back upstairs – in the lift – to see how his colleague had fared. No lasting damage! Feeling sheepish in the extreme, they reluctantly called their *capo* to tell him what had happened. He was not asleep and had been waiting in his office for developments. Confusingly for the two young officers, all the *commissario* had said was: "I'll be there at once." His voice was unnaturally calm and held no indication of his state of mind. Gino and Danilo found this very off-putting. "He'll nail us to the wall!" said Gino. They had still some way to go before they understood the manner in which their new *capo* dealt with his team.

Beppe Stancato arrived at the same time as the *carabinieri* car did. Puzzled, he ran up the stairs in the company of his 'rival' colleagues.

"Who called you out, *capitano?*" he asked.

"Some lady in Flat 32," replied the *carabiniere* officer.

"Ah! That would be the Little Nun, as we call her," he said. "We have an ongoing problem in the flat opposite hers - just a domestic incident."

Beppe Stancato did not want to involve the national police force at this stage. "Can I call you tomorrow, *capitano?*" he added. "I'll explain what is going on in case we need your help."

Sure enough, Beppe and his two crestfallen young colleagues heard the *carabinieri* going downstairs a few minutes later. They made far more noise than the 'charging buffalos' of a few minutes earlier, thought an anxious Little Nun as she closed and locked her front door with a heavy chain.

Disconcertingly for Gino and Danilo, their *capo* remained totally unruffled. He had insisted that they describe events precisely as they had occurred, omitting not the slightest detail.

"We're so sorry we let you down, *commissario...*" Danilo said at the end of their account.

Their chief shrugged his shoulders and said nothing reassuring but equally did not accuse them of failing in their duty.

"You got his mobile. That was something, *ragazzi.*"

By now, the 'doctor's' mobile phone was in a clear plastic bag in Beppe's pocket.

"By the way *capo,*" said Gino out of the blue. "The 'doctor' got into a black Audi Q7. I'm pretty sure the registration plate began **KP22**. It disappeared a bit too quickly to see the rest of the *targa.*"[20]

---

[20] Number plate

"And this doctor, if he really is one, is Spanish – or Latin American," added Danilo. "He called our girl *señorita* and said *por favor* instead of 'per favore'.

Beppe Stancato looked at his junior officers with his lop-sided grin and patted them lightly on the shoulder.

"Well, we seem to have got somewhere after all. Now you two go home and get some sleep. We will all meet tomorrow morning – no, *this* morning – at 08.30. *Buonanotte, ragazzi!*"[21]

Gino and Danilo went off feeling bewildered yet relieved. The absence of criticism of their failure by their chief was worrying. No doubt they could expect a verbal drubbing tomorrow – in front of all their colleagues.

Beppe's phone rang. It was Sonia calling from the hospital.

"Can you come to the hospital, *capo?* It's the Sleeping Beauty. She seems to be waking up."

* * *

Beppe drove directly to the hospital. He would hand the confiscated mobile phone to the technical team at headquarters after his visit to the hospital. He informed his colleagues on night shift where he was going and told them to try and track down anyone with a black Audi Q7, possibly with KP22 in the registration number. You never could tell - maybe they would get lucky.

He found Sonia by the Sleeping Beauty's bedside holding the girl's hand in her own. She was talking quietly to her, while a young officer called Remo was watching from a

---

[21] Goodnight lads – and lasses if women are present.

distance. Remo had been a waiter for a number of years before being accepted into the police force at Pescara. In his slightly over-large uniform – they had been promising him a closer fitting one for weeks – Beppe thought privately that he still looked more like a waiter. He often wore a slightly subservient smile on his face and looked as if he would be happier with a corkscrew in his hand rather than a pistol. "I'm sure he will shape up well in the long run," Beppe had once observed loyally to somebody who had expressed reservations about his suitability as a police officer.

From the Sleeping Beauty's bedside, Sonia turned to Beppe and said:

"She seems to have drifted off again, *capo*. She is a bit disorientated. But apart from saying "Where am I?" she kept going on about her uncle. *"È colpa di mio zio.* It's all my uncle's fault... Please don't let him anywhere near me..."

"We managed to get some water down her, *capo,* and I went and fetched some soup from a machine downstairs. We wanted to get her to a toilet but it seems to be on the next floor down," explained Remo.

"Tomorrow morning, we shall have to move her somewhere less public," said Beppe thinking out aloud. He went on to relate what had happened to Gino and Danilo back in the apartment where the girl had been found.

"We are up against one or more persons who are involved in something more serious than a private family row of some sort," added their chief. "Are you two alright to stay on here for another few hours?"

They nodded and said there was no hurry. Beppe Stancato told them about the meeting the next morning at 08.30 hours. "Be careful and very vigilant, *ragazzi.* We're not dealing with a group of bird-watchers here."

Sonia gave her *capo* a warm smile which contained a hint of regret that he was leaving them. The smile almost made him go up to her and plant a *bacio*[22] on her cheek. To his alarm, he found he had to check the desire quite consciously. An image of Laura, his *fidanzata,* briefly came to mind to aid his resistance.

On his way down to the ground floor, Beppe was distracted from his private thoughts by his mobile phone ringing. It was the doctor, Bruno Esposito.

"Ciao, Beppe," he began. "Well, my guess was right about the concoction of drugs; mainly Diazepan to keep her relaxed but with a 25% touch of Rohypnol to make sure she stays confused about what has happened to her when she wakes up. Very nasty, I would say, and very carefully balanced to achieve the desired effect. Strange though, it is difficult to get Rohypnol readily in Italy - quite easy, however, in Latin American countries, for example."

Beppe Stancato's mind was working quickly, piecing together the bits of scant information they had gleaned.

"Thank you, Bruno. Will it be alright to move our Sleeping Beauty out when it's daylight to somewhere less public?"

"*Buonissima idea, Beppe!* She should only need a couple of hours before the effects of the drugs begin to wear off. *Buonanotte!*"

"*Buonanotte, Bruno... e grazie mille.*"

* * *

---

[22] A 'friendly' kiss

The two officers, Sonia Leardi and Remo Mastrodicasa – a real mouthful of a surname for which he was frequently ribbed - prepared themselves mentally for another few hours' vigil before they would be relieved later on in the night. They kept a constant check on the Sleeping Beauty, who was at least no longer lying like a marble statue on the bed. She would utter sighs and shift her position from time to time in her state of sleep – as if she was reacting to a disturbing dream.

The two officers spent a few desultory minutes trying to imagine what was behind this abduction but could come up with nothing convincing.

"If only we knew her name, we might find out who her uncle was," said Remo to his colleague.

"If the phone trick works, maybe we shall know who the uncle is before we know who our Sleeping Beauty really is."

It must have been around two o'clock in the morning when Sonia Leardi needed to find the *bagno*.[23] She excused herself, promising to be as quick as possible.

"The nearest toilets are on the floor below," explained Remo, who had had the wit to notice their whereabouts when he had gone off to fetch the hot soup. "If you turn left instead of right down our corridor, you'll find a fire escape route to the next floor down."

Sonia was loath to leave her junior colleague even for five minutes, but she checked to make sure the corridor was empty before heading off towards the stairwell.

Officer Remo Mastrodicasa was surprised to see a doctor walk into the room. He was wearing a green coat. He

---

[23] Bathroom – a euphemism for 'toilet'

had a stethoscope around his neck and a white medical mask which covered the lower part of his face. The doctor was abnormally tall.

"I'm Doctor Bruno Esposito," said the man reassuringly. "I am in charge of this patient. I'm coming to check how she is before I go home. Is that alright with you, officer?"

Remo had, of course, heard Doctor Esposito's name in connection with this case, but had no idea what he looked like. This doctor spoke softly but Officer Remo could hardly fail to detect the accent, which sounded Spanish to his untrained ear. Remo shrugged his shoulders but he had unclipped the pistol in his holster instinctively – somewhat to his own surprise. As soon as the doctor drew out a plastic-coated syringe, Remo was alert.

"Stop that, doctor," he said nervously. "I'm going to phone my *capo* before you do anything to that girl!"

He was relieved to hear the door opening behind him. Sonia Leardi must be back. He felt the vicious crack on his head as he sank down to the floor, semi-conscious. An accomplice must have been waiting in the wings.

When Sonia came into the room seconds later, she found her colleague groaning in pain. Of the Sleeping Beauty there was no sign. Sonia let out a cry of anger mixed in with despair.

* * *

As soon as his mobile rang, Beppe had a presentiment of disaster as he registered the caller's name and number. The desperate sound of tears, magically transmitted by an invisible stream of electro-magnetic waves, confirmed his worst fears.

"Stay where you are, Sonia. I'm coming over now."

As Beppe stepped into the room, so recently vacated by its precious occupant, Sonia ran towards him in a state of deep distress. What else could he do but put consoling arms around his colleague and hug her, rocking her gently from side to side? Remo Mastrodicasa, staggering to his feet, was looking exactly like a downcast waiter who had just been told that the fish course was a culinary disaster.

"I'm so sorry, Beppe! It was all my fault," sobbed Sonia. "They must have been waiting in the dark for one of us to leave the room." Wasn't the *sostituto commissario* supposed to be called *capo* at the very least by his subordinates? He chose to let it go, however. What harm was there in omitting a title just for once?

"It was all *my* fault, *commissario*," began Remo, "you mustn't blame *agente* Leardi for all this." He went on to explain what had happened and how it was his lack of vigilance that had been the true cause. Beppe Stancato was looking very thoughtful during Remo's account.

"Now we're back to square one," said Sonia still sobbing. *"Anzi[24], we're even worse off than before... and our girl is now in greater danger than ever."

"*Ragazzi, ragazzi!*" said Beppe calmly, regretfully unwrapping his arms from around his junior officer. "Stop blaming yourselves. It is my fault, not yours. I have really underestimated the complexity of this case right from the outset."

---

[24] On the contrary

Both Sonia and Remo were quite unnerved by his quiet, unruffled words. It was a new experience to come across a *commissario* – even a substitute one - who, in the face of disaster, did not off-load blame on to his subordinates.

"Don't worry," he said as they went their separate ways later on. "We shall get to the bottom of this...*and* find our Sleeping Beauty alive and kicking."

Sonia arrived back home still feeling her body tingling slightly at the invisible pressure of her superior officer's arms around her. *"O Dio!"*[25] she muttered. "Did I really call him by his first name?"

---

[25] Goodness me!

4: Picking up the pieces

At half past eight the following morning, a very subdued gathering awaited the arrival of their chief in the briefing room. Those who had been involved in the previous day's events were filling in the others in hushed voices. They were shocked that the as yet nameless young woman had been violently abducted – presumably for a second time. Remo, the waiter, had redeemed himself when he had tentatively announced to Beppe Stancato much earlier that morning that he had taken a photo of the girl lying on the makeshift hospital bed.

"Well done, Remo. You acted with great foresight," he had complimented the young officer, whose self-esteem was, understandably, at low ebb.

The police officer had sheepishly confessed to his *capo* that it was because of her beauty rather than because of any foresight on his part that he had taken photos of her – three he had blushingly admitted.

"Well, it amounts to the same thing, Remo," Beppe had added kindly, suppressing the malicious suspicion that this officer might have been hoping for a unique news scoop. Beppe had 'borrowed' the smart phone to download the photos, explaining he would have posters made up so that everybody would be able to identify the girl.

Apart from the male contingent, plus Sonia Leardi, the youngest member of the team had returned from leave. She was only in her mid-twenties. She was slim and wiry in build, with long black hair tied into a single plait that came half way down her back – contrary to regulations someone had once rashly ventured to tell her. She was graced with the lovely name of Oriana Salvati. But the younger males in the team had nicknamed her *'La Spinosa'* – the 'Prickly One' – because of her terrifying ability to resist every advance, verbal or otherwise, that any of them had dared to make in the vain hope of currying an iota of favour. Most of the team, except Sonia and Beppe himself, had been on the receiving end of her viper's tongue on one occasion or another. The person who had rashly said she should cut off her plait of hair had been told that her hair was her own problem and that the police force of Pescara would be without their youngest recruit if anyone suggested that she should part with it. It was rumoured that she had practised martial arts from the age of eight and had a black belt in all of them. Some of the more malicious members of the admin staff had suggested amongst themselves that she had obtained the post by means of a *raccomandazione*,[26] thanks to the mediation of an influential relative. Nobody, however, had dared to suggest this to her face.

To Beppe she had once confided that she felt the need to establish respect from this male dominated crew before she could afford to drop her defences.

Beppe had smiled at her and reassured her that even Godzilla would think twice before crossing her path. Oriana Salvati had inwardly sworn total allegiance to her chief after his colourfully flattering response.

At this moment in time, Oriana was listening to Sonia as she filled her young colleague in on the details of the Sleeping Beauty case. Oriana, naturally enough, felt an immediate affinity with the victim of this abduction, if only because of her age and her long, flowing hair.

---

[26] A 'recommendation' from a high-placed friend or relative to help one jump the queue of applicants. It happens a lot in Italy. We call it 'nepotism'.

This was how *Sostituto Commissario* Stancato found his team when he walked into the room. They had never seen him looking quite as pale as he did at that moment of time. He had a saintly, ascetic appearance about him as his eyes darted over the gathered police officers, who were transformed into a state of instant attentiveness. Had they known him as an inspector back in his native Calabria, they would have recognised the symptoms of an uncompromising concentration on the case in hand.

"*Buongiorno ragazzi.* We have a great deal of work on our hands," he began. "I shall begin by summing up everything we have discovered so far."

There were no recriminations, no veiled accusations and no sarcasm. Beppe had simply accepted that the previous day's mishaps were a thing of the past. There were a few murmured sounds of protest when he quietly reiterated that it was he who had underestimated the implications of this case. The murmurs of protest became audible gasps of surprise from many of the police officers as their chief pinned up an enlarged photo of the Sleeping Beauty.

"Yes, this is the young woman who is at the centre of this enquiry," began Beppe. "We need to find her quickly. She was abducted – for the second time, we assume – in the early hours of this morning. It is almost certain that the perpetrator is a man who is not far short of two metres tall. He is very strong and athletic. He claims to be a doctor. We know this because, by Remo's description of events; he was about to administer an injection into her arm before she was abducted from the hospital. He was also the man who came to the apartment earlier, expecting to find his 'patient' waiting for him. Gino and Danilo can tell you all about that encounter. But anybody with a bit of know-how can stick a needle into a person's body, so we can't assume he's a doctor. Anything else anybody wants to add?"

"Yes, *capo*, we think he might be Spanish or Latin American. He spoke with an accent and used a few Spanish words," was Danilo's contribution.

"Yes, that's important," continued Beppe Stancato, whose sense of team leadership led him to encourage the others to participate. "This supposition could be supported by the fact that the girl had been injected with drugs which included Rohypnol, the so-called 'date-rape' drug, which is still readily available in parts of Latin America. But these are just possible indications at present. Anything else I've missed out..?"

"Yes, *capo*," added Danilo. "He's a vicious bastard," he said massaging his bruised and swollen chin.

A brief smile from Beppe before he added unexpectedly: "That's right. You should all be aware when we come across him again that he is left-handed."

"What makes you think that, *capo?*" asked Gino puzzled.

"You two guys told me," said Beppe as if he was stating the obvious.

Gino and Danilo looked puzzled.

"Did we, *capo*?" asked Gino.

"You, Gino, were the one who recovered quickly enough to chase after the Spaniard in the flat. Danilo was on the man's left. Danilo took the phone out of his left hand, didn't you, Danilo? And it was you who received the hardest blow to your chin."

"*Bravo capo!*" nodded Gino.

"And I would bet that Remo would confirm that the 'doctor' was administering the injection with the syringe in his left hand. *Vero*[27] Remo?" said Beppe directing the comment to the back of the room where Remo was standing, looking self-conscious.

There were titters from the floor when, swivelling round to look at Remo, they saw him with his eyes tightly closed, gesturing with his two hands alternatively as he tried to picture mentally the image he had of the scene at the hospital just before he was slugged from behind.

"Yes, *capo*," he finally replied opening his eyes. "That is correct..."

The smirks vanished as they noted the severe expression on their chief's face.

"This may or may not have any importance," said Beppe sharply. "But one never knows. Now I'm going to assign tasks to each of you. You should work in pairs as far as possible. And we need results quickly. So, I want all of you back here this evening at 19.00 hours. *D'accordo?*"[28]

"But do you believe we shall find the girl alive?" asked Oriana anxiously.

Beppe looked at her unsmilingly. She was regretting her interruption. "I'm sorry *capo*... I shouldn't have..." she began before the words froze on her lips as she saw the intense look of something akin to fury on her chief's features.

The younger men were secretly amazed to find that *La Spinosa* seemed to be exhibiting evidence of gentler feelings. Beppe, as *Agente* Oriana Salvati would understand on further acquaintance, needed to sift through his inner

---

[27] True
[28] Seeking someone's agreement

thoughts before he could make a considered judgement. The process took an alarming fifteen seconds of deep concentration during which Oriana looked increasingly perturbed.

"Don't be sorry, *agente*," said Beppe finally. "You are right to be concerned. The answer to your question is 'yes', I believe she is alive. It is becoming increasingly obvious that she represents some risk to some person, or persons, unknown. She knows something or is threatening to expose something that would cause great embarrassment. I suspect we shall find a family link between her and this individual. Otherwise, she would have been eliminated already. Sonia…?

"Yes," said Sonia, taking this to be her cue to share with everybody present the few words which the Sleeping Beauty had uttered before slipping back into unconsciousness. "The young woman kept on talking about her uncle and how it was all his doing. She seemed scared of him. She kept on saying: "No, no, I don't want to see him again".

"So, you see, we have everything to hope for," concluded their chief. "And now *ragazzi – al lavoro!*[29] Down to business!"

Officer Remo Mastrodicasa approached his chief shyly and said: "May I have my smartphone back, *capo?*"

"Of course, Remo! Sorry, it slipped my mind. *Eccolo,*"[30] he said, fishing the phone out of his trouser pocket and handing back to its owner. "I'm sorry to tell you, Remo, that I considered it necessary to delete the photos of the girl – for security reasons." The nostalgic look that stole across

---

[29] Down to work!
[30] Here it is

Remo's face was enough to tell Beppe that his previous suspicions of this naïve young officer had been ignoble on his part. He gave the lad's arm an affectionate squeeze and said: *"Grazie mille Remo...e buon lavoro.* See if you can get somewhere with tracking down that black Audi Q7."

Whatever shortcomings 'the waiter' might have, he was adept at using the police computers, Beppe had discovered.

* * *

Beppe Stancato had been struck by the inescapable fact that the tall man with the Spanish accent had taken only a matter of hours to discover the whereabouts of the Sleeping Beauty, tucked away in an obscure unused room in their local hospital. It was as good as certain that the man in the apartment was the same as the 'doctor' who had abducted the girl again in the hospital room. Bruno Esposito had phoned Beppe at seven o'clock that morning. He had been astonished to find the room on the top floor of the hospital unoccupied when he had gone up to check on their patient.

"So you've managed to find a safer location for our Sleeping Beauty already?" asked Bruno in surprise.

Beppe had to tell his friend what had happened, apologising for not phoning him beforehand.

"So the abductor knew exactly where to find the girl," stated Bruno Esposito immediately. "That would imply he really is a doctor and connected to this hospital."

"Appunto! Precisely, Bruno!"

"Give me a few hours, Beppe. I'll make a few enquiries. It should not be hard to track down a two-metre tall, left-handed Spaniard."

They had agreed to meet up at the hospital at ten o'clock that morning.

***

Before leaving for the hospital, Beppe Stancato headed for the technical laboratory, where he had left the Spanish doctor's confiscated mobile phone in the hands of the two non-uniformed officers in charge of electronic gadgetry. Marco Pollutri and a married lady in her forties, rejoicing in the gloriously alliterate name of Bianca Bomba, greeted Beppe with a smug expression on their faces.

The two technicians had honed to perfection the act that they put on to any police officer, regardless of rank, who presented themselves in their laboratory - an act based on the confident assumption that their specialist know-how rendered them immune to dismissal in a world dominated by ever more sophisticated technology. In his native Calabria, Marco and Bianca's counterparts had usually adopted an annoyingly secretive façade – as if to assert their superiority by emphasising the presumed ignorance of ordinary policemen. *Commissario* Stancato found the *pescarese* version preferable and was happy enough to play along with their wry banter.

"Ah, there you are at last, *commissario!*" began Marco with a mischievous twinkle in his grey eyes. "We were wondering what had become of you – since you told us it was so urgent."

"I take it you've managed to winkle out something useful, you two clever people?" he began, with mild irony.

"Yes, *commissario*," piped up the equally buoyant Bianca. "Your man is very tall and he's left-handed of course."

"How did you manage to work *that* out?" asked Beppe, impressed despite himself.

Bianca Bomba smiled like a conjuror pleased with a trick she had just pulled off to perfection. It was obvious that the two technicians were enjoying themselves. He would have to indulge them for a few minutes longer.

"Finger smudges on the screen, *commissario*. Not clear enough for fingerprints, however – there are someone else's prints on top..."

"*Agente* Simone's, when he snatched the phone from him, I would think," said Beppe as if to himself.

"The owner has fingers that are too large for such a small screen and he holds the device in his right hand while he types with his left hand. He could have just had big fingers, but I guessed correctly about his height, didn't I?" added Bianca Bomba.

"So would you be able to tell me something I *didn't* know already?" asked Beppe anxious for new information.

"Oh, yes, *commissario*." Marco took up the narrative. He picked up a transparent envelope with several sheets of printed paper inside. "All the numbers he's dialled and a list of incoming calls since April, plus an enlarged set of fingerprints for you, just in case. Oh, and there are some very interesting photos that he's taken too."

"Well done, you two," said Beppe with unreserved sincerity as he held out his hand for the envelope. But obviously, the two technicians had not finished with him yet.

"We get so cut off from things, down here on our own, *commissario*," began Bianca with an expression of yearning on her face. "Can't you give us just some little hint as to what this is all about?"

Beppe sighed in resignation and told the two technicians briefly about the Sleeping Beauty. He looked at his watch. It was already twenty to ten and his doctor friend was expecting him at the hospital at ten.

"Ah," said an enlightened Marco. "I suspect that it's *her* photo on this device."

Beppe registered surprise. So, the tall Spaniard had a photo of his victim on his smart phone's camera. Interesting!

"Yes," continued Bianca. "It was taken in L'Aquila, by the way - before the earthquake. We recognised the cathedral in the background."

"It was a clever idea of your colleague to allow the man to begin his phone call before confiscating it," said Marco Pollutri. Beppe had previously told him the importance of the last dialled number. "I'm not so sure you'll be happy when I tell you the number belongs to a gentleman from Naples – going by the illustrious name of Gianluca Alfieri."

Marco handed the envelope over to Beppe Stancato in the certain knowledge that his *coup de théâtre* had struck home. Gianluca Alfieri was the *boss* of a mafia clan belonging to the notorious *Camorra.*

Beppe Stancato drove thoughtfully to the hospital and arrived there at ten past ten.

* * *

Dr Bruno Esposito was waiting for him in the entrance foyer.

"I'm sorry I'm late, Bruno," said Beppe.

"Ten minutes late for an Italian is better than a German arriving ten minutes early!" exclaimed the doctor with a dismissive shrug of his shoulders. "You look upset, Beppe. I'm not surprised. I share your sympathy for that poor girl."

"The galling aspect of this is that I intended to move her somewhere safe today. My colleague, Sonia, you know whom I mean, Bruno, had even offered to hide the girl in her own apartment. But…I left it too late." He spoke quietly with apparent calm. But Bruno understood that he was hiding his self-reproach only by exerting a great deal of will-power.

"Well, maybe I can offer you a crumb of comfort, Beppe. This 'doctor' appears to be a qualified anaesthetist working here in this hospital. He is Colombian, apparently qualified at the University of Bogotà. But, perhaps not surprisingly, he has failed to show up today. I gather that the rest of the team are more than slightly relieved. He's only been employed here for a week – on the minimum salary. Long live spending cuts! One of my female colleagues, who's an anaesthetist too, found him 'a bit sinister'.

"I don't suppose you have a name for him?" asked Beppe.

"Oh yes, I do! He claims to be called Diego Ramirez."

"What do you mean – 'claims' to be called…?"

"Well, it was strange. They told me that, during his interview, someone came in and asked him if he wanted a coffee. The person called out to him, 'Doctor Ramirez', but he acted just as if he hadn't recognised his own name. Then he looked startled and turned round to the person who had called out to him. You see where I'm going, don't you Beppe?"

Beppe Stancato *did* see. He briefly squeezed the doctor's arm and, looking preoccupied with his thoughts, took his leave.

"I suppose I had better go and have a word with the *carabinieri*. I might be needing their help at some stage."

"Keep me posted, Beppe and *in bocca al lupo*.[31] Best of luck!" added Bruno Esposito. "Oh, I nearly forgot, Beppe," said Dr Esposito in all innocence. "I stole a photo of Ramirez from his personnel records. I thought it might prove useful to you."

He received a quizzical look from the *commissario*.

"I thank you, *dottore;* very helpful of you."

* * *

An hour later, Beppe was back at his desk. He had paid his courtesy visit to the *carabinieri*. The senior officer he had spoken to had offered cooperation if it was ever needed.

"Let me know if anyone gets murdered, *commissario*," had been the *colonnello's* ironic parting words.

Beppe was assimilating the snippets of information that he had gleaned. He drew no comfort from his thoughts. A half-eaten mozzarella and tomato sandwich lay discarded in front of him. He tossed it distractedly into the rubbish bin and drank deeply from a bottle of mineral water. Shaking his head as if to clear it of negative images, he stood up purposefully and went in search of anyone from his team. He was tempted to call Sonia Leardi, who was out and about with Pippo. They had both been assigned the task of seeing if

---

[31] 'Best of luck'. Lit: In the mouth of the wolf. Not even Italians seem to know the origins of this phrase.

they could find out who owned the apartment where they had found the Sleeping Beauty.

"Estate agents, public records at the town hall and so on," he had told them. "Find out all you possibly can."

He resisted the temptation to call Sonia, realising that what he really wanted was the comfortable feeling of her presence. He needed to tell someone about the disturbing revelation that the tall Spaniard had phoned a man who bore the same name as a mafia 'boss'. Surely, there must be a mistake, he tried to convince himself. It must be a mere coincidence of names. But he knew, beneath the surface of this vain hope, there lay the one certainty about life in Italy – the mafia is involved in every walk of life and in every corner of his beautiful country to a greater or lesser extent. It was better to face up to this probability than to take refuge behind misplaced optimism.

But the doubt, which he most wanted to share with his colleague, was precise; if the anaesthetist had immediately phoned the mafia *boss,* Gianluca Alfieri, it hardly tied up with what the Sleeping Beauty had briefly talked to Sonia about from her bed in the hospital - unless the girl's uncle and Don Alfieri were one and the same person. *"Non mi quadra,"* he muttered. "It just doesn't add up."

Until his team, including Sonia, turned up again, he felt the need to do something practical. He should automatically have asked the two technicians if they could trace the whereabouts of the mobile device which apparently belonged to the *mafioso*. He went in search of the two technicians down in the basement of the police station. Frustratingly, they were not there. He looked at his mobile phone screen – he refused to wear a watch – and realised that normal human beings were all at lunch. He had to kick his heels for another thirty minutes before Marco Pollutri and Bianca Bomba strolled nonchalantly back to their laboratory.

"Sorry, *commissario,* our simple technicians' stomachs require some rudimentary form of sustenance to see us through the day. How can we help you?" said Marco with what appeared to be unfeigned willingness.

Beppe Stancato explained his earlier omission.

"Oh, that's no problem, *capo,"* replied the voluptuous Bianca with a smile. "It was our fault for not telling you. We set up the call tracing computer and I made a call to that number. We don't think it was Don Alfieri who replied – maybe just his stooge. But I kept him on the line just long enough for Marco to trace their whereabouts. It was touch and go though. Subsequently we noticed that the mobile device had been switched off – just as we thought would happen."

There was a pause in which nobody said anything. Beppe broke the silence with something resembling impatience. These two were enjoying making him work for the information he needed.

"Well...?" he asked. "What did you discover?"

"Ah sorry, *commissario.* It must be the thought of those *arrosticini* that were distracting me," replied Marco, savouring the memory of the marinated mutton kebabs which he had eaten for lunch.

"Thank you for reminding me that I have not had time for a proper lunch," said Beppe in a nostalgic voice. "Now will you two good people put me out of my misery... please!"

The technicians relented with good grace.

"It was in a place just outside L'Aquila, *commissario*. Probably in a village called Monticchio."

Beppe's eyebrows had shot up in surprise.

"But a *boss* from Naples near L'Aquila?" he said in disbelief.

"They get everywhere, *capo*," said Bianca. "Any place where they smell the sweet scent of money."

Beppe thanked the two technicians, shaking them by the hand. He left, looking pensive.

"I shall have to get someone to check up on the movements of Don Alfieri," he thought. "I just can't believe that…" But he knew that anything was possible as far as the mafia was concerned.

* * *

When he arrived back upstairs, he was agreeably surprised to find that everyone was back in the police station. His sense of foreboding was alleviated by a smile from Sonia Leardi, which he guardedly returned, aware that a number of officers were looking expectantly in his direction. She looked pleased with herself which meant that she had not had a wasted day. Pippo Cafarelli suggested they bring the meeting forward since everyone was present. Beppe Stancato nodded his approval.

The team of police officers in front of him looked at him so expectantly that he launched into a detailed account of everything that had transpired during the day. Nothing was omitted as he spoke non-stop for nearly an hour, his eyes roving from one member of the team to the next. They did not once attempt to interrupt the flow of words from their leader's lips. There were occasional nods of agreement or gasps of surprise during the narrative. Only Sonia thought how his Calabrian accent added to the aura of quiet authority that emanated from him.

"And now," concluded Beppe Stancato, "you tell us what progress you've made today, *ragazzi.*"

There was a reluctant pause before *Agente* Remo began explaining that the black Audi Q7 had been traced to an Audi concessionaire in Pescara. Officers Danilo Simone and Gino Martelli had gone to check out the details in person.

"So, does the car belong to a Diego Ramirez?" asked Beppe.

The two officers shifted in their seats.

"No, *capo,* the concessionaire assured us the driver's name was Daniel Rojas. That was the name on his passport, so it seems. But it had to be our doctor. The description of him was exact – including being left-handed. The Audi man remembered him signing his name on the documents. And the car was leased out to him, not sold. He certainly signed his name Daniel Rojas.

"That confirms what Doctor Bruno Esposito told us. Our Colombian friend has at least two sets of documents. It's remarkable how criminals who wish to go under more than one name *inevitably* choose the same initials for each name."

"By the way, *capo,*" added Danilo Simone, "the Audi agent told us that the Colombian exchanged cars this morning as soon as the place was open. He said our 'doctor' seemed to be in a big hurry. He's now driving a modest red Audi A1 – registration number AP 115 CK."

"And you won't be surprised to learn, *capo,* that he's given the address of the flat where we found the Sleeping Beauty as his official residence," added Gino Martelli.

"Well done, *ragazzi*. We'll get that car registration number circulated immediately."

It was now the turn of Sonia Leardi and Pippo Cafarelli.

"You'll find this interesting, *capo*," she began. We got lucky with the public records. That apartment belongs to a gentleman with the memorable name of Donatello Altadonna, who has an address in L'Aquila. We managed to track down the estate agent in Pescara who sold him the apartment for €102 000 about two years ago…"

"And guess what, *capo*," said Pippo taking up the narrative. "This guy has instructed the agent to put it back on the market this morning."

"He couldn't remember much about his client. But he thought he was some kind of scientist – a distinguished-looking man with wavy salt-and-pepper hair."

Beppe Stancato was frowning at some connection which had stirred in his mind. A scientist? L'Aquila? It prompted some vague but recent memory.

He closed the meeting at 18.30 hours.

"Well done, everybody," he said. "Go and get some rest as soon as you can. We shall reconvene tomorrow at 08.30." He went back to his office and sat down at his desk. That name… Altadonna. It was annoying him. He would check it out on the internet. It did not take him very long. Donatello Altadonna was a seismologist. He was a member of the High-Risk Assessment Commission who had been summoned to L'Aquila with a team of scientists to assess the likelihood of an imminent earthquake. There *was* a connection with L'Aquila. And then there was the photo of the young woman resembling their Sleeping Beauty on the

Colombian anaesthetist's smart phone, showing L'Aquila's undamaged, pre-earthquake *duomo*[32] in the background.

Beppe had been sitting at his desk for nearly an hour. He looked up and, to his astonishment, saw Sonia Leardi walking into his office. She was no longer in uniform. He suspected that his jaw had dropped slightly before he felt his mouth forming a smile.

"Come on *capo*," said Sonia. "I knew you'd still be here. Please take me to a pizzeria. I'm starving and I need some company."

* * *

It had been the first time he had seen her out of uniform. Strange, he thought, how those police trousers managed to disguise the shape of a woman's legs. And how the tight-fitting jacket seemed to crush the shape out of a woman's... Sonia was wearing jeans and a close-fitting top which was having a decidedly positive effect on his imagination. They were both hungry - and thirsty. Like him, Sonia preferred drinking red wine with her pizza, rather than beer. Beppe's mobile began ringing. It was, inevitably, his fiancée, Laura calling from 'home' in Calabria.

"Quite amazing," thought Beppe, "how women invariably sense when one is in the company of another woman. It's enough to make one believe in telepathy."

"It was my sister," he explained to Sonia as he sat down again at their table after a very brief dialogue.

---

[32] cathedral

But Sonia was looking at him quite openly with a knowing look in her eyes and a broad smile on her face. "Ah," she said. "So you have a sister, do you?"

He smiled sheepishly and said, aware that he was blushing despite himself: "Yes, in point of fact, I do have a sister called Valentina."

"Don't worry, *capo*," she said. "We all have a past life that catches up with us on occasions."

And that was it. He knew in that instant of time that coming to Abruzzo was not just a temporary stage of his life. It was Sonia's tacit assumption that his life in Calabria belonged to his past that had shaken him. They began – inevitably – to talk about the Sleeping Beauty case, as Sonia called it. His phone rang again. "Your sister again...?" asked Sonia with a malicious sparkle in her eyes.

"No," he told her, with surprise in his voice. "It's Pippo." He stayed at the table this time to take the call.

"*Capo*," he began breathlessly. "I was just watching the news on RAI 1. There's some industrial protest going on in Milano. They're all chanting and waving banners about..."

"Pippo," interrupted the *commissario*. "It's good of you to share your viewing experiences with me but..."

"Sorry, *capo*. The point is... I've just remembered where I saw our Sleeping Beauty before. She was on the TV news a few days ago – during that big student protest in L'Aquila, against those scientists who told everyone there was no risk of a major quake. She talked to a reporter, *capo*, and I remember she gave her name during the interview."

5: *A glimmer of light*

Beppe and Sonia had continued to discuss the implications of Pippo's revelation until they were the last customers left in the pizzeria. Unfortunately, Pippo had not been able to recall The Sleeping Beauty's name, but it would be a simple enough step to find out. Beppe had even ordered desserts and coffees in order to prolong their time together. Whether out of generosity or because he wished to signal to this couple - whose desire to converse seemed insatiable - that it was approaching midnight, the owner offered them a final coffee and a golden-yellow *genziana*[33] liqueur 'on the house'.

Beppe ignored his colleague's protests that she did not need walking back to her apartment. A silence descended on them as they walked along the streets of Pescara; a silence born out of the unspoken awareness that there was an untimely but irresistible bond developing between them. The silence, which lasted an eternal sixty seconds, was broken in an unexpected manner.

"Do you believe in...?" they both said simultaneously.

They laughed, embarrassed, yet recognising the significance of the spontaneous coincidence of words. They continued to walk along in silence, but now Sonia's arm was tucked discreetly under that of her *capo.* They each avoided asking the other what the end of the question would have been – for fear of breaking the intimacy that it had engendered.

Beppe watched Sonia disappear through the main entrance of her *palazzo.* She had stood on tiptoe to brush his mouth with her lips before walking away without a

---

[33] A liqueur made from the gentian flower. A speciality of Abruzzo.

backward glance, perhaps preparing herself in advance for the need to become detached once again the following morning.

Beppe, walking home, felt he was no longer alone in this town He conceived a plan to give them time together whilst still pursuing their investigation. He was often quite disturbed by his own capacity for deviousness. He was also acutely aware that, if he chose to follow this path, it would more than likely lead him away from his past life and any chance of returning to it. The realisation caused him more than a twinge of guilt, as he felt old and familiar heartstrings being tugged. Now was not the moment for self-analysis, he concluded.

* * *

Despite the lateness of the hour, a meeting was about to take place, some distance away, high up in the spectacular and unspoilt mountain town of Sulmona, some fifty kilometres to the south-east of the stricken city of L'Aquila.

Four men were sitting round a table in a darkened dining-room, which was lit by a few subdued lamps placed at strategic points around the room. They were waiting for their chief, *Professore* Donatello Altadonna, who had reluctantly agreed to drive down from L'Aquila at their behest to discuss the implications of the looming crisis in their collective lives.

The four men looked more like resistance fighters during the war, huddled in silence round the table, nervously fingering little glasses of *grappa*, waiting for the arrival of the secret police. Nobody spoke. The man whose house they were in tutted impatiently whilst looking at his watch.

"Where the hell has he got to?" Romano Di Carlo muttered to himself.

Romano Di Carlo was the only one who was not a scientist in the group. He was in charge of the Civil Protection Agency[34] for the whole of Abruzzo. The other three men were scientists who also belonged to the High-Risk Commission – Corrado Viola, Raimondo Leonti and Salvatore Manca. The three of them were highly qualified seismologists who held teaching posts in various Italian universities. Their expertise had been called upon as soon as tremors had been felt in the area of L'Aquila in the weeks before April 6th. They looked exactly like the academics they were – in their late thirties to early forties – intelligent and serious. The tension within them was apparent as they looked surreptitiously at one and another, as if to be reassured that they were not isolated in their suffering.

They stirred in their seats as they heard the sound of a car arriving in the drive outside the house, followed by the sound of a doorbell being rung impatiently. Romano's wife went to open the front door, the heels of her shoes clicking as she crossed the marble-tiled floor. There were muted greetings in the hallway before the lady of the house ushered Donatello Altadonna into the dining-room without a word.

The atmosphere changed in a trice. The chief scientist of the High-Risk Commission breezed into the room, apologising for his lateness.

---

[34] 'Agenzia per la Protezione Civile.' A nationwide organisation which can be called upon in times of natural disasters such as earthquakes and floods.

"As you can imagine, gentlemen, the roads are a bit difficult at the moment."

"You seem to be remarkably unperturbed by the turn of events, *professore*," remarked Romano Di Carlo, a note of asperity in his voice. It was the first time they had met together since their previous meeting just a few days before the earthquake.

The chief scientist sighed patiently and sat down at the head of the table. With his crop of wavy salt-and-pepper hair and a look of unruffled calm on his imposing features, he exuded an air of natural leadership within the group. He looked at each of the members of the team in turn with the hint of a reassuring smile for each of them. He understood the mixture of dread for their own futures and the deep sense of remorse which afflicted them, but he was determined not to be sucked into the morass of collective guilt which threatened to overwhelm his colleagues. Nor did he wish to put his own long-term projects into jeopardy because his colleagues seemed to be acting like condemned men waiting for the executioner to finish them off.

"I share the fears and self-doubts that you are all, quite naturally, experiencing," he began. "But we must focus on the facts of this singular tragedy, which has deeply affected the whole of Italy."

Inevitably, like a tightly coiled spring suddenly freed, his placating words released the flood of sentiments that had been bottled up inside each member of his team. It was Romano Di Carlo, whose house they were in, who uttered the first words of what would become a bitterly accusatory debate. The words of frustration were inevitably aimed at their leader as, one by one, they vented their pent-up frustrations on Professor Altadonna.

Romano DC: This 'singular tragedy' - as you euphemistically call it - was predicted by all of us present here right now, professore. We were called to the city of L'Aquila, as I am sure you remember, because there had been a series of tremors which were thought to be a precursor to a severe seismic event.

Donatello A: You said it yourself, Romano... 'thought to be a precursor...' All of us present in this room – a beautiful dining-room by the way, Romano – know how impossible it is to make accurate predictions in our line of business. Seismic events on various scales have been happening in this part of Italy for five million years and more. It is quite impossible to predict to the minute when such an event will occur – let alone its magnitude. It is in the nature of earthquakes to be unpredictable. We can only offer our considered opinion.

Corrado V: But there were very distinct signs that an earthquake was imminent, professore. Even some minor lab technician at the University of L'Aquila had warned that there was an increase in radon gas escaping into the atmosphere only weeks before...

Donatello A: Come now, Corrado! You know as well as I do that the presence of radon gas is never a 100% indication of an imminent earthquake. It is a very unreliable indicator – especially in a zone like this where there are more gaps in the Earth's surface than holes in a colander. Radon gas can escape through a worm-hole if it so wishes. Just like the reports of flashing lights during the lead-up to the...event. We just don't know enough about earthquakes yet to consider such phenomena as clear indicators.

Raimondo L: But you remember perfectly well, professore, that on the very day before this tragedy, we sat round a table in L'Aquila and came to the conclusion that a serious earthquake was a distinct probability in the near future. Just how near that future was now makes your reassuring words to the people of L'Aquila seem like callous indifference and professional incompetence. An incompetence that reflects on us all...

Romano DC: And, professore, I have to tell you quite unequivocally, that it was NOT your brief to publicly announce to the people of L'Aquila – even via the mayor of the city - that they should stay in their homes that night. It should have been MY decision as the representative of the Civil Protection Agency to make any public announcement.

Donatello A: For which I truly apologise, Romano. But I would remind you, with respect, that you were showing all the signs of a calamitous lack of decisiveness at the time. What would you have done differently, Romano? Would you have announced to the mayor that he should evacuate all the one hundred thousand inhabitants of L'Aquila within the space of one afternoon? Don't forget, there were a host of foreign students at the university too. Can you visualise the logistical chaos that would have ensued? And what if every inhabitant of L'Aquila had descended on Pescara overnight - only to be told the following day that they could return home again because nothing had happened on that particular night? The mayor had already taken the initiative of moving the primary school children to another site. He is already anxious that the funding for this decision won't be forthcoming. Imagine his dilemma if he had decided to move the whole population out of the city. What effect would that have had?

Salvatore M: Well, most of the inhabitants would have been alive today, capo. I spoke to a very angry and deeply traumatised man whom I came across by chance in a bar after the earthquake. He was attempting to drown his sorrows in liquor. On the strength of our reassurances, he had decided not to take his family to relatives in Penne that night. He lost his teenage son and daughter, as well as his own father. They were crushed to death as their house collapsed on top of them. All I could do was to offer him another drink.

The stark reality of Salvatore Manca's words coupled with the gentle, conciliatory tone of his voice brought about a momentary pause in the onslaught of words directed against Professor Donatello Altadonna. But the tightly coiled spring of anger and remorse was still too powerful to have dissipated all its force. Instead, the lull merely signalled a change in direction. It was Romano, the Civil Protection agent, who initiated the debate yet again, speaking as if his words were having trouble escaping into the open from a constricted throat.

Romano DC: And now, just as I predicted during our earlier telephone conversation, professore, there is a growing certainty that we shall have to appear in court in the immediate future. We shall be tried for gross professional negligence. I have even heard it reported that they will put us on trial for manslaughter. And this threat comes, not from

Rome, but from the people of L'Aquila. It's the brainchild of a respected local lawyer. They are looking for a scape-goat.

The other three scientists were looking expectantly at their leader to see how he would react. He shook his head sadly and his answer, when it came, was delivered with a total calm that amazed them. In the silence that had preceded his considered reply, the anxious voice of a young girl could be heard speaking in the hallway.

"Is *papà* alright, *mamma?* What are those men doing to him?"

Romano's wife could be heard uttering reassuring words to their daughter as she led the girl upstairs again. Romano's face was registering a mixture of remorse at having upset his daughter and frustration that he was unable to give full vent to his ire. There was a brief but conscious effort from the scientists to subdue the level of their voices. Finally, the chief scientist resumed what sounded like a rehearsal for his defence.

Donatello A: You said it yourself, Romano; they need their 'capro espiatorio'.[35] They have lost their loved-ones. They have lost their homes. They have lost their beautiful city - all in a matter of minutes. I do not blame them. I suspect we would have reacted in precisely the same way had we been in their shoes. But the simple fact remains that, as much as they would like it to be otherwise, we cannot be punished for an act of God, or more to the point, a violent manifestation of nature over which we have no control.

---

[35] A scapegoat

Raimondo L: But, professore, we could have prevented most of the deaths that occurred. It was you who stated publicly that, I quote: "a few minor tremors do not necessarily indicate that a major earthquake is about to occur." I suspect those words will haunt us for many years to come.

Corrado V: And how can we go about our normal professional and family lives with the threat of prosecution and even a lengthy prison sentence hanging over our heads? Just because you...

Romano DC: And I have been reliably informed, professore, that you were in Rome on the night of the tragedy attending a performance of Verdi's Aida. How fortunate for you, some might say!

Unconsciously, they were beginning to raise their voices again. Salvatore Manca came to the rescue.

Salvatore M: Just a minute, Corrado, Romano. We are all equally to blame for our act of disastrous over-cautiousness. There is nothing to be gained by pointing an accusatory finger at Donatello alone. He had every right to be in Rome – for whatever reason.

Donatello A: Thank you, Salvo. Your support is much appreciated in this time of trouble. But the others are right. In the end, it is I alone who must shoulder the blame. You must all go about your daily business as best you can and leave the worrying to me. Before we part company tonight, I would like to show you these letters of support that we have already received from various scientists and seismologists round the globe. Many of these letters state that the authorities should be concentrating on ensuring that, in future, the proper anti-seismic building techniques are more rigorously applied. Other letters stress that it should not be 'science that is on trial'. Any public prosecution of us will mean that seismologists all over the world will be reluctant to make any predictions at all, for fear of legal recriminations. No, I think you should all defend our profession as vigorously as you can. Do not give way to the temptation to beat your breasts in public. I believe that a criminal conviction is very unlikely.

After a desultory discussion round Romano Di Carlo's dining room table, the meeting began to break up. Romano himself remained seated. Only after the others had taken their leave and were heading back towards the stricken city of L'Aquila, did Donatello Altadonna make as if to get up from the table.

"Just five more minutes of your time, *professore*," said Romano with a degree of authority that had been lacking during their meeting. The timbre of his voice took Donatello by surprise and he sat down again with the first hint of anxiety on his face.

"There is one more matter we need to talk about before you go. I did not think it advisable or diplomatic to bring it up whilst the others were present," he stated ominously.

Donatello had already succeeded in reassuming his air of unshakable self-assurance.

"Oh yes, Romano? And what might this matter involve?" he said with an edge of disdain in his voice. Romano, however, was not to be unnerved, it seemed.

"I wish to talk about your niece, *professore*."

A brief flash of anger crossed Donatello's face, to be replaced by an attempt at a rueful smile.

"You seem quite obsessed by my niece, Romano. I realise she's a very attractive young woman but..."

"I have spoken to your niece at some length, *professore* - immediately after the demonstration that she was instrumental in organising. Against us, in case you hadn't realised."

Donatello Altadonna made a dismissive gesture with his hand to indicate this information was nothing new to him. He attempted to bluff his way out of the situation by putting on an act of avuncular outrage.

"How dare you permit yourself to approach my niece – a girl little more than twenty-two years old, Romano. You should know better than to..."

"Oh, believe me, she was the one who approached *me*. She was only too willing to communicate what was on her mind. I understand she is studying *giurisprudenza*.[36] I am certain she will make an excellent lawyer, *professore*."

"That is as maybe, Romano. At this moment in time, she is a hot-headed young woman full of idealistic notions of justice. You shouldn't give too much credence to what she says. I had strong words with her after that demonstration. Fortunately, I dissuaded her from pursuing her political activities in the future.

"That is strange, *professore*, because she seemed quite determined to give an interview on *TV-Tavo*[37] the following day. She told me it was already arranged with a reporter from our local television station."

---

[36] Law
[37] A made-up name for the local TV station. The River Tavo is just north of Pescara

"Yes, I know. I managed to persuade her not to go ahead with it."

"She did not seem to me to be the sort of girl to be put off so easily. She was planning on approaching *Rai Uno*[38] later on. Where is she at the moment, by the way, *professore?*"

"She has gone back to Orvieto to be with her parents – my brother and sister-in-law. She told me she needed to spend some time at home - to get over the shock, you understand. Don't worry. I can assure you that she will not be putting us all in an embarrassing position, Romano. I have her solemn word that..."

"You are missing the point, *professore*. She was less concerned about the High-Risk Commission's shortcomings. She talked to me about something far more sinister."

"Well, I am happy that my niece considered you sufficiently trustworthy to confide her misguided suspicions to you, Romano. But I repeat, she is a passionate believer in her notions of justice. Whatever else she might have told you should really be taken with a pinch of salt. Now Romano, it really is very late..."

"She told me, *professore,* that she had discovered you had some kind of deal set up with a certain *uomo d'onore*[39] called Gianluca Alfieri. Something to do with rebuilding contracts..."

Donatello Altadonna's anger did not need to be feigned. His face had turned a livid puce colour as his voice dropped to a menacing whisper.

"Your disloyalty and impertinence to me have been noted, Romano. I will try my very best to forget the absurd

---

[38] Channel 1 on the national TV broadcaster RAI = Radio Audizioni Italiane
[39] 'A man of Honour' as mafia bosses call themselvesRisk

accusation you just made. But I fear our relationship will never be the same again from this point onwards. You may no longer count on my whole-hearted support."

He strode angrily out of the front door without acknowledging the presence of Romano's wife. Husband and wife stood hand in hand in the hallway. They heard Donatello's car being revved hard as he shot across the gravelled driveway out into the night.

"What in heaven's name did you say to him, *amore?*" asked Romano's wife fearfully.

"Whatever it was, it obviously struck a raw nerve, Mariangela," said Romano, whose face had turned very pale.

* * *

Beppe Stancato was back at his desk early the following morning. He was looking pensive as he mapped out in his mind what he would be telling his team at their 8.30 morning briefing. There had been an obscure memory niggling in the back of his mind most of the night - which had been spent on his boat, whence he had headed on leaving Sonia. The 'niggle' was something that Officer Gino Martelli had said during the previous day's meeting. He had tried for hours to recall Gino's words, but they had eluded him.

He firmly believed that the gentle rocking of the waves was far more conducive to thought than lying on a bed in his poky little apartment. The bed in his boat was hard but comforting to his back. When opened up, the bed filled most of the cabin space. He had slept for little more than a couple of hours and was drawing heavily on his reserves of energy, supplemented by a jam-filled *cornetto* and a series of espresso coffees. But now his mind was lucid and he wanted to get on with the business in hand. He was just wishing that he had assembled his team for eight o'clock, when Officer Giacomo D'Amico walked into his office and saluted smartly.

"We're all here, *capo,* should you wish to get started a bit earlier."

Beppe looked at Giacomo gratefully. His team were worth their weight in gold, he reckoned.

Beppe flashed a brief smile of appreciation which encompassed all of the assembled police officers. He noticed that Sonia was dressed smartly in civvies as he had suggested to her over the phone earlier that morning. As he entered the briefing room, Giacomo D'Amico had obviously just asked her why she was not in uniform. Beppe had caught her shrugging her shoulders with a look that said "Don't ask me!" before the group fell into an expectant silence.

Before his arrival, everyone present had been talking or privately wondering what the next step in their search for the Sleeping Beauty could possibly be. Beppe was painfully aware to what extent his team relied on him to know what direction the investigation should take. It was quite daunting. As always on such occasions, he was suffering from something akin to stage fright. If anything, the frank expression of optimistic confidence on Sonia's face made matters worse – an alarming indication that he did not want to let her down. He visibly shook himself free of these emotions as he began talking, as if to dispel the mists of self-doubt.

"I've been turning over in my mind something that one of you said yesterday," Beppe began. "It took me most of the night to identify what it was. Excuse me all of you if I seem a bit weary today..."

There were polite titters as his team made the inevitable connection with the word 'weary' and their chief's surname. He smiled almost shyly in acknowledgement of his unintended slip of the tongue. "I slept for about two hours – on my boat," he added by way of explanation. "As soon as I woke up, though, I remembered what the connection was. It was something *you* said to me Gino..."

Gino Martelli felt the eyes of everyone upon him. He squirmed uncomfortably in his seat.

"*Me* chief?"

"You might – albeit unintentionally – have set us off on the right track, Gino. When you told us about the Colombian doctor – whatever his name really is – you said: 'You won't be surprised to know that...' You went on to tell us that he had given the address of the flat in Pescara where we found the drugged girl – sorry, our Sleeping Beauty."

Everyone present nodded without actually understanding what their chief was getting at.

"I couldn't work out why your words stuck in my mind, Gino. Then I realised that I *was,* in point of fact, *very* surprised that he had given that particular address. Do you see what I'm getting at?"

They didn't, but they were all thinking very hard. After a pause that seemed endless but was, in reality, no more than six or seven seconds, the nervous voice of Remo Mastrodicasa, the ex-waiter, was heard. As usual, he had remained standing unobtrusively behind everyone else, as if by remaining upright, he could make a quicker getaway when the time came. Everybody swivelled round to look at him. One or two of the younger officers had the hint of a smirk on their face, more out of habit than anything else. Remo, inevitably, had turned a bright red, but he stammered out the words as best he could. The smirks soon vanished to be replaced by a look of covert admiration.

"You think there must be a link between the Colombian anaesthetist, the scientist who owns the flat, *and* Don Alfieri, the mafia boss, don't you, *capo?*"

The subdued applause that followed was born out of a touch of envy as much as by the unexpected revelation that Remo had more nous about him than they had hitherto given him credit for. The team had just made the discovery that their 'waiter' was not so dumb after all. To Beppe Stancato, the revelation did not altogether come as a surprise.

"*Bravissimo,* Remo," said Beppe quietly. "That is precisely the conclusion I came to. By implication, our Sleeping Beauty must also fit into this triangle too. Last night, round about 11 o'clock, Pippo phoned me with another vital piece of information...Pippo?" said Beppe by way of invitation to his young colleague.

"I remembered seeing the girl on the TV some nights ago – last week in fact. She was taking part in the demonstration in L'Aquila against the High-Risk Commission's failure to tell everyone the earthquake was imminent. She gave an interview to a reporter on our local television station, you know, *TV-Tavo*. She said she had something shocking to reveal and was promised a studio interview the following day. Her name had slipped my mind, I'm sorry to say."

"Well done, Pippo. You should easily be able to track her down through the TV station."

It was Pippo Cafarelli's moment of triumph and he had been savouring it.

"I said it *had* slipped my mind, *capo*. I spoke to a girl I know who works for *TV-Tavo* just before I came in this morning," he added smugly. "I can tell you all that our Sleeping Beauty's name is Serena Vacri."

6: *The unconvincing seismologist*

The whole team broke into a round of spontaneous applause at Pippo's announcement, accompanied by cries of *'Bravo, Pippo'*. There were smiles of pleasure on the faces of nearly everyone present. It was as if, by assigning a name to the Sleeping Beauty, she had been brought one step nearer to salvation. Their *sostituto commissario* was applauding alongside his team but he was not smiling. He could not help but think that Remo Mastrodicasa's contribution to the proceedings had been more deserving of such public acclaim. But theirs was an understandable reaction, he had to admit. He had no wish to diminish the impact of Pippo's discovery.

"And now, we have to roll up our sleeves, *ragazzi*," said Beppe, bringing his team back down to earth. "We still have a long way to go."

He spent the next fifteen minutes designating tasks to everyone with an air of self-assurance that he did not altogether feel. They were still groping in the dark.

"Pippo, I want you to go to the TV station in person and see if anyone has gleaned any information as to what Serena Vacri was going to reveal. You never know. Try and talk to the reporter who interviewed her during the demonstration in L'Aquila. She might well have said something off the record. If that doesn't take you too long, come back and get in touch with the national channel, Rai Uno. You said something about her intending to give them an interview too – although I somehow doubt she had enough time to contact the Rai before her abduction. When you've done that, you can help the others."

As things turned out, Pippo's visit to the local TV station was overtaken by events.

"Remo, I want you to find out all you can about the people on the High-Risk Commission – you can concentrate on the one who belongs to the Civil Protection Agency.

Giacomo, get your little team working on the scientists. I want to know their names, where they live, where they work and where they are staying at the moment. Above all, find out about Donatello Altadonna's background, his family connections. He is, I am certain, crucial to this investigation.

Finally, Gino and Danilo, I'm giving you the pleasant task of finding out all you can about Don Gianluca Alfieri – our mafia connection. The call that the Colombian doctor made just before you confiscated his mobile phone was to a village just outside L'Aquila. The village is called Monticchio. It is just possible that our friend from Naples has a hideout there. See what you can discover. Phone up the police in Naples – they should know better than us what the movements of the *Camorra* are, even beyond the confines of Campania. If our surmise is correct, we should find all the elements of this investigation under one roof so to speak - hopefully, including our Sleeping Beauty, Serena Vacri. I am still convinced that she must be alive – especially since there seems to be a link between Altadonna and the *mafioso*.

Now if this all seems like inaction to you, don't worry. After today, we should all be out in the field. Be ready to do a lot of travelling out towards L'Aquila – or what is left of it. Any questions…?"

"Yes, *capo*," piped up Oriana Salvati. "May we ask what *you* will be doing today?"

"Ah yes. *Agente* Leardi and myself are hoping to pay Professor Altadonna a visit in L'Aquila, where that gentleman is living according to his estate agent. We will present ourselves as a couple in search of an apartment."

"Shouldn't be too hard to fake," said Oriana Salvati. The words had just come out of her mouth quite spontaneously. There was a gasp of astonishment from the other officers, amazed that *La Spinosa* had dared to exercise her sharp tongue on their leader. Sonia Leardi had her head down to conceal her blushes - which had begun when Beppe had revealed his plan for them to go to L'Aquila together.

Oriana Salvati, realising she might have committed a *faux pas* of career-threatening proportions was looking horrified.

"I'm so sorry, *capo*," stammered Oriana. "I didn't mean... It's just that you two seem to work so well together, but I..." Her voice tailed off in emotional confusion.

Beppe realised in that instant that the rapport between himself and Sonia must be more apparent to everyone than he had supposed. He would have to engineer a quick cover-up if he wanted to throw the officers in his team off the scent. He considered it important to maintain an air of professional impartiality.

"Ah, yes *Agente* Salvati," Beppe began without a hint of a change of expression on his face. "I almost forgot to tell you. I have a special assignment for you. You are coming with *Agente* Leardi and myself to L'Aquila. I'll explain what I want you to do on the way."

"You would make a very good poker player, *capo*," commented the older officer, Giacomo D'Amico amicably. His comment produced a burst of laughter from the team and a rueful grin from Beppe in acknowledgement of his officer's back-handed compliment.

"Thank you, Giacomo. I should put it to the test one day. Now, *ragazzi,* let's get started. The success of this operation depends on what we find out today."

* * *

The first stop was at Donatello Altadonna's estate agent; 'to establish our credentials', explained Beppe to Sonia. They left Oriana Salvati behind to do some research with the others, telling her to be ready by ten o'clock for her ride to L'Aquila.

On the way to the estate agency – imaginatively called *Case da Sogno,* Dream Houses – Beppe apologised to Sonia for his botched attempt at engineering an occasion for them to be together.

"If only to be able to talk freely during the drive up to L'Aquila," he explained.

"It was a good plan, *capo,*" she said. She had taken the unilateral decision to call Beppe 'chief' when on duty. "Otherwise, I shall slip up in public," she had clarified.

"Taking Oriana with us was the only way out I could think of on the spur of the moment."

"That's fine. It will do her good to get out of the police station. We shall have plenty of time to rectify the situation when all this is over," replied Sonia quietly. "By the way, what are you going to do with Oriana in L'Aquila?"

"Send her to the University – or what bits of it are still standing – to find out all she can about the Sleeping Beauty. I mean, Serena Vacri. I am very curious as to why she has not been reported missing by her parents. Normally, a missing girl would find her way on to the national television in no time at all."

"Yes, that is unusual," agreed Sonia. "Obviously, her parents must be unaware that she has disappeared."

They had arrived outside the offices of *Case da Sogno*. As they walked in, Sonia linked arms with Beppe with a broad grin on her face.

"Just for the sake of realism," she explained.

The estate agent introduced himself as Andrea Cataldo. Like so many young men and women in this profession, he was already sizing up this couple to assess whether he would be able to increase the monthly rent by €100 or, in the case of a potential sale, whether the asking price would be accepted without bargaining. "A junior vulture," thought Beppe.

"I phoned you earlier to enquire about the apartment along the seafront," began Beppe.

"*Sì, signor...?*" began the estate agent, who had forgotten the surname of the person who had called him a little after eight that morning.

"Filetto, and this is my partner, *Signorina* Bellisario," Beppe improvised.

"Like the American TV film producer," said the estate agent trying to impress the lady with the breadth of his general knowledge.

"My grandfather," lied Sonia with a smile that was as forced as she could make it. She had taken an instant dislike to this individual. She was not enamoured of estate agents at the best of times.

Beppe and Sonia had had to agree to go and see the flat in question. Sonia was praying fervently that the 'Little Nun' would not appear as soon as she heard people outside her door. Sonia did not want to be recognised during this play-acting scene for the estate agent's benefit.

They made intelligent noises of approval about the newly fitted, modern kitchen and the luxurious tiled bathrooms. It occurred to Sonia that Beppe might genuinely be interested in this apartment for himself. It might explain why he was managing to sound so convincing in response to the estate agent's sycophantic platitudes. She would ask him when they were on their way back to the police headquarters.

"I believe you mentioned that the owner might even be interested in selling this property," said Beppe.

"Yes, that is definitely a possibility, *Signor* Filetto."

As soon afterwards as he dared without being too obvious, the estate agent asked:

"Would it be indiscreet, *signori,* to enquire what your professions are?"

"Yes, it would…" Sonia was on the point of replying bluntly. She was halted in her tracks by a stern look from her *capo.*

"We work together for the Provincial Tax Office in L'Aquila," lied Beppe smoothly.

"Oh!" said the estate agent, instantly abandoning any hopes he had entertained of making tax-avoiding deals. At least, they would be in receipt of a reliable state income.

Back in the agency, Beppe skilfully managed to extract the address out of the estate agent.

"What did you say the owner's name was? Belladonna?"

"No, Altadonna. He lives in L'Aquila – at least for now."

"We will go and visit him, *signore*. Don't be concerned. I can assure you we would not dream of making a deal behind your back. But, since he lives in L'Aquila too, we would feel more comfortable knowing what kind of man we shall be dealing with. Please make a phone call to this *Signor* Altadonna to arrange for us to see him. Shall we say at midday? I am sure he too would like to meet the people who may want to rent, or even buy, his apartment in Pescara."

The estate agent was obviously reluctant to take the risk of allowing potential buyers to visit his client, without getting them to sign the standard contractual agreement that would protect him from the couple making a private deal with his client.

Beppe was secretly fingering his police ID document, hoping that he would not be forced to reveal his hand. But the estate agent felt under some inexplicable pressure; there was something disconcerting about the manner in which this client was staring at him. This 'tax inspector' succeeded in giving the impression that he was aware of every shady aspect of his life as an estate agent, which could be used against him if he did not comply with the request. In the end he made the phone call.

"*Professore* Altadonna will see you at 2 o'clock at his home," said the estate agent. "Would that be convenient for you?"

* * *

"Why couldn't we just have looked up Altadonna's address, *capo*? We could have avoided having dealings with that obnoxious little estate agent," asked Sonia as they were getting into their car.

"Simple," replied Beppe, "I don't want to alert him that we are police officers. This way Altadonna will be completely off his guard."

"Clever, *capo*. Good thinking," she said in admiration as they drove off. "I reckon you would quite like to live in that apartment, wouldn't you?"

Beppe nodded. "Was it that obvious, Sonia? I seem to be overestimating my ability to conceal my true intentions these days."

"I think the people whom you work with are beginning to suss you out, Beppe… sorry, *capo*. And it is a lovely, light and spacious apartment."

"I can see my boat from the window," he added nostalgically.

"Ah, your boat! Of course!" said Sonia quietly. She looked at him and smiled. "Yes, one day soon, I would like to show you my boat," he said, having read the clear message on her face.

"By the way, what were you going to say after we left the pizzeria? You remember… when we both said, 'Do you believe in…?' at the same moment.

"No, you write down on a piece of paper the word *you* were about to say. *Then* I'll tell you."

She took a pencil and a note-pad out of her handbag and scribbled down a word.

"Now, tell me," she said holding her breath.

"Telepathy," said Beppe.

Sonia showed him the notebook, grinning triumphantly.

"Let's go and pick up Oriana," sighed Beppe, for whom this revelation provided an all too inviting glimpse into his future.

* * *

The three police officers set out on the road to L'Aquila just before midday. The ride would take well under two hours. There was one positive aspect of having a uniformed Oriana Salvati in the back of the car, thought Beppe; her presence served to keep their minds focussed on the task in hand. Sonia was driving her Lancia Ypsilon with Beppe and Oriana as passengers.

"I know the roads to L'Aquila, *capo*. We'll get there quicker if I drive."

At one point, Oriana began to apologise for her *faux pas* earlier on in the day. Since her words were greeted by a stony silence, she had the sense not to continue. Instead, she asked her chief what it was she was expected to do when they reached L'Aquila.

By way of response, Beppe handed her a copy of the photo of Serena Vacri which they had extracted from the Colombian anaesthetist's cell phone.

"We are going to drop you off at the University – the admin building is still just about intact, I understand. I want you to find out all you can about where Serena's home is, Oriana. Invent some pretext for asking questions but take great care not to imply she is missing. If you have time afterwards, try and find any of the remaining students who she hung out with to see if you can glean any information about her. Find out what she was intending to tell the local

TV station, if you can. Sonia will phone you when we've finished – but that won't be until three o'clock, I imagine.

By the secret smile on Oriana's face, Beppe, glancing at her in the rear-view mirror, understood that Sonia had been correct in her supposition; Oriana was delighted to have been entrusted with a useful assignment at last, without having to put up barriers between herself and her male colleagues.

"*Grazie, capo,*" she said as if to herself a minute or two after Beppe had handed her the photo. She felt the emotional need to re-attempt an apology for her earlier gaffe but managed to swallow the words before they - and their consequences - could escape into the public domain.

Once the car began climbing upwards towards L'Aquila, Beppe became increasingly overawed by the mountain scenery, so different to the rugged slopes of his native Calabria.

"It's all so green!" he exclaimed. "And everywhere seems quite deserted after being in Pescara."

"Yes, *capo,*" said Sonia. "Abruzzo is the greenest and lushest region in Italy with more National Parks than any other part of our country."

"What's the population of Abruzzo?" asked Beppe. "Do either of you know?"

Sonia shook her head. It was Oriana who supplied the answer.

"We Abruzzesi are a rare breed, *capo*. There are only 1.3 million inhabitants in the whole of Abruzzo – and most of us live squashed between the coast and the foothills of the mountains. Even more so now - since half the population of L'Aquila have had to come and join us."

They were mentally prepared for the fact that they were heading for an earthquake zone. But nothing prepared them for the scenes of desolation that greeted them as they drove into the outskirts of the town itself. It resembled a war zone. The few inhabitants out and about were picking their way through the rubble of collapsed buildings. Presumably, they were looking for shops still open where they could buy food to stay alive. Beppe and company were stopped from driving any further by a couple of uniformed police who looked with surprise at the occupants of the car, which included one young uniformed police woman who was looking at them challengingly.

Beppe briefly explained their business in the city. It turned out that Donatello Altadonna's street was not that far from the university building.

"One of us will accompany you, *commissario*," said the officer in charge, impressed by his discovery that this unassuming looking man in the front passenger seat was waving a police inspector's ID badge under his nose.

"What did you think, officers?" said Oriana sharply, "that I had arrested a couple of escapees all by myself?"

The young officer, who got into the back seat of their car and guided them through the stricken town, looked warily at the dark-skinned beauty sitting next to him, her hair tucked tightly under her kepi.

"It's alright, officer," said Sonia smiling reassuringly. "She only attacks police officers when seriously provoked."

The car pulled up outside the university admin building. It looked shaken but was more or less intact. The officer who had accompanied them pointed out the street where the scientist lived.

"*Signorina,*" he suggested tentatively to Oriana, "would you like me to accompany you?"

There was a stony silence.

"*Dai,* Oriana!" said Beppe stepping in quickly. "It might be a very good idea to have a local officer with you. You can do all the talking."

To Sonia and Beppe's surprise, Oriana Salvati broke into a smile and thanked the officer graciously. They watched the retreating figures disappear behind the massive wooden entrance doors. "She's actually talking to him!" said Sonia in mock astonishment.

* * *

"This is the street," said Beppe, after they had been walking for little more than a minute. They had both been struck by the havoc caused by the earthquake, especially when they had walked in front of what had been a fashion boutique. The window panes had been shattered and shards of glass littered the display area. Two denuded mannequins stood in petrified shock, slender plastic fingers pointing in mock horror at the scene beyond the window frames. A desultory bar was open but deserted except for a couple of old-timers sitting speechless at one of the metal tables. The owner served Beppe and Sonia a coffee like an automaton, going through the motions of tamping down the coffee and operating the giant *Gaggia* coffee machine out of sheer habit.

Now they were standing in front of the entrance to an apartment block. Beppe looked at his watch. It was three minutes past two. He found the button marked 'Altadonna' and pushed it briefly. Sonia put her arm through Beppe's.

"Well, we *are* supposed to be a couple!" she reiterated with a radiant smile and mischievous eyes. "We should act the part."

"I'm sure young Oriana would be delighted, if she was here," said Beppe, giving her arm a gentle squeeze of affection.

On the instructions of the authoritative male voice that bid them come up, they climbed the stairs to the second floor. Professor Donatello Altadonna led them into the spacious lounge and they sat down side by side trying to look like a shy couple venturing into unknown territory. It was difficult to keep a straight face when their quarry picked up a small silver bell which tinkled daintily in the vast room. A pleasant-looking girl in her twenties, dressed as a maid, came in deferentially and greeted them with a subdued *'Buongiorno, signori'*. Although she had addressed them both, she was looking intently at Sonia.

"Bring us some coffee, Marta, and some little biscuits," he ordered, without saying 'please'.

Sonia found herself with a forced smile on her lips, which was necessary to prevent herself laughing out loud at this elaborate, lordly performance, apparently designed to impress such lowly mortals as themselves.

"So, I understand from my estate agent that you are interested in my apartment in Pescara," began the scientist.

Sonia nodded, biting her tongue. Beppe had instantly understood the nature of the man whose house they were in - an arrogant man, too full of his own importance. He had often come across this type of individual. He would take great delight in undermining Altadonna's presumptuous self-assurance.

"*Sì, professore,* we are very interested."

"Did my estate agent give you a price?"

"No, he didn't," lied Beppe. "He said he would leave it to you to discuss the price with us."

"The rent will be in the region of €650 per month, *signori*."

"Lie number one," thought Beppe. The estate agent had intimated the rent would be in the region of €550, judging by what the previous tenant had been paying. Beppe was beginning to enjoy himself.

"How long would you be looking to live there, *signori*?" asked Altadonna smiling with all the charm he could muster.

"Oh, at least a year, *professore*. We are moving to Pescara because of our work. We shall eventually be looking for an apartment to purchase."

Beppe was waiting to be asked what his job was. Altadonna did not ask the question at all. It was inevitably an indirect way of finding out how much the tenant or purchaser could afford, before one adjusted the price accordingly. The fact that he did not ask the question was a sure sign the 'obnoxious little estate agent' had phoned him again after they had left.

"I may be able to help you there too, *Signor* Filetto," said the scientist with the sincerest of smiles.

Beppe looked suitably pleased. Sonia was beginning to wonder whether her chief had forgotten the reason for their visit. She shifted imperceptibly on the sofa. Sonia's 'partner' laid a hand gently on her knee for an instant as if to reassure her. Unfortunately, Sonia was so taken aback that she started as if she had received a mild electric shock. To cover that brief second of astonishment at the intimacy of the gesture, she found herself grinning insanely in the scientist's direction, placing her hand on Beppe's thigh as if the gesture was intended to be reciprocal – which it was, in point of fact, she realised.

Beppe carried on, seemingly unperturbed by the little drama that had been enacted in those few brief seconds. Beppe's next words alerted her immediately to what her *capo* was up to. She listened with growing admiration to his skilful interrogation tactics.

"But how soon would we be able to move in, *professore?*"

"Straight away, *Signor* Filetto, once the formalities have been addressed."

Sonia was still tempted to giggle at the absurd surname that her *capo* had landed himself with. 'Filet of beef or filet of chicken?' she wondered. But an instant later, she was watching carefully to detect any unconscious reaction on the part of Donatello Altadonna to Beppe's subtle line of questioning.

"Oh, I see," said Beppe with mock surprise. "I was under the impression that you already had someone staying there – your daughter, I was told…"

It was a shot in the dark, but it was instantly apparent that it had found its mark. For a brief second, a flash of something akin to panic crossed his face. His eyes darted wildly round the room as if he was fearful that there might be another presence there overhearing the conversation. It confirmed one of Beppe's deepest suspicions. The scientist recovered his aplomb with remarkable speed. If Beppe and Sonia had not been observing him constantly, they would have missed the brief slipping of the mask. The genial smile was back on Altadonna's face in an instant.

"Oh, that was my niece, *dottore.*" Altadonna had unconsciously upgraded his social perception of Beppe, addressing him as *dottore* instead of plain *signore;* a clear indication of an unconscious desire to placate this inscrutable man.

"She was only there for a couple of nights before she went back home to her parents. Before that, there was a doctor from the hospital staying there."

An interesting psychological phenomenon, considered Beppe - people who are concealing the truth always take refuge in half-truths to make their lie more convincing. He had observed it countless times during the course of investigations in Calabria.

"How did you know...?" Altadonna began, but decided it would be better not to complicate the issue. He stood up and asked if he could be excused for a second. He left the room and could clearly be heard ordering the maid to go and collect the tray.

In a trice, Sonia had a pen and notebook in her hand and was scribbling something on the little piece of paper. Beppe looked at her quizzically but she was entirely focussed on what she was doing. Sonia slipped the note under a coffee cup. It was a gesture which the girl could not fail to spot. To Beppe's surprise, the girl gave Sonia a brief complicit smile. A look of gratitude shone momentarily in her eyes as she whisked the tray out of the room. The scientist reappeared, his composure and aloofness firmly back in place. He shook Beppe by the hand and addressed him as *'signore'* again as he dismissed them at the door leading on to the landing.

"*Buona fortuna!*"[40] he said to their descending figures. "My estate agent will arrange everything if you decide to go ahead."

Beppe took Sonia's hand as they descended the stairway. He smiled a broad smile in her direction and put a warning index finger over his lips to ensure that she did not let off steam too soon.

* * *

"I thought you were never going to get to the point, *capo!*" said Sonia explosively as soon as they were safely back inside the car. "Talk about beating round the bush!"

"Obviously, you have never been fishing, *mia cara!*[41] You learn to make one move at a time until the moment when you can stop playing the fish's game and begin to reel him in."

"I would just love to go fishing one day," added Sonia, irrelevantly, in a nostalgic voice.

"And so you shall, Sonia, I promise."

He had understood immediately that a boat ride out to sea was uppermost in her mind.

"What did you make of our *professore*?" asked Sonia.

"He was making a valiant attempt at disguising his guilt. He was lying about almost everything, as I am sure you noticed."

"But, excuse me, *capo*. We didn't really learn anything we didn't already know… did we?"

---

[40] Good luck
[41] My dear

Beppe smiled that slow, lopsided smile that always appeared when he had made some devious deduction from scant empirical evidence.

"Oh, I know for certain that he is involved in some way with our *mafioso* friend, Don Alfieri. We can now follow up that lead with complete confidence."

"How can you possibly know that?" asked Sonia.

"I've seen that panicky look of terror on countless seemingly honest faces during my time in Calabria. It's an instinctive reaction to cast your eyes around the room when your most deep-rooted fear is that a mafia informer may be lurking beyond your line of vision."

Sonia was thoughtful for a minute before she said:

"One up for your experience, *capo* - you are absolutely right, of course. I didn't like him at all..." she added.

"He was covering up an awful lot of guilt. He is very vulnerable. Don't forget he has the public disgrace to contend with – as well as a possible trial for manslaughter."

"But if we pull him in for questioning, the wrong people might get to know. We would be putting Serena Vacri's life in great danger."

"Precisely, Sonia."

Sonia was waiting for Beppe to ask her the obvious question. Instead, he merely looked at her with a quizzical eyebrow raised.

"Aren't you glad you brought a woman along with you, *capo?*" she said with a provocative glint in her eyes.

"Well...? said Beppe, wishing to force her to reveal what he knew she was secretly dying to tell him.

"*Bastardo!*" she said with feeling.

"Alright, Sonia. I was truly impressed! How did you know Marta wanted to talk to us?"

"As soon as she came into the room, I caught the look of desperation in her eyes. She was pleading with me silently. Only a woman would have read the signals. Maybe she intuited that we were not whom we claimed to be."

"But what could a servant girl such as Marta know about all this?" asked Beppe, genuinely puzzled.

"If Serena Vacri is Altadonna's niece..."

"...she must have been to the house dozens of times – or even lived there. She's the same age as Marta. Of course, she must have told her something! Maybe, they're friends. Marta must be from a local family."

"Precisely, Beppe," said Sonia, imitating his previous tone of voice.

Beppe conveniently forgot where they were, leant over and kissed Sonia on the mouth. He had a sudden vision of Police Officer Oriana Salvati, hands on hips with professional indignation, peering at them through the car window. He broke away from Sonia with a sigh.

"*Brava*, Sonia. I couldn't have done it without you. Now could you please give Oriana a ring to see if she's ready to be picked up?"

Beppe could hear Oriana's voice without being able to make out her words. She was talking animatedly to Sonia, who was smiling.

"Alright, Oriana, let's say in thirty minutes time outside the University where we dropped you off. *Ciao. A presto.*"

"I take it she is not ready to rejoin us just yet?"

"She was telling me that 'Giovanni' – the young policeman – is taking her to the campsite outside the city.

You know – for those who didn't want to leave L'Aquila or haven't got relatives to go to."

"So our Oriana is on a sight-seeing tour?"

"No, Beppe. Apparently, they are going to find a student who hung around with Serena Vacri. She sounded very pleased with herself."

"I have a presentiment that some of her pleasure comes from having discovered Giovanni." Sonia nodded in agreement.

"But what are we going to do for half an hour, Beppe?"

"I think we ought to pay a courtesy call to the local police. I am pretty sure we are going to need their help before long."

Sonia Leardi had hoped her chief was going to suggest finding somewhere to eat. But she knew that Beppe was different to almost any other Italian she knew in that he seemed to be able to ignore signals from his stomach entirely when he was in the middle of an investigation – even at lunchtime, which had been over a couple of hours ago. She sighed audibly. Beppe misconstrued the sigh.

"Don't worry. It won't take long, Sonia. Then we'll be off home. I need to have a chat with the *Questore* as soon as we return to bring him up to date and enlist his aid in setting up phone taps on Altadonna. For a chief of police, he seemed to me to be quite an amenable type on the few occasions I have met him."

"You're indefatigable, Beppe Stancato!" exclaimed Sonia resignedly.

7: One step forward...

The three police officers were speeding back towards Pescara along the route which would take them past Penne and Loreto Aprutino.

"There's usually less traffic on this road, *capo*," explained Sonia.

They had picked up Oriana at the appointed time. She had seemed very reluctant to drag herself away from *Agente* Giovanni Palena. It had required a discreet beep on the Lancia Ypsilon's horn to recall her to the present time. To Sonia and Beppe's surprise, Oriana had given her companion an affectionate *bacio* on each cheek before running over to the waiting car. She looked distinctly pleased with herself.

"I could arrange a transfer if you like," Beppe had remarked drily. Oriana had smiled radiantly before replying:

"I'm happy where I am for now, *capo*."

On the way back to Pescara, Beppe found himself assailed by both women begging him to let them stop to eat something. Oriana even tried blackmailing Beppe by saying she could not possibly impart any information she had gleaned about the Sleeping Beauty until she had something solid in her stomach.

"There won't be anywhere open at this hour, *ragazze*," Beppe pointed out. "It's siesta time."

"We are about to pass a restaurant called *La Bilancia*[42] on the left, which is owned by my uncle," stated Oriana triumphantly. "He'll give us something to eat if I ask him nicely."

---

[42] 'The Scales' This is a real-life restaurant outside Loreto Aprutino on the road from Pescara to Penne. It is at least as good as it sounds.

Beppe reluctantly gave way to the overwhelming odds. He suspected there had been a degree of collusion between the two women. Maybe they had anticipated being hungry at some point and knew from experience that their chief could easily survive without food throughout lunchtime and beyond. The choice of their home-coming route might well have been planned in advance. He had to admire their tactical skills.

"Alright *ragazze,* but no more than a thirty-minute stop. Agreed? We have a severe case of abduction to resolve should it have slipped your minds."

"It won't be solved at all if our brain cells are dying off!" retorted Oriana with a brief return to her usual acerbic tone.

Her chief turned round to look at her severely but she fancied his eyes were smiling.

"Mi scusi, capo," she said with a grin. "I always get a bit ratty when I'm hungry."

"Then you should definitely keep eating, Oriana," said Beppe.

* * *

The restaurant was big enough to seat a hundred diners and seemed vast with all the empty tables. It was a traditional restaurant, with a glowing wood fire in a wide stone fireplace behind the counter, where the grilled meat dishes were cooked. Rows of hams and salami hung on hooks above the food counter.

Oriana's uncle, it transpired, was fast asleep. It was left to the head waiter, Lorenzo, who greeted Oriana with suitably avuncular pleasure, to coax a bit of late food out of the kitchens. To their surprise, just behind the central wine rack, there was still a family, with two young children, at one of the tables, chatting and laughing.

"Hotel guests," explained Lorenzo. He was introduced to Sonia and Beppe by a proud Oriana as 'my new colleagues'.

"This is *Commissario* Stancato," she said when it was Beppe's turn to be introduced.

The importance of Beppe's rank produced three plates of something which Beppe, from Calabria, looked at suspiciously – unable to come to terms with the unusual combination of ingredients. Lorenzo explained that it was a local dish consisting of lamb stewed in rosemary and white wine and garnished with scrambled eggs. After tasting a few mouthfuls, Beppe vowed it would not be long before he was eating it again.

"It's called *Agnello Cacio e uova*,"[43] Lorenzo informed him.

"You see, *capo*, what a lot Abruzzo has to offer you," said Sonia slyly.

Oriana, her pangs of hunger diminished, needed little encouragement to relate what had happened to her while her colleagues had been with Donatello Altadonna. To Beppe's growing surprise, Oriana's account tied up very neatly with what they themselves had discovered. Oriana had opened up and neither Beppe nor Sonia attempted to stop the flow of her enthusiastic narrative:

It really helped having Giovanni with me, capo, you were quite right. I got information about Serena Vacri without any trouble at all. She comes from Orvieto where she lives with

---

[43] A traditional dish from Abruzzo. See recipes on line and in cookery books by Valentina Harris.

her mum – I've got the details here. There was no mention of her father, so I can't tell you whether they're divorced or whether, you know... Anyway, officially she is living with her uncle who, as we suspected, is the scientist called Altadonna – I guess you both know his address by now. As you can imagine, there was a bit of an atmosphere in the admin office at the mention of his name – 'That so-called scientist' the admin secretary called him. There's going to be a preliminary hearing in L'Aquila next week, she tells me. The lawyer for the prosecution is a local man, it seems – Avvocato Torrebruna, he's called.*

"Then you went sight-seeing with your young police officer," interposed Beppe with only mild irony in his voice. His most junior officer gave him a fleeting look of withering scorn before continuing:

If you can call going to see a few hundred people living in flimsy tents in a football stadium miles away from the nearest shop 'sight-seeing', capo, yes! But the real reason we went there was to find a student called Gabriele Rapino who, we found out from someone in the admin office, is one of Serena Vacri's fellow law students. Apparently, about a week or so ago, Serena begged Gabriele to let her stay with him – not as a boyfriend or anything, but just as a friend. When we found Gabriele, he told us that Serena had fallen out badly with her uncle...

"Did he say what the row was about, Oriana?" asked Sonia.

He didn't know the details but Serena told him that it wasn't just to do with the fact that the scientist had put everyone's life at risk, but something to do with Altadonna's brother-in-law, who is a local builder. Apparently, this brother-in-law has put in a bid to work on the reconstruction of some of the historic buildings – including the cathedral dome..."

"That's it!" exclaimed Beppe, enigmatically failing to enlighten his two colleagues as to his mental processes. "Well done, Oriana. You've just filled in a huge missing part of this puzzle."

"Can you tell us exactly what this discovery means, *capo*? We must have missed the obvious," said Sonia.

"It's the link between Altadonna and the *mafioso*, Alfieri. Altadonna must be in cahoots with Gianluca Alfieri. He's the middleman between his brother-in-law and the mafia setting up an illegal contract through a genuine local builder. It's a bit of a leap of faith, I know, but I would bet a year's salary – no, better still, my boat - that this is what's behind the abduction of Serena Vacri."

"I've got you, *capo!* Our Sleeping Beauty is a kind of hostage to make sure that Altadonna doesn't get cold feet over the next few months," said Sonia. "Poor girl! She's really put herself into great danger."

Beppe looked over the table at Oriana with admiration in his eyes, his lips forming the words to compliment her.

I haven't quite finished yet, capo. There's something else we discovered from Gabriele. Serena Vacri made a friend while she was living with her uncle. Her name is Marta Casoli. I'll bet neither of you can guess how she fits into this set-up?

Sonia looked at Beppe with an imploring look in her eyes which said clearly: "Don't spoil Oriana's moment of triumph." Beppe's face remained expressionless as he looked at Oriana.

"Go on, Oriana. Don't keep us in suspense."

This Marta Casoli works as a kind of house-keeper for Donatello Altadonna. Maybe she and Serena Vacri had long talks about everything.

"*Brava*, Oriana, *bravissima!* You've really done brilliantly today. All we need now – urgently – is Altadonna's phone number and then I can set up a..."

"Oh, I've got his mobile numbers and a landline number too, *capo*," said Oriana waving a sheet of printed paper in the air. "The university had them, of course, because officially that is where our Sleeping Beauty was staying. Altadonna is one of the people who need to be contacted in an emergency."

"How ironic!" commented Beppe.

"You're a star, Oriana," said Sonia.

"Just one more important thing that Gabriele told me, *capo*," added Oriana, looking at Sonia too as she spoke. "Serena Vacri was supposed to go round to Gabriele's improvised home but, of course, she never turned up. Gabriele has become really worried because she never got in touch with him at all. We know why, of course. She must have been abducted before she managed to go and stay with Gabriele. Even a campsite must have been preferable to living with her uncle, I reckon."

"Thank you, Oriana," said Beppe. "You've done a great job."

Beppe signalled to the head waiter to give them the bill.

"You are not being serious, of course, *commissario*," said Lorenzo. "That meal was on the house. It has been our pleasure to meet you."

Sonia drove rapidly back to Pescara. The only other question that Beppe asked Oriana was about the young police officer with whom Oriana had apparently formed an attachment.

"Did Giovanni Palena ask you any awkward questions about our Sleeping Beauty, Oriana?"

"No, *capo,* but he guessed she might have gone missing. He's obviously bright," she added with a note of secret pride in her voice.

"He mustn't say anything indiscreet, Oriana. That might well put Serena Vacri in peril of losing her life," said Sonia.

"Oh, he won't! Don't worry! I told him he would never see me again if he breathed a single word to anybody about our visit to L'Aquila – even to his commanding officer."

Beppe and Sonia laughed at this revelation.

"I should think he will be too petrified to take that risk," said Beppe seriously, omitting to tell her that Giovanni Palena's commanding officer was already in the know thanks to their brief visit to the police headquarters before picking Oriana up.

"Thank you both for everything today. We can really get moving on this case now. I knew from the outset this was going to be a complex business," he sighed.

The three officers had no idea at that moment in time just how complex the investigation was about to become. Before many hours had elapsed, they would be shaken to the core by a further sinister turn of events.

Looking out through the back window of the car, Oriana remarked to her colleagues how the *Gran Sasso,* retreating behind them, looked just like a normal mountain range. The illusion of the sleeping girl had vanished being this close to its rocky slopes stretching up towards the sky.

"Where has our Sleeping Beauty gone, I wonder?" she added wistfully.

* * *

Back at headquarters, the whole team was ready and waiting for their evening briefing. There was an air of expectancy in the meeting room as they exchanged snippets of information they had gleaned during the course of a very industrious day. Everybody was trying to piece together a fuller picture of the case of the missing girl. Out of habit – or sentimental preference – she was still referred to as The Sleeping Beauty.

The arrival of their chief, some fifteen minutes after the scheduled time for the meeting, was marked by an ironic burst of applause.

"I'm sorry for keeping you all waiting, *ragazzi*. I was summoned by the *Questore*[44] suddenly deciding that he wanted to be brought up to date. You know how he is when he gets the feeling that events are overtaking him. He's agreed to set up phone taps on Altadonna immediately. Alright, we'll begin with our trip to L'Aquila, which has certainly proved to be fruitful. Sonia? Oriana? Maybe you would like to fill everybody in?"

Everybody was listening intently to their description of the day's events. The younger male officers were visibly taken aback by the transformation in Oriana's demeanour. She was speaking with confidence, no longer on the defensive. Only Pippo picked up on the full significance of her frequent mention of the police officer from L'Aquila, Giovanni Palena.

---

[44] Chief of police – in charge of a Questura

"I wonder if the shrew is about to be tamed!" he thought mischievously.

Beppe outlined his conclusions about the link between the *mafioso,* Gianluca Alfieri, the scientist, Altadonna and his brother-in-law who had put in a tender for L'Aquila's rebuilding project.

"I believe we must go all out in our search for Serena Vacri, *ragazzi.* If I am correct in my thinking, her chances of survival depend on our speed and Alfieri's belief that his scheme is still going according to plan. At the moment, I would guess that Serena is being used as a lever to ensure that the scientist and his brother-in-law don't renege on any deal they have worked out – as well as making certain she doesn't compromise their position by going public. Right, now let's hear what everyone else has been up to today… Danilo, Gino, you first."

"You wanted us to check out the *mafioso,* Don Gianluca Alfieri, *capo."*

"We phoned the police and the *Carabinieri* in Naples.

"They confirmed our worst suspicions. Don Alfieri 'retired' from his *Camorra* clan a year ago. Just as you feared, *capo,* he bought a house in Monticchio, just outside L'Aquila. The *Carabinieri* captain whom we spoke to said Alfieri claimed he wanted to lead a blameless life in the mountains well away from the scene of his many previous crimes. The Captain wished us luck!"

Gino continued:

"His house is more like a castle. It's surrounded by a high wall and an automatic wrought-iron gate. The house itself has been virtually rebuilt – earthquake proof, would you believe! And the builder's name was Antonio Breda…"

"What's the betting that Antonio Breda turns out to be Altadonna's brother-in-law," Sonia chimed in.

"Just what I was thinking," said Beppe, further enlightened. He explained his deductions to the gathered team. "I think we can safely assume that Antonio Breda and Altadonna's brother-in-law is one and the same person," he concluded. "Remo, can you check this Antonio Breda out more thoroughly? We know he's involved in the post-earthquake rebuilding contracts. But it's not clear if he's in on the scam or just an unwitting victim of an illegal set-up involving Altadonna and Don Alfieri. While you're at it, Remo, could you get a copy of the building plans of Don Alfiera's house? They must have been approved by the local planning department at some point – with or without a back-hander. If, as I suspect, we shall need to raid our mafia friend's hide-away in a day or so's time, it would be invaluable to have an exact idea of its lay-out. What about the Civil Protection agent, Remo? Did you find out anything about him?"

Beppe was aware of just how many tasks he had assigned to this one officer.

"That was easy, *capo*. His name is Romano Di Carlo. He lives with his wife and daughter in Sulmona. I've got the address and landline number."

"*Bravi, ragazzi,*" Beppe complimented the team of three. "And finally, Giacomo... What did you find out about the other scientists?"

"Well, apart from Altadonna, who's the chief scientist as you know, there are three more scientists belonging to the High-Risk Assessment team: Viola Corrado, from Bologna, Leonti Raimondo, a seismologist from Padova and Manca Salvatore, a geologist from Rome. Then of course, there's the Civil Protection agent from Sulmona, as Remo just told us. It's interesting, though, *capo*... I've been talking to an acquaintance of mine in Sulmona; apparently there is a measure of disagreement between this guy, Romano Di Carlo and Altadonna. It's just local gossip at the moment. You know how it is in villages and small towns like Sulmona – word spreads quickly. Romano Di Carlo, it seems, was all for warning the people of L'Aquila that they should make other arrangements until the risk of an earthquake had subsided. But he was overruled by the chief scientist – who took it upon himself to speak to the *sindaco* [45] in L'Aquila. The mayor, of course, took Altadonna's word that a major quake wasn't imminent – with the tragic consequences that we are all too familiar with by now..."

"But surely, it should have been the Civil Protection agent who made the official announcement anyway. That's how it works, isn't it?"

"Precisely, *capo* - it looks as if this Romano character is going to be a great asset to the lawyer for the prosecution."

"Do we know exactly when the preliminary hearing is going to be held?" asked Beppe.

"Next Wednesday morning, *capo*, the eleventh of June." It was Remo who had supplied this piece of news.

The meeting broke up at about eight o'clock, even though nobody seemed inclined to let matters go without deciding what to do next.

"We'll meet tomorrow morning, *ragazzi*, when we're all fresh. I need time to sort a few things out. But I shall be asking for volunteers to go to L'Aquila over the next few

---

[45] A mayor

days. We need to put Don Alfieri's house under covert surveillance. Any ideas about that... you can tell me tomorrow morning," he added hurriedly. Out of the corner of his eye, he had noticed Oriana Salvati's arm being raised as he was speaking. His first volunteer, he realised, amused and impressed.

"Get some food and sleep, *ragazzi*," were the Chief Inspector's final words to the assembled officers. He interpreted a raised eyebrow from Sonia to be an invitation to eat out together. He nodded curtly in her direction by way of acceptance.

* * *

"Let's get out of Pescara, Beppe. I'll drive you down south for a few kilometres - towards Vasto. We could eat fish by the sea. That should make you feel more at home."

"What worries me most, Sonia, is that I am beginning to feel that Abruzzo *is* my home," replied Beppe quietly. "Thanks to you."

"Then I would guess you are feeling a bit guilty about your family - and the *fidanzata* you left behind."

"Laura, yes, I feel guilty every time she phones – which she does three or four times a week. I can genuinely tell her that work stops me going home at present. But she's beginning to suspect that I don't want to go back. She's looking after a sick father at the moment. I can't escape the feeling that there's something she wants to tell me but she's holding back..."

"Well, I shall go along with whatever you decide, Beppe. But it would be better to tell her how you feel rather than prolonging the agony."

Beppe sighed.

"Ah, but what *is* the truth, Sonia? You see I'm not only a shallow man but I take ages to make up my mind about anything to do with my personal life. I'm a coward too..."

"No, you're not, *commissario*. You are neither a coward, nor are you shallow – as you like to make out."

There was a pause in the conversation as they drove out of Pescara. The mountains were in darkness but the lights from fishing boats bobbed about on the waters of the Adriatic Sea to their left. A waxing moon hung over the silvery waters. Sonia said nothing for half a minute before saying quietly:

"We've got plenty of time, Beppe. Life is long!"

He put his hand on her thigh and the firmness of her flesh and warmth of her skin excited his senses.

"What about you, Sonia?"

"Nobody. There hasn't been anybody for nearly..."

Beppe's mobile phone rang – as if to emphasize his moral dilemma.

"We're nearly there, Beppe. If it's Laura, you can call her back when we stop."

Beppe shook his head before answering the caller.

"*Ciao, mamma,*" he said resignedly. These were the only words Beppe uttered before both he and Sonia's ears were assailed by a torrent of words which filled the confined space of the Lancia Ypsilon. His mobile was not in loudspeaker mode but his mother's voice overcame this obstacle with little difficulty.

Sonia was smiling in amusement as her *capo* attempted to ward off a variety of accusations and recriminations spoken in a dialect that she had great difficulty understanding. Only his answers made it possible to guess what Beppe's mother was saying.

I'm fine, mamma... Yes, I'm with a colleague... No, I'm not in my flat... Because it's only nine-thirty...Yes, I'm in a car...No, my colleague's driving...Of course, he's a man! All policemen are men, mamma! No, I haven't eaten yet, I'm... Mamma, I promise I'm not starving myself. They do have food in Abruzzo, you know. Another barrage of words. *Listen, mamma. I can't really talk right now, I'm working...No, it's not a dangerous job. We're chasing a man who's running round Pescara in his pyjamas.* Sonia burst out laughing. *No, mamma. It's a male colleague – he's got a high pitched laugh, that's all. Ciao mamma. I'll call you back later...I promise.* Beppe's mother continued talking and Sonia caught the mention of Laura's name.

"I'm sorry, Beppe. I didn't help matters, did I? But it was so comical listening to your elaborate excuses!"

Beppe realised that the car had stopped along the seafront outside a restaurant called *L'Alta Marea*. With a name like 'High Tide', he felt safe in assuming that it was a fish restaurant.

"Where are we?" he asked.

"Ortona. It's just down the road from Pescara. I would have loved to take you all the way down to Punta della Penna, where there's this beautiful, unspoilt beach. But we have to start early tomorrow, don't we?"

"I think tomorrow will be the start of our real search for Serena Vacri.

They sat down in the restaurant which, unlike *La Bilancia*, was full of diners at this hour.

A young waiter, looking remarkably like Officer Remo Mastrodicasa, came and took their order. Beppe had a mixed seafood grill and Sonia asked for skate cooked in capers, olive oil, lemon juice and black olives. They exchanged forkfuls across the table once or twice. Beppe said he wished he had chosen the skate.

"The simple things are always best in this life," added Sonia.

"I would hardly call you *simple*, Officer Leardi," said Beppe. As usual with her *capo,* the smile was in the eyes.

"Are we going to have an affair, *capo?*" asked Sonia with an inviting glint in her eye.

It was merely an instinctive gesture on Beppe's part to look at his watch. Sonia laughed amusedly.

"I wasn't necessarily thinking within the next few minutes," she said amused.

Beppe apologised, explaining that his mind was focussed on the investigation in hand. He apologised for being too aware of pressing events.

"You don't have to apologise. I like you just the way you are."

"I've changed my mind about you, Sonia. I think you would make an extremely proficient catcher of fish! You are succeeding perfectly in luring this one to take the bait."

Sonia sighed happily as she looked across the table with that intensity of expression in her eyes which showed profound contentment. Beppe stood up and walked round to Sonia's side of the table. He kissed her on her surprised lips and enjoyed the electric thrill of that first real kiss. There was a round of applause from the neighbouring table, graciously acknowledged with an ironic bow from *Commissario* Stancato as he sat down again, with his dignity intact, and resumed eating.

They continued to talk idly about the events of that long day while they finished the food on their plates. Sonia was sipping from her glassful of *San Pellegrino*. Beppe was making his quarter litre carafe of white wine last as long as possible. Their cosy intimacy was interrupted by the sound of Sonia's mobile phone ringing and vibrating somewhere in the depths of her handbag. By the time she had fished it out, it had, frustratingly, stopped ringing, as if the caller had given up, discouraged by the lack of response.

Sonia stood up and headed for the main door.

"That could be her, Beppe," she explained. "I'd better go and ring her back immediately."

Beppe understood instantly and nodded his approval. If it was Marta, Altadonna's young housekeeper, it was too vital a call to miss.

As he was sitting on his own, his attention was caught by the inevitable television in the corner of the dining room. It was time for the local news on *TV-Tavo*. Suddenly Beppe was up on his feet. He peremptorily demanded that the owner of the restaurant behind the counter should turn up the volume. The momentary hesitation to react on the part of the owner was transformed into instant obedience as Beppe flashed his police badge in the man's face. It was the name Romano Di Carlo that had woken him up from the pleasant sensations engendered by the prospect of future intimacy.

Romano Di Carlo, the Civil Protection Agent on the High-Risk Commission had been reported missing by his wife. She was tearfully explaining to a local reporter that her husband never failed to be home on time. A pallid-looking girl of nine to ten years of age was standing by her mother's side, her face rigid with anxiety. A captain belonging to the local *carabinieri* was briefly interviewed, assuring viewers that the report of the missing Civil Protection Agent was being taken very seriously. Beppe thrust a €50 bill into the surprised owner's hand and headed for the exit. The restaurant owner ran after him telling him he had paid too much.

"Keep the change, *signore*. The food was excellent. We'll have a bottle of wine on the house next time we come here," he told the astonished proprietor over his shoulder.

"That *was* Marta, Beppe. She's coming into Pescara tomorrow on the early morning coach. It's her day off. I told her I'd meet her at the bus station at 7.15. Is that alright, Beppe?"

Beppe merely said: "Of course", and told Sonia about the missing Civil Protection agent in an urgent whisper.

"I'll drive you back to base, *capo*," she said, all business-like again, knowing full well that the man she had singled out as her new 'partner-for-life' would be unlikely to go to bed until the early hours of the morning.

8: Blood in the mountains

The group of English trekkers, who had spent the night in an *agriturismo* just outside Sulmona,[46] were all up by half past six and waiting with obvious relish for their breakfast. The proprietor of *L'Agriturismo*[47] *'Il Portico'* finally appeared, bleary eyed, at quarter to seven. He prayed fervently that this group of keen English walkers would not be asking him for a bacon and egg breakfast. In his experience, English, Dutch and German tourists seemed to think it was essential to eat 75% of their day's calorific intake before eight o'clock in the morning.

Inevitably, his version of an English breakfast, consisting of crisply fried *pancetta* and deep yellow scrambled eggs – not on toast – produced ill-concealed expressions of disapproval. Many of his English clients would ask him, as politely as English people do, if he had something that sounded like *'bike-ed beentz'*. When he got his teenage daughter to research this item on Google, he was astounded to discover that they wanted something that he only ever served up as an *antipasto*, but with no hint of the beans wallowing in a wholly unappetizing-sounding tomato sauce. But the proprietor need not have feared on this occasion; the men and women who made up this motley crew belonged to a stratum of English society whose virtues he could not possibly have appreciated without having lived in England. He himself had never left Sulmona – let alone the Italian Peninsula.

---

[46] A spectacular mountain township – famous for its sugared almonds.
[47] A splendid Italian invention! Usually a farmhouse-style restaurant – often with guest rooms. What you eat has to be locally sourced.

These holiday-makers were desperate to 'blend in' with the natives and would have eschewed any suggestion that they should want copious cups of tea and mounds of sausages. He was pleased to discover they all wanted *cappuccini* and *cornetti*[48] – just like normal people.

Their local guide, obligingly named *Guido*, walked nonchalantly into the dining room just as the walkers were assembling in the entrance hall shouldering their bulky ruck-sacks with tea pots and compasses dangling from the straps. Guido led them out to the minibus which would take them to the foot of the mountain slopes just beyond Sulmona.

The trekkers had had time, the previous evening, to visit Sulmona with its wide and stunningly picturesque *piazza.* Many of them had spent twenty euros or more on the brightly coloured sugared almonds which represent one surprising aspect of the town's economy.

They had then been treated to the local cuisine prepared by the staff of *Il Portico. The "oohs" and "aahs"* of appreciation for the food and wines had been pretty well continuous. They waved a cheerful farewell to Sulmona and to the proprietor of the *agriturismo,* with his wife and daughter standing in front of the rustic farm house. Their love of this beautiful land was expressed clearly by their smiles as they drove the short distance out of Sulmona.

Today, they were going to set out on the second leg of their trek. Their destination was a spa town to the north east called Caramanico Terme.

The minibus drew up in a lay-by where there was just one lonely white Alfa Romeo parked. Of the owner there was

---

[48] croissants

no sign whatsoever. Only Guido frowned in a puzzled manner and walked over to the car before leading his group up the mountain path. The car door was not locked and he noticed a sheet of note paper on the dashboard. He picked it up and read it before replacing it. His frown had deepened perceptibly.

The English group was too overwhelmed by the beauty of the scenery on that warm day in early summertime to notice that their chief guide looked preoccupied.

Guido called the walkers to some kind of order and outlined the itinerary to the attentive group in very passable English. One advantage of dealing with English tourists, he reckoned, was that everybody listened to what he was saying. When the group consisted of Italians, most of them continued their conversations *sotto voce* during his talk. English people were far more disciplined as a race than his compatriots. Germans would look daggers at anyone who dared even to whisper two words and would ostracize them for the rest of the day.

"We shall have a lunch break at an *osteria*[49] about ten kilometres up in the hills," he explained. Their minibus drove off, heading for a strategic point between Sulmona and Caramanico Terme, in the unlikely event of anyone falling by the wayside.

The trekkers set off happily along a well-marked path which headed gently up a grassy slope with clumps of trees generously dispersed on the hillside. The Maiella Mountains, their peaks still white with unmelted snow, glowed in the morning sunlight.

---

[49] A hostel – a country-style restaurant offering a more limited menu

"This is as close to paradise as one can get on Earth…" said somebody.

"I was told Abruzzo was beautiful, but this is better than I ever imagined," gasped Dorothy in amazement.

"I want to buy a house here and live out the rest of my days here…"

"This part of Italy is all so breathtaking…much more spectacular than those awful house-buying programmes on English TV seem to imply…"

"Do Italians realise they live in the best country in the world, I wonder?"

"It's perfect here. So clean, so unpolluted and the air smells so pure…"

"Not to mention the food…"

Their conversations continued in this vein for at least 500 metres. One man, Clive, was walking a little behind the others. He had a pair of powerful binoculars slung round his neck. A second Italian guide, a taciturn individual called Efisio, originally from Sardinia, was following at the tail end to collect stragglers. He spoke no English and looked as if he would rather be walking a lot faster and on his own.

Clive was looking up at a little copse of trees two hundred metres or so above the path. He had spotted something out of place near the trees. He looked through his binoculars to check what it was. What he saw made him stop in his tracks, which forced Efisio to do the same - with a tut of impatience.

"*Andiamo avanti, signore,*"[50] he urged crossly.

Clive passed him the binoculars and pointed up the slope. What the guide saw looked like a pile of old clothes

---

[50] Let's get a move on

but there was something sinister and inappropriate about the way they were lying on the ground. It looked like a motionless tailor's dummy.

"Guido!" shouted Efisio to his leader. The whole group stopped in silence, wondering what had brought them to a sudden halt just as they were getting into their stride.

"Che c'è, Efisio?"[51] shouted Guido to his fellow guide. Efisio handed the binoculars back to their owner and began to walk up the hillside, beckoning Guido to join him. Guido already intuited the worst-case scenario. As soon as he had read the hastily scribbled note left on the dashboard of the white Alfa Romeo, he knew there was something wrong. It had been written in poorly spelt, unpunctuated Italian. It had said simply: *"no posso continuar mi vergonga troppo scusami"*[52]

The English walkers had fallen silent. Their previous mood of elation had evaporated in a trice. They had all turned to face the two guides who were looking at the shapeless form on the ground. They were talking and gesticulating. Guido fumbled inside his jacket pocket and retrieved his mobile phone.

"Maybe it's just a dead animal," suggested Dorothy hopefully.

"What? With clothes on?" replied Clive sharply.

"Oh dear God!" muttered another woman. "You mean it's a dead body, don't you?"

"I'm going up to have a look," said Clive, taking his first steps up the slope. Guido and Efisio saw him and waved their arms wildly at him in a gesture that plainly told him not to come any nearer. There followed another rapid

---

[51] What's up? *kay chay*
[52] I can't go on - I'm too ashamed-sorry

exchange of words and Efisio came down the hill purposefully.

"*Andiamo più avanti, signori!*"[53] he said curtly, leading his unwilling flock further along the track. They followed him submissively at first, disorientated by the sudden change in atmosphere. Although the sun was warm on their faces, it felt as if a cloud had cast a deep shadow on their former feelings of exuberance. After a few hundred metres a reaction began to set in. They came to a halt because those in front decided they would not follow this surly substitute guide any further. Those behind them closed up so they were huddled together in a compressed body of humans.

"Excuse us, *signore,* we don't want to walk any further without your colleague."

Efisio understood the sense of the words by their body language. He shrugged his shoulders indifferently, sat down on the grassy verge and lit a cigarette. One by one, the trekkers sat down on the grass – leaving a good-few metres between them and the other guide. A silence had fallen. Suddenly, Italy did not seem such an idyllic country after all. Then, in the distance, a chilling sound was heard.

"What's that noise?" asked Claire, a pretty woman in her mid-thirties who was accompanied by her boyfriend. "It sounded for all the world like a…" The sound was heard again. It came echoing off the rocky mountain slopes from some distant valley higher up in *La Maiella* mountain range.

"*Lupi,*[54]" said Efisio indifferently. "*Ce ne sono tanti qui.*"[55]

---

[53] Let's move further on
[54] Wolves. The animals were reintroduced in Abruzzo – to regenerate wildlife in the region. The inhabitants are divided as to this move. There are bears as well.

Charlotte had learnt some Italian in the past and translated for them in a strangulated whisper: "He said it was wolves and that there are lots of them in these mountains."

The secret dread of the wild struck them all dumb. A more mundane harbinger of disaster was clearly heard approaching from the nearby road; a police car's siren shattered the last vestige of the former tranquillity and beauty of the spectacular countryside.

"*Viva l'Italia!*" muttered Charlotte with bitter irony.

* * *

As soon as Beppe had been deposited back at police headquarters the previous evening by a reluctant Sonia, after a speedy drive back to Pescara, he had telephoned a very grouchy *carabiniere* captain in the town of Sulmona. The call had been forwarded automatically to the captain's mobile phone. Apparently, this senior police officer was one of those who held the view that emergencies must only be permitted to occur when he was officially on duty.

"I was in bed with my wife," said the *capitano* gruffly.

Beppe had to stop himself from replying that he was relieved not to have interrupted the man whilst committing an act of adultery.

"I do apologise profusely, *capitano*. I can only assure you I would never have called you at this time of night had it not been very important. I shall soon need your help and close cooperation, you see."

---

[55] There are loads of them here.

Beppe's rank and the hint of obsequious flattery seemed to mollify the captain enough to allow Beppe to explain the reason for his late-night call.

"When I saw the report of the missing Civil Protection Agent from Sulmona on the TV just now, I knew that his disappearance must be tied up with an ongoing investigation that we are conducting here in Pescara. Just so you realise how delicate this case is, *Signor Capitano,* I have to tell you that it is all bound up with the abduction of a twenty-two-year-old girl from L'Aquila. We are ninety-nine percent sure that there is an underworld connection."

"Romano Di Carlo's wife only reported him missing a few hours ago, so I don't quite know how you can be so certain of that. I told her not to worry too much. He has probably been delayed on business in L'Aquila – what with the impending trial and so on…"

"Yes, of course, that is the most likely explanation, *capitano.* All I ask is that you contact me – at any time of the day or night – if there are any developments. With your permission, I would like to come over to Sulmona tomorrow morning and fill you in on the details of the case. I am sure you will find them fascinating."

The captain grunted his consent and hung up. Beppe's main reaction was a sense of stifled outrage at the irresponsible indifference on the part of a minority of officials when it came to doing the job they were paid for. "Why bother to be a policeman at all if you are not on the side of the angels?" he thought angrily. It was a personal reaction he had constantly had to battle with in his native Calabria. He was saddened, but not altogether surprised, to come across the same level of indifference here in Abruzzo. He felt disappointment at being let down by a fellow officer.

He consoled himself with the thought that his own team were not tarred with the same brush. He might have considered the possibility that this was because of his particular style of leadership. But he also suffered from a degree of modesty unusual for his rank.

He was much more successful when he woke up his opposite number in L'Aquila, whom he had met earlier on that day. He looked at his watch. Yes, it was just a few minutes short of midnight. He and his colleague had instantly agreed a policy of mutual cooperation. His faith in the system was partly restored. He would be sending Oriana, Danilo and Gino to L'Aquila the next day. Officer Giovanni Palena, he was informed by his opposite number, would welcome the opportunity to team up with Oriana Salvati.

"No uniforms for the next few days, *ragazzi*," he had told the three officers. "You should take your own cars, too. You're going undercover," he added with dark humour.

He would have liked to call his technical duo, Marco Pollutri and Bianca Bomba, to see how the phone tapping was progressing, but he decided he had woken up enough police officers for one night. The indefatigable Beppe Stancato decided he should get some sleep and headed instinctively for his boat with images in his mind of Sonia fast asleep in her bed.

***

The following morning, a uniformed Sonia failed at first to recognise the smartly dressed, smiling young woman who had alighted from the 7.15 bus from L'Aquila on to the crowded concourse in front of Pescara's railway station. The girl, however, walked straight towards Sonia without a second's hesitation.

"Marta!" exclaimed Sonia placing her hands briefly on the girl's arms. "You look different."

"So do you...Officer Leardi!"

"Ah, you mean the uniform, don't you? Out of curiosity, how did you know we were from the police back in the professor's house in L'Aquila?"

"Well... I didn't know about you being from the police until I read the message you left me. But when you looked at me as I brought the coffee into the room, I felt you were more interested in something other than wanting to rent that creepy man's flat."

"That was very perceptive of you, Marta," said Sonia, being careful to hide her surprise at the unexpected epithet that she had used to describe her employer.

"But if you are the police, that means HE has done something bad, doesn't it?"

"Come on, Marta. I'm sure you could do with a cup of coffee and something to eat. Let's find a quiet coffee bar somewhere – and you can tell me why you find our *professore* such a 'creepy man' – as you put it."

Marta let out a quiet groan as if to indicate that it would be difficult to know where to begin.

As they spoke over cups of coffee and jam-filled *croissants,* Sonia had the increasing conviction that Marta was impressionable and probably relatively innocent in the ways of the world. In the same instant that these thoughts occurred to her, she knew instinctively that the girl would only be able to confirm their suspicions as to what Donatello Altadonna was up to, rather than add anything new. But Sonia Leardi understood the importance of having potential first hand witnesses. Sometimes, insignificant details assumed greater importance later on. At the present moment, Marta needed a friendly arm to lean on – someone who would listen to her story.

Thus, Sonia quickly learnt that Serena Vacri had confided in their young housekeeper once only in a hurriedly whispered conversation only hours before she had disappeared out of Marta's life. Despite providing no new evidence, the story which Marta had to relate left Sonia Leardi with her mouth open in astonishment as the narrative progressed.

It was about ten days ago, I suppose. I sometimes stay at his house overnight rather than drive out of L'Aquila in the dark – especially after the... earthquake. I live with my brother and my mother in San Gregorio; it's about 5 kilometres outside L'Aquila. I have quite a nice room at the top of HIS house – with its own bathroom. Well, I was already in bed because it was about eleven. I had the TV on. I was watching something silly on Canale 5 when I thought I heard someone tapping on my door. At first, I thought it was on the TV – I was half asleep by then. Then the tapping got more urgent. It was Serena. I only opened the door a crack because I was afraid it might be HIM.

"Why, Marta? Has he ever...touched you or anything? Because if he has, you should not stay there any longer..."

No, he's never...done anything like that. But I always have the creepy feeling that he would like to. Serena says she feels the same way too.

Sonia noticed the fact that Marta used the present tense when talking about Serena. She did not even realise that Serena had gone missing. Surely she must suspect something?

"Go on, Marta," she said encouragingly.

Well...Serena pushed her way in to the room. She looked pale-faced and scared – as if she thought she might be followed. She spoke in a whisper. "I've got to talk to someone, Marta," she said. She gave me an envelope and told me to hide it somewhere. "If anything happens to me, then take this to the police." I asked her what was in it. She told me something about her uncle. She said he was involved with some evil man – a mafioso from Naples – who lives in a big house in Monticchio. That's just a kilometre away from where we live out in the country. I could hardly understand what she was saying, Officer Leardi...

"Please call me Sonia, Marta. We're friends and you are just helping me find... someone." Obviously, Marta was not entirely without some understanding of the situation because she immediately asked:

It's Serena, isn't it? She's not...? She had a look of dread on her face.

"We hope she's alright, Marta. But what you tell me could be vital. Please carry on telling me what happened that night."

We heard footsteps coming up the stairs. Serena managed to shove the envelope under the pillow. She looked petrified. "He mustn't find me here, Marta". I pointed to the bathroom door and she only just made it there in time. HE knocked on the door and came in without waiting. He pretended to be all embarrassed and said he thought Serena had come upstairs to my room. The TV was still on quite loud. I was scared. I thought I must distract him somehow, so I got out of bed. I only had a skimpy nighty on and I could see him looking at me while pretending not to. He made his way to the bathroom, Sonia. I just said the first thing that came into my head. I told him I had a period on and that my soiled knickers were rinsing in the basin. I told him I would not be able to continue working for him if he embarrassed me like that. It's amazing how so many men are put off by that kind of thing.

"She's not so naïve after all," reckoned Sonia, smiling knowingly at this slip of a girl.

Well, he left me and went downstairs. I thought Serena was never going to come out so I went and told her the coast was clear. She gave me a 'bacio' and was out of the room. "Don't let me down, Marta," she said. Well, the horrible thing was that HE was waiting for her in the dark. I heard her let out a little scream of shock. I heard him saying: "You've been to see the girl, haven't you? What have you been telling her?" Then Serena – who's got a lot more bottle than me – told him to leave her alone and asked what he was doing creeping round the house spying on her anyway?

Marta had stopped talking, her story out in the open at last.

Sonia, with her heart in her mouth, asked:

"Do you happen to have that letter with you, Marta?"

The girl looked puzzled as if she had not been expecting such a question. Sonia had to remind herself that it might not have occurred to Marta to collect the secret letter before setting out that morning for her rendezvous with a police officer. But, to Sonia's relief, she opened her handbag and ferreted around for the envelope.

"Good job I keep it on me all the time," she said, handing the slightly crumpled envelope over to Sonia with an obvious sigh of relief.

"Why didn't you take this to the police sooner, Marta?" asked Sonia gently.

"I didn't know anything was wrong, Sonia, did I? *HE* told me she had gone home to Orvieto to be with her mum. I *did* wonder why none of her clothes seemed to be missing though. I'm sorry. I've been a bit stupid, haven't I? As usual..." she added sadly.

"You've been an enormous help, Marta, really."

"Thank you for saying so, Sonia. I'm really glad we met."

"By the way, isn't there a *Signora* Altadonna somewhere?"

"She went on a round-the-world cruise – at least, that's what *he* says. That's why he needed a housekeeper!" added Marta ruefully.

"She's left him, in other words," thought Sonia to herself.

"*Cara* Marta – there's just one more favour I must ask you. I need you to come with me to the police station so that we can take down your statement. All you'll have to do is tell an officer what you just told me."

"So something bad has happened. *HE*'s done something to her, hasn't he?"

"She's gone missing, Marta. We want to find out what's happened to her as soon as possible. There, I've told you more than I should. Now I must trust you not to say anything to anyone. *I* shall be in big trouble if you do – and what's worse, you would be putting Serena's life at risk too. So... lips sealed, alright?" Officer Leardi put on her sternest glare.

"I won't say a word, Sonia. I swear."

"When you've signed your statement, we can drive you back home if you want."

"Oh no, don't worry about that. I'm staying with a girlfriend until tomorrow. I'll take the bus back again."

Sonia left Marta with Officer Remo Mastrodicasa – thinking he would be the least intimidating officer in the station. Marta had, somewhat to Sonia's surprise, planted a *bacio* on each of her cheeks.

"We'll keep in touch, Marta. I'll let you know what happens," Sonia promised her. She was dying to open the envelope that had been entrusted to her. As she walked away in search of Beppe, she could just hear Marta saying: "You don't look like a policeman, Officer Remo." She smiled and wondered if she might inadvertently have done them both a more personal kind of favour. She looked briefly back over her shoulder. Yes, Officer Remo was blushing and he had a broad grin on his face; the same reaction he would have had as a waiter if he had just received an unexpectedly generous tip, thought Sonia maliciously.

"*Forza,*[56] *Remo!*" said Sonia under her breath, as if she had been saying a prayer on his behalf.

* * *

Beppe and Sonia were heading for Sulmona. For a change, it was Beppe driving the police car with the words *POLIZIA* painted in blue and white lettering on the door panels. They had set off round about the time that the English trekking group had arrived at their departure point – where Guido had noticed the abandoned, white Alfa Romeo.

---

[56] Go for it! Lit: strength

"Why are we going to Sulmona, Beppe?" asked Sonia, curious.

"I think we need to go and talk to Romano Di Carlo's wife – before that *carabiniere* captain has a chance to visit her. Your ability to put people at ease will make it easier for her to tell us anything she knows. If that *capitano* gets there first, she probably won't want to speak to another policeman in her life," explained Beppe drily.

Until the phone call arrived from the aforementioned *carabiniere* captain, the conversation in the police car was relaxed and light-hearted. It was Sonia who was the main instigator, wishing to begin breaking down the barriers to their intimacy. The ensuing conversation took both of them by surprise, revealing as it did two diverse perspectives – destined, sooner or later, to meet somewhere in the middle ground.

"We haven't had sex yet," stated Sonia gaily in a way that was designed to provoke a reaction.

Beppe turned his head towards her, taking his eyes off the road for no more than a couple of seconds. Sonia could have sworn that he had rapidly checked the driving mirrors before looking at her. *Was it impossible to catch him off his guard?* she wondered. She had a glimpse of that solemn, sensuous mouth and the sad brown eyes that appeared to be concealing a smile. She loved his face, which reminded her of an undergraduate philosophy student's - rather than that of a forty-four-year-old police inspector.

He was looking at the road again, but his profile showed a rueful smile.

"I *had* noticed the omission, Sonia," he replied wistfully.

He paused before continuing, his eyes now glued on the road ahead. The female voice of the on-board Satnav was telling him to turn right at the next roundabout. "But you know the main reason why?"

"Yes, I do – and I promised not to interfere, Beppe. I apologise."

"Besides which, making love requires a great deal of concentration."

"Does it?" she asked, genuinely taken aback by the idea. Beppe looked at her again for a split second. In that blink of an eye, he took in her high cheek bones, her blue eyes flecked with tints of gold and the pouting lips pushed forward as if in invitation.

"Che bellezza!" he said quietly, once again looking at the road. "Yes, it does! And so does this investigation!" he added, bringing Sonia – and himself – back to order.

Sonia was smiling happily to herself.

"Do you have a middle name, Beppe? Just out of curiosity, of course."

"Yes, thanks to *mamma's* crazy ideas about life. But if I told you what it was, you would be able to blackmail me at any point in the future by threatening to tell the rest of the world."

"It can't be that bad, surely? *Dai!* Go on – tell me what it is. I promise never to reveal it."

After a pause, he reluctantly replied: "Calogero."[57]

"I see," was all Sonia said. "It's a very southern Italian name, isn't it?"

"Do you know what it means?" asked Beppe.

---

[57] Ka-LODGE-ero

"Yes – considerable embarrassment whenever you have to tell anyone, I would imagine."

"It actually means *'graceful in old age'* – it's from the Greek, I believe," explained Beppe, laughing at Sonia's comment. "And what about *your* middle name?"

"It's just plain and simple Fran..." she began.

That was as far as their conversation got. Beppe's hands-free phone was ringing. It was the *carabiniere* captain from Sulmona, who was standing on a hillside just outside Sulmona, looking at the bloody remains of a dead man.

"Well, you asked me to phone you, *commissario*," said the *carabiniere* officer, gruffly. "We've found the body of *il dottor* Di Carlo. It appears that he's committed suicide."

* * *

Following the crude directions of the *carabiniere* captain and with the aid of an activated emergency siren, Beppe and Sonia arrived at the point indicated by their colleague within the space of twenty minutes.

"Now, it's a murder case," were almost the only words spoken by the duo during their headlong rush to reach their destination. Sonia Leardi did not query her senior officer's interpretation of events – largely because she knew instinctively that he was correct.

"Let's hope we get there before that *carabiniere* and his crew trample all over the scene of the crime!" Beppe had added tartly. Sonia nodded in agreement. Their previous jovial mood had been shattered in an instant and replaced by an urgent need to reach their destination.

They spotted the white Alfa Romeo parked in the lay-by with the midnight blue and red-striped *carabiniere* car behind it.

"Here we are!" said Sonia in relief after the most hair-raising car journey in her ten-year-long career as a police woman.

Commissario Stancato and *Agente* Sonia Leardi walked solemnly up the mountain path side by side. They quickly drew level with the group of three uniformed *carabinieri,* standing on the hillside in front of a small wooded area. Beppe and Sonia had obviously beaten the forensics team to the scene; they would have to come from L'Aquila, he remembered. As they approached the group of men, Beppe had no difficulty in identifying the surly *capitano,* who had been interviewed on the TV the previous evening. He was in his late fifties. "One of the 'old school'," Beppe said to himself.

Introductions were curt and business-like.

"May we go and look at the body?" asked Beppe who was, in point of fact, already walking up the slope. There were no objections but the *carabiniere* captain told Sonia that she should stay where she was.

"It's no sight for a woman!" he said in a peremptory manner.

"I'm a police officer first and foremost, *capitano,*" Sonia snapped at him. The captain merely shrugged indifferent shoulders.

Romano Di Carlo was lying on his back. His face was recognisable from the photos they had seen. His chest was a mangled and bloody mess. A shotgun lay a few steps away from him. Sonia was looking pale-faced and horrified but kept tight control of the physical nausea which risked erupting from within her. There was a tree just a few centimetres behind the victim's head. Beppe had taken one look at the body. It was enough for him. He walked thoughtfully up towards the tree and then did a slow tour of its trunk and took a couple of photos on his iPhone. He rejoined his fellow officer and looked at her with that meaningful gleam in his eyes that she was beginning to recognise so well.

"Come on, Sonia," he said quietly. "We should leave this to forensics."

Beppe put on his most conciliatory manner as he addressed the *carabiniere* captain.

"What led you to believe that this is a case of suicide, *capitano?*" he asked in a quiet voice, which concealed the suppressed anger that he felt towards such obvious incompetence.

The *capitano* nodded at one of the junior officers who, to Beppe's consternation, handed him a sheet of paper with his bare hands.

"Why isn't this inside a plastic folder, *capitano?* It's evidence, for heaven's sake!"

The policeman bridled and went instantly into defensive mode

"It's just a suicide note. It's of no forensic interest at all. We found it on the dashboard of his Alfa Romeo when we arrived."

"Have you read what the note says, *capitano?*" asked Beppe sternly as he handed the sheet of paper to Sonia.

"Of course I have. It's obvious – he is too ashamed to go on trial in two days' time. He took his own life to avoid the public disgrace."

Sonia was biting her lower lip in a futile attempt to control her mouth. She had a look of enraged indignation on her face. Beppe knew she would be unable to contain herself but did nothing to stop her next words, which were addressed scornfully in the direction of the police officer.

"*Il Dottore* Di Carlo is an educated man. Just look at the writing on this note. It's unpunctuated and badly spelt. He never wrote that letter – somebody else did."

"It might just be physically possible to shoot oneself in the chest with a shotgun at that range," added Beppe, his anger now well hidden. "But it does not seem likely that he would take such a drastic step just before he was on his way home to his wife and daughter."

"You can't know he was returning home," retorted the *capitano*. "Besides which," he added with a note of defiant triumph in his voice, "his Alfa Romeo was pointing away from Sulmona!"

"That is another aspect which is highly suspicious, *capitano*. The TV report stated that his wife was worried because he had not come home on time. She was expecting him back from L'Aquila. In other words, the car was pointing in the *wrong* direction.

"But if he did not write that note, then we are dealing with…"

"Precisely, *capitano*!"

"You should have put that letter in a plastic evidence folder immediately," said the captain, turning on one of his junior officers. "Do it now!" he added angrily. A crestfallen officer walked down the hill with the piece of paper in his hand. The forensic team was arriving and he gave the letter to one of them.

"I need to have a word with you, *capitano,* about our investigation. May I come and see you at your base in Sulmona? Let's say in about an hour's time?" Beppe's tone of voice was all sweetness and light. The captain nodded and managed to shake Beppe by the hand as he and Sonia set off back down the hill. The couple noticed with curiosity a group of trekkers further up the wide mountain path. They kept looking backwards over their shoulders until their dwindling figures disappeared into the blue, sunlit distance.

* * *

Beppe had not said a word until they were both inside the car, heading slowly back towards the little town of Sulmona.

"Che stronzo!"[58] said Beppe, finally allowing his true feelings to become apparent.

"Well done for your diplomatic handling of that man, *capo!*" said Sonia in admiration. "I'm sorry I let fly but…"

"Don't be sorry, Sonia. I wanted you to let off steam. Your rebuke must have been far more humiliating coming from a woman. *Hai fatto benissimo."*[59]

"Grazie, Beppe. Apart from the obvious, what made you reject the suicide idea? You had that knowing glint in your eyes as you walked round that tree."

"Didn't you notice his body, Sonia? There were burn marks on his wrists which that idiot didn't spot – and behind the tree, I found a length of electrical flex. They tied him to the tree and shot him at point blank range."

---

[58] What a complete arse-hole – or words to that effect!
[59] You did brilliantly

9: *On the offensive*

Neither Sonia nor Beppe uttered a word for the first few minutes in the moving police car, the grizzly memory of the dead Civil Protection agent haunting their imaginations. Unlike the journey from Pescara to Sulmona, Beppe was driving at what seemed like a snail's pace, in a vain attempt to defer the grim task in front of them.

"I guess our visit to see Romano Di Carlo's wife is even more important now, isn't it, Beppe?"

"Yes, indeed. We would be neglecting our duty as human beings if we were not the ones to break the news to her first. Do you remember her name, Sonia?"

She had had the foresight to check up with Remo before setting out that morning after leaving Marta to make her statement.

"Mariangela Abate – and they have a ten-year-old daughter called Tiziana. Poor girl," added Sonia with a catch in her voice.

"Let's go and get something strong to drink before we go and see them," suggested Beppe, who always dreaded the ordeal of breaking the news of someone's death to close family members. It did not matter how many times he had had to carry out this duty in the past. It never got any easier.

* * *

An hour later, their faith in human nature – inherent but not always apparent reckoned Beppe – had been fully restored. They were heading for the *stazione dei carabinieri* with a renewed and entirely focused sense of purpose regarding the harrowing case in which they were involved.

Romano Di Carlo's wife had been very strong and had a clear insight as to the circumstances leading to her husband's murder. She had utterly rejected the notion that her husband would ever have taken his own life. She poured scorn on the facile interpretation of events when Beppe told her about the conclusion that the *carabiniere* captain had jumped to.

"Besides which, he has never owned a gun in his life. He was opposed to the law which allows anyone to own a firearm – even for hunting animals," she had stated angrily.

The only moment when she had looked as if she would break down was when she opened the front door and saw a police uniform. She turned pale and her lips began to quiver as tears formed in her eyes. But then she was back in control, thinking only of her daughter standing by her side.

"Why don't you go upstairs, *tesoro*, and carry on reading your book?" suggested her mother gently.

With a gesture which swept away any vestige of doubt Beppe might have had about the virtues of his future companion, Sonia squatted down in order be on the same level as the bespectacled little girl. She held out her arms and said:

"Why don't you take me to your room and tell me all about the book you're reading, Tiziana?"

The invitation was irresistible. They went hand in hand up to the first floor, talking quietly.

"How did you know my name?" asked the little girl.

"It's written all over your face," replied Sonia.

Tiziana let out a little giggle as she instinctively wiped her hand over her forehead.

"You've got an exceptional colleague there, *commissario*," said Mariangela Abate quietly. "Come on into the kitchen and let's get this over with."

Mariangela Abate listened attentively to every word that Beppe said. He restricted himself to relating how he had come to the conclusion that her husband had been murdered. Only her eyes registered the horror of what he was saying.

"Now I must tell you exactly what my husband told me a couple of days ago. All the scientists belonging to the High-Risk Commission had a meeting in this house late at night. Afterwards, Donatello Altadonna, drove off in a fury. There had been a heated argument between him and my husband – it even woke Tiziana up. I asked Romano to put me in the picture because I knew that something was seriously wrong. That's when he told me Altadonna's niece had confided in him a week or so ago. She told him she had overheard her uncle talking to his brother-in-law about a building contract which would be organised by a man called Gianluca Alfieri. Apparently, the brother-in-law, Antonio Breda, had already spent months renovating a house outside L'Aquila for this man. But the niece said that she suspected this Alfieri character belonged to a criminal organisation. Everybody in and around L'Aquila guessed as much, but of course, nobody would talk openly about it..."

"You have just confirmed our suspicions, Mariangela," said Beppe. "Now what I am about to tell you must remain between these four walls. Altadonna's niece, Serena Vacri is her name, has been abducted – almost certainly by Alfieri's mob. We assume that she is being held at Alfiera's house as a kind of hostage against any wavering on the part of Altadonna to see this business through – there will be huge sums of public money involved in rebuilding L'Aquila, as you can imagine. I am not going to publicly contradict the interpretation of events put out by your local *carabiniere* captain. If *they* know we suspect as much as we do, then Serena's life will be at risk. There would be no point in keeping her alive if they think she is a liability. We need a couple more days..."

"I understand you perfectly, *commissario*. Trust me. And now, if you would be so kind as to leave us to grieve in private, I should be eternally grateful."

Beppe shook her hand, held between both of his. Sonia was coming downstairs with Tiziana, who was crying.

"I didn't have to tell her," said Sonia with tears in her own eyes. "She is bright. She understood all too well..."

Tiziana, her face rigid with fear, ran into her mother's arms.

"Why, *mamma*? Why?" she sobbed uncontrollably.

"Will you be alright, Mariangela?" asked Sonia, feeling they could not leave without some consoling words.

"I'll be alright, officers. Thank you both for being so kind and understanding. Don't worry - my brother and sister both live in Sulmona. We won't be alone."

Mariangela Abate ushered them towards the front door, knowing she would be unable to suppress her grief and shock for more than a few seconds longer.

* * *

Beppe and Sonia drove in silence towards the *carabiniere* station to forestall any gauche move on the part of the captain. It was Beppe who broke the silence just as they arrived.

"We shouldn't be too hard on the man, I suppose," suggested Beppe. "I would guess he has only a year to go before retirement. He just doesn't want to face up to a very public murder enquiry after, one can imagine, years of nothing worse than coping with English and American trekkers getting lost in the mountains."

"Or petty disputes between rival sugared almond producers," added Sonia wryly.

The charitable intentions they might have harboured before arriving at the police station were rendered futile by the discovery that the *capitano* was not there. The two junior officers, looking embarrassed, informed Beppe that their *capo* had gone for an early lunch, saying that he could not wait any longer. Sonia openly gasped in disbelief.

The young officer, who had been berated by the *capitano* for not putting the 'suicide note' in a plastic evidence bag, introduced himself as *Tenente* Nardini. He apologised for being remiss and handed a copy of the document to Beppe.

"I thought this might be useful to you, *commissario,* in case you need to compare handwriting or something. The forensics team did a scan for me and e-mailed it over to us. I wanted to put the original in an evidence bag as soon as we found it, but I was told not to waste time – or resources. I suppose he meant the plastic folder," the officer added caustically.

Both *Tenente* Nardini and his colleague were looking appealingly at Beppe, torn between official loyalty to a superior officer and the desire to distance themselves from his incompetence. Beppe decided to risk taking them into his confidence.

"I would like you to do me a small favour, *ragazzi.*"

They both looked eagerly at him, relieved that they were not going to be berated – or worse – reported to a higher authority. The favour he asked left the two officers – and a shocked Sonia – with their mouths open in astonishment.

"Please inform your *capitano* that I apologise for jumping to conclusions about Romano Di Carlo's death. I think suicide is a far more likely scenario."

"But..." stuttered Lieutenant Nardini, "didn't you notice the length of flex behind the tree and those burn marks on his wrists? It looks more likely the *dottore* was..."

"*Bravo, tenente.* You noticed that too," interrupted Beppe smoothly. "The truth is, I need a couple more days – three possibly – to complete an ongoing operation that involves a twenty-two-year-old girl..."

Beppe went on to explain about the missing girl, Serena Vacri, to the two officers, whose faces expressed growing concern.

"I'm hoping that, by the time the autopsy report comes out, we shall have found the girl and brought her to safety. It's a delicate situation. We don't want to alert her captors in any way because it will put them on their guard. I'm counting on your total discretion, *ragazzi.*"

His closing words were expressed with a precise mixture of trust and the merest hint of menace in his voice – a technique which Sonia had come to recognise as one of her *capo's* specialities.

Beppe shook the two officers warmly by the hand.

"*Grazie ragazzi e buon lavoro.* We'll keep you posted," he promised, leaving them with a sense that they had a role to play, which would effectively leave their commanding officer out of the equation.

"You can rely on us, *commissario*. And thank you."

"It always works," he confided to Sonia as they drove off towards L'Aquila.

"What are we going to do in L'Aquila, *capo?*" asked Sonia.

"Oh, we shall check to see how Officers Salvati, Simone and Martelli are doing…"

His voice tailed off as he had to swerve to dodge a wobbling Vespa scooter on the rutted, earthquake damaged road.

"Is that all?" asked Sonia with something akin to disappointment in her voice.

"Oh no, *Agente* Leardi - we're going to arrest Donatello Altadonna and take him in for questioning," stated Beppe, as if their first offensive move in this investigation was the most self-evident course of action in the world.

Sonia smiled and shook her head in silent awe at her chief's spontaneous and apparently random decisions.

"Of course we are!" she said in a matter-of-fact tone of voice. "Why didn't *I* think of that?"

* * *

At more or less the same time as Beppe and Sonia were negotiating the bends on the winding N17 road to L'Aquila, officers Danilo Simone, Gino Martelli, Oriana Salvati and Giovanni Palena were perched on a hillside in a vacant house which overlooked the 'fortress' belonging to the ex-mafia boss, Gianluca Alfieri. They already seemed to be working as a coherent team. At present, the 'local boy', Giovanni, was the natural leader – if only because he knew the terrain well. But Officer Palena was marginally older and his additional years as a policeman had bestowed a measure of maturity which Danilo and Gino would acquire over time. That, at least, was how Oriana Salvati explained to herself the attraction that she was decidedly experiencing towards the officer from L'Aquila. In the past, she had, when provoked, turned on her colleagues in Pescara, uttering such scathing words as: "That's the only trouble with working here – you are all either too old or plain immature!" She had thoroughly earned her nickname, *La Spinosa*. But Gino and Danilo could hardly fail to notice the softening of her features as soon as Giovanni Palena appeared on the scene. It was a trifle galling, they decided, but since they all had to work together, it was more appropriate to feel relief about her mellowing attitude towards her male colleagues.

It had been thanks to Giovanni Palena's initiative that a house for sale, overlooking the Alfieri property, had been commandeered from a reluctant estate agent. Like so many properties around L'Aquila, it had suffered minor earthquake damage to parts of the house. The owner could not afford – or was unwilling to fork out for - the necessary repairs. He was living in the hope that he could dupe some wealthy Milanese buyer, wishing to fulfil a bucolic dream, into acquiring the property. A German buyer would be even better – there already was one waiting in the wings, his estate agent had optimistically hinted. It was, therefore, very irritating to be told that the police were insisting on taking the property over at short notice; "for as long as it takes", the estate agent had been informed. "And not a word about this to *anyone*, *Signor* Tomei," he had been warned by Giovanni Palena's officer-in-command, *Ispettore* Fabrizio De Sanctis. "If you're lucky, it should only be for a couple of days, but if you tell a single living soul about it, I can promise you we shall arrest you for obstructing the police whilst carrying out their duties. *Sono chiaro,*[60] *Signor Tomei?"*

The estate agent assured him that the message was abundantly clear.

"But what shall I tell the owner?" pleaded the estate agent.

"Nothing at all, *signore.* If there's a problem, contact me and we will deal with the owner. We understand he is living in his house in Montesilvano, so there is no need to tell him anything."

* * *

The immediate problem which faced the four police officers was that the wall surrounding Don Alfieri's estate was so high that, even from their vantage point further up the hill on the opposite side of the road, they could only see a limited area of the courtyard and one corner of the house. Furthermore, the double wrought iron gates were fitted with sheets of black painted metal, which obscured the front of the house from view. Beyond the house, further down the hill, they had an unobstructed view of the estate descending to the lower road, which followed the contours of Don Alfieri's estate as far as the tree filled valley below. It was very frustrating to know that Serena Vacri might be concealed somewhere in this house, out of their sight.

Since their arrival, earlier on that morning, they had taken it in turns to man the look-out post. They had selected one of the upstairs bedrooms whose window marginally afforded the best view of the *mafioso's* house. They had

---

[60] Am I making myself clear?

equipped themselves with a powerful pair of binoculars whose lenses were coated with a blue filter to lessen the risk of the glass catching and reflecting the sunlight. The team had decided that each one of them should do a one-hour shift. Gino had gone first, followed by Oriana – who had seen a portly lady in her seventies walking across the visible section of the courtyard, carrying a laundry basket full of washing, which she hung up on a drying rack in the sunshine. Nobody else crossed Oriana's line of vision during her watch.

11.35h Stout lady - aged about 75? Probably housekeeper – or a relative, Oriana wrote down in the notebook which Giovanni Palena had provided for the purpose.

Well before it was time for his 'watch' to begin, Giovanni appeared, carrying a fresh cup of coffee, and set it down on the window sill where Oriana was standing. She smiled her thanks in his direction. What struck her most was that Giovanni never seemed to do or say anything at all to try and impress her. She had the sensation that he was just being himself. For this reason, she never felt the need to deploy her usual prickly, defensive tactics. "He knows how to approach women," was Oriana's instinctive analysis of *Agente* Palena's character. She smiled appreciatively in his direction before concentrating again on the seemingly lifeless house opposite them.

"Nothing seems to be happening in there, Giovanni. I've seen a rather plump housekeeper and that's it. We're going to have to find some pretext or other to get inside the grounds – or at least make sure they have to open the gates," added Oriana. "Otherwise…"

"Have you ever seen the film Crocodile Dundee, Oriana?"

"One or two?" she asked smartly.

"I can't remember which one it was. But he got a gang of local youths to create a diversion outside the gangster's house while Crocodile Dundee sneaked inside."

"That's number two," she said. "I've seen those films at least six times each. They're my baby brother's favourite films. Are you suggesting that we create a diversion using local teenagers?"

"I wasn't being entirely serious, Oriana. In any case, I bet Alfieri keeps a couple of Dobermans running wild in those grounds," said Giovanni.

Oriana gave a start and then passed the binoculars to her companion.

"There's one of them, Giovanni," she said. He peered through the lenses, adjusting the focus.

"That's a Rottweiler," he said. "They always come in hungry pairs."

"Crocodile Dundee just had to talk to dogs to disarm them!" remembered Oriana. "We shall have to drug them – or shoot them. Unless you've got hidden talents in that direction, Giovanni!" she said disarmingly.

He smiled, shaking his head.

"Never been put to the test," he replied.

The hour passed without any other incident. Oriana wrote down "Rottweiler" on the note pad and they chatted to each other about their families, their favourite pastimes and their respective bosses, to while away Giovanni's watch, whilst he kept the binoculars trained on the target.

"Thank you for staying with me, Oriana," said Giovanni. "It would have been very dull without you."

They were looking at each other directly in the eyes. They might have kissed there and then but the spell was broken by Danilo coming up the stairs for his watch.

"I think it must be nearly lunchtime," said Danilo. "Bring me up a sandwich if you get a moment," he said pointedly. "It will be getting on for one o'clock by the time I finish my watch. I'm feeling hungry already."

"We've only seen one human being and one Rottweiler so far," said Giovanni. "I hope your watch proves a bit more exciting, Danilo."

Oriana and Giovanni went downstairs together. Danilo picked up the binoculars and dutifully peered at the seemingly deserted house. After no more than twenty minutes, during which time hunger and boredom were beginning to take their toll, Danilo's attention became riveted by something that had fleetingly caught his eye further down the hillside. Suddenly, his hunger and boredom vanished as the significance of what he had glimpsed sank in. He let out a cry of victory.

* * *

Beppe and Sonia's first port of call was the police station in L'Aquila. Diplomacy and good manners demanded that they should inform the inspector of the events that had taken place in Sulmona and how they intended to proceed with the investigation by taking the chief scientist, Donatello Altadonna, into custody. Even though Beppe outranked the inspector by a grade or so, he had already proved to be a pleasant and cooperative officer, who deserved to be kept in the picture.

"We would very much appreciate your presence when we go round to Altadonna's house, *ispettore*," Beppe requested.

"Thank you, *commissario*. I will accompany you with pleasure. By the way, don't forget that Altadonna is on trial in two days' time."

"Oh, we shall ensure that he attends the trial – have no fear!" said Beppe.

"If you can give me a minute or so, I must try to contact the defence lawyer. Romano Di Carlo's death will put a totally different perspective on things," said Inspector De Sanctis.

The defence lawyer, he was told by the secretary, was too busy to be disturbed. The inspector was wise enough not to leave such a delicate message with the secretary.

Beppe told his fellow officer that on no account should he make it public that Romano Di Carlo had been murdered before the official autopsy made the revelation inevitable. The inspector looked long and hard at Beppe and Sonia before nodding and saying wearily:

"*Santo cielo!* This is becoming a truly complex investigation, isn't it?"

"That's why we need you in with us, *ispettore*," added Sonia, hoping to emulate her chief's unfailing ability to get everybody on his side. Beppe looked at her with his customary poker-faced neutrality and nodded in the direction of Inspector De Sanctis. This was as close as he was prepared to go to indicate that he agreed entirely with his junior officer.

Fabrizio De Sanctis merely nodded in return. He had already decided that he trusted this *commissario* from Pescara.

For *Commissario* Stancato to utter the words, *"I really don't like this Altadonna individual"* would have been quite out of his professional character. But his request to his two colleagues, as they drew to a halt some fifty metres before Donatello Altadonna's house, revealed a streak of mischievousness beneath his official front.

"Could you give me a minute or so alone with our friend?" he asked Sonia and the Inspector. "I would just like to string him along for a minute or so. I'll beckon you over when I'm ready for you."

And so, the plain-clothed *commissario* strode towards Altadonna's house, while his two uniformed colleagues looked on, fascinated, through the windscreen of the stationary police car.

"I wish we could be flies on the wall during *this* conversation," she said to her colleague.

Donatello Altadonna opened the door almost immediately as if he had been on the point of going out. The look of surprise on his face at seeing the man who was supposed to be renting his flat in Pescara gave way quickly to an expression of mild irritation.

"I thought I suggested that you should sort things out with my estate agent, *Signor...?* Altadonna had paused briefly while he tried to remember the preposterous surname which this man with the disconcerting stare had given him two days ago.

As Beppe merely continued to stand there in silence, the chief scientist was forced to continue speaking.

"Look, I have an appointment to meet my colleagues with our lawyer. I have to appear in court in two days' time, so if you would just ask my estate agent any questions you might have, I'm sure he will be only too willing to help you,

Signor... I'm sorry. I cannot recall your surname for the moment."

"*Commissario* Giuseppe Stancato, *professore*," said Beppe, holding up his ID badge a few centimetres away from the scientist's astonished face.

Donatello Altadonna's capacity for assuming the pretence of outraged innocence was impressive. It might well have fooled a man with lesser experience than Beppe Stancato. As ever, the tell-tale signs of panic could always be detected in the unconscious, shifty movement of the eyes, over which there is little control. This police officer was, once again, fixing him with that impassive stare, forcing him to search for words.

"What's this all about, *commissario?* There had better be a good reason for your visit – and your previous childish play-acting!"

"It's about a vanishing girl, *professore.*"

There was a brief look of shock on Altadonna's face followed, Beppe noticed, by an inexplicable expression of relief which crossed the scientist's face. Beppe had to control his impassive stare in order to maintain his grip on the situation and cover his surprise at this apparent set-back.

"Oh, you mean Marta, my young housekeeper, *commissario!* I'm sorry - I should have reported her missing when she didn't turn up this morning. But honestly, I didn't want to bother the police at this time. I expect you'll find her somewhere in Pescara. She must have decided to stay on with her friends. She can be a bit unreliable at times. Don't worry about her. I'm sure she'll turn up."

Beppe had realised almost immediately how the confusion had arisen. Surely, it couldn't possibly be that *Agente* Remo had plucked up the courage to ask Marta out and kept her with him the following day too - just as Sonia, the match-maker, had hoped? Beppe almost smiled with inner pleasure. The joker card was still safely in his hand.

"I'm sorry, *professore*. There seems to be a misunderstanding. I wasn't referring to Marta. Shall we just say that I was very disturbed, a few days ago, to find your flat in Pescara occupied by your niece, Serena."

The chief scientist suddenly became flustered but still put up a defiant, last-ditch attempt at bluffing his way out of the dilemma.

"Oh, you need not be concerned about my niece, *commissario*. She'll be out of the apartment within the next few days..."

"I should have said, *professore*, that we found her deeply asleep on the bed. She was the worse for wear from a hefty dose of some drug."

"I knew nothing about this, *commissario*," replied Altadonna. "I have no idea what she got up to when she was not in my house in L'Aquila."

"We have reason to believe otherwise, *professore*," stated Beppe calmly. "Now, if you would like to go and pack a hold-all with the things you will need overnight, I am placing you in custody for complicity in the abduction of your niece."

"This is absurd, *commissario*. I have to appear in court in connection with the tragic events that have struck this town. My solicitor and colleagues are waiting for me as we speak. There is no way you have a right to take such a course of action at this moment in time. You will have to wait until after the hearing this Wednesday. Then I will help you if I can," stated Altadonna defiantly.

"*Professore*, I have *every* right to take you in for questioning. I would advise you to cooperate with me, and allow me to accompany you to the police station. It is in your own interest to do so."

Beppe was holding the news of Romano's death in reserve as well as deliberately understating the seriousness of his niece's situation.

Donatello Altadonna briefly entertained the thought that this singular police officer was acting alone. He contemplated making a run for it. But the unwavering and implacable lack of expression on the *commissario's* face was disconcerting. Reading his mind, Beppe signalled with his hand for his two colleagues to make an appearance.

Donatello Altadonna had not spotted the police car down the road. He knew his ordeal was not over.

"I will not cooperate unless my lawyer is present," he said in a surly manner.

"It strikes me your lawyer will have to be in two places at once, *professore*. He will certainly have his work cut out over the next few days, don't you think?" said Beppe affably.

Donatello Altadonna's lawyer was a woman, but he didn't bother pointing this out.

"Officer Leardi will accompany you upstairs again to pack your things, *professore*," said Beppe. To Sonia, he whispered a few words, inaudible to the other two men.

"Don't forget Pippo's trick!" Sonia nodded with a brief, complicit smile on her face.

"Oh, it's *YOU!*" said Altadonna rudely. He had just recognised the uniformed police officer who had fooled him into believing she was *that* police inspector's partner!

"After you, *professore*," she said in her most ingratiating manner.

* * *

Agenti Gino, Oriana and Giovanni plainly heard Danilo's cry of triumph from the floor above them, echoing round the sparsely furnished house. They were in the kitchen preparing a rudimentary lunch and discussing how they could get a better view of Don Alfieri's house – and eventually gain access for a reconnoitre. Oriana and Gino had decided they must talk to their chief as a matter of urgency. He would be able to supply them with a plan of the house at the very least.

"Colombo is bound to come up with some ingenious idea about how to get in there!" had added Oriana loyally. She then had to explain to Giovanni how their new *capo* had come to earn his nickname.

Danilo's shout interrupted their conversation. They looked at one another and, as if they had been joined together, headed for the stairs.

They could tell by the way he was holding the binoculars, with his elbows sticking out, that he was concentrating on a specific target. All he said in answer to their eager questions was:

"Just a minute, *ragazzi*..."

After what seemed an interminable interval to the three police officers, who were peering out of the window at the seemingly deserted countryside, trying to see *anything* that had provoked their colleague's excitement, Danilo uttered the words "Gotcha, you bastard!"

"Come on, Danilo! Stop messing us about," pleaded an impatient Oriana.

"It just caught my eye because it didn't fit in with the green of the countryside – otherwise I would have missed it altogether..."

"WHAT?" the three others shouted in chorus.

"Look, right down the bottom of the hill. You can just spot a red Audi parked under the trees," he said, passing the binoculars to the person standing nearest to him, which happened to be Giovanni.

"I can just see it... but so what?"

Gino had to explain about the tall, Latin American doctor who had abducted Serena Vacri.

"We know that he rented a red Audi on the day The Sleeping Beauty was abducted from the hospital," added Oriana. "But, Danilo, you can't assume that the red Audi belongs to him just because...it's a red Audi. You've got us all excited over nothing!"

"I haven't finished telling you the rest of it yet," Danilo said smugly. "I've just seen Doctor Diego Ramirez – or whatever name he goes by. He appeared in the courtyard just now and disappeared into the house."

"You mean, you saw him walking up the hillside and you wouldn't let us have a look too!" exclaimed Oriana sharply.

"No, Oriana. That's just the point – I *didn't* see him until he appeared just outside the house," explained Danilo.

It was Giovanni who cottoned on first. His expletive was a measure of his surprise.

"*Porca puttana!*[61] Don Alfieri has got an escape route! There must be a tunnel leading down the hillside!"

The three of them let out a spontaneous cheer.

---

[61] A pithy way of expressing surprise. 'porca' = pig : puttana = whore. I know – it doesn't make sense!

"Just wait till we tell Colombo what we've discovered!" said Oriana with a broad grin spreading across her face.

It was revealing, thought Gino, how everybody – without exception – genuinely did not want to let their new *capo* down. A credit to his unobtrusive style of leadership, no doubt. It did not matter that the discovery of the escape route did nothing to prove that a twenty-two-year-old girl was being held prisoner in this house against her will, with every chance that her young life had already been maimed for good.

Gino dismissed these sombre reflections. It was not the moment to harbour negative thoughts. The discovery had certainly given them the necessary motivation to persevere with their vigil, he conceded.

The next minor breakthrough, which happened on Oriana's afternoon watch, was so obvious in its quotidian simplicity that it took them by surprise.

10: *Reeling in the catch*

Commissario Beppe Stancato placed a cup of coffee on the table in front of the seismologist.

"I thought you might like this, *professore*. We didn't put sugar or milk in but we can get you the sachets if you like."

"No – thank you!" replied Altadonna brusquely. "Let's just get on with this charade."

The more intractable Altadonna became, the more polite and gracious was Beppe's response – all with the intention of disarming his adversary from the outset. Beppe was a firm believer in the principle that the more aggression an interrogator displayed, the less the truth was likely to emerge. Altadonna had regained some of his aplomb and was beginning to harbour the secret belief that this policeman could not possibly have any concrete evidence against him. Beppe knew this to be partly true – most of his 'proof' was based on hearsay and reasonable deduction. But he had no intention of allowing such a minor drawback to deter him from winkling the truth out of this arrogant man.

"My lawyer and my four colleagues are quite undoubtedly waiting for me in my lawyer's studio as we speak..." continued Donatello Altadonna agressively.

"Three," interjected Beppe, so unobtrusively that the seismologist failed to notice the numerical correction for several seconds.

"Pardon me, *commissario,* but you are ill-informed. There are the three other scientists and the Civil Protection agent, Romano..."

"I am so sorry to have to break this news to you, *professore*," Beppe interrupted quietly, "but one member of your team has tragically departed from this life."

Beppe's dramatic but deliberately imprecise declaration had the desired effect on the seismologist. The swift transition from fear to guilt which flashed across his face while he tried to master his reactions told Beppe all he needed to know. He maintained an expression of sympathetic concern on his face while Sonia, sitting by his side, remained vigilant but impassive.

"Poor Romano!" said Altadonna under his breath.

Beppe knew he was on firm ground from that point onwards. Sonia had had time to tell Beppe that the "Pippo" phone trick had worked as planned. Altadonna had informed her that he needed a visit to the *bagno*[62] before being escorted to the police station. He had made a phone call - just as the Latin American doctor had done, whilst sitting on the toilet seat. Sonia had made no attempt to take his phone from him, which would assuredly have put him on his guard. On Beppe's instruction, she had phoned the technicians at their Pescara headquarters. She was able to establish that Altadonna *had* made a call to an 'unknown' number just outside L'Aquila.

"It went like this," said Bianca Bomba, reading from a transcript.

Altadonna: "The police have taken me in for questioning about the disappearance of my... little sparrow"

Man's voice: "Get off the line immediately. Deal with the problem – professore. And change your mobile phone again."

There could be little doubt whose voice it was.

---

[62] Bathroom – a euphemism for 'toilet'

"It must be to the new number Don Alfieri is using, Sonia," Bianca Bomba had told her. "We've got some very interesting conversations for you to listen to when you get back."

Sonia had slipped into the interview room and passed Beppe a note which said simply:

Yes, he did. 329 666008 – they are referring to Serena as the "little sparrow".

"What makes you think it was Romano Di Carlo who died, *professore?*" continued Beppe, with what appeared to be a tone of innocent curiosity in his voice. Sonia experienced a sudden rush of admiration for her *capo*. It was a privilege to be working next to someone who was so skilled at manipulating words to achieve the ends of justice. She had to stop herself placing a hand on his thigh under cover of the table. She remembered that there was another young officer standing directly behind them on guard by the interview room door. His presence just saved her from an embarrassing gaffe.

Altadonna was looking flustered but he still regained sufficient composure to attempt to stave off the inevitable collapse of his case.

"Well...naturally, I assumed it would be Romano who had... Was it a heart attack? He has been suffering from unbearable stress ever since...that night," the seismologist finished in a lame attempt to cover up his blatant *faux pas*.

Beppe was staring impassively at his adversary again, forcing Altadonna to fill the hiatus with words – any words.

"Or maybe it was Corrado... *I* don't know, do I?" he concluded, sounding rattled again.

Beppe let out a long sigh, as if to say: "Do we *really* have to keep up this pretence?"

"You were right first time, *professore* – as I am sure you had every reason to suspect."

"What do you mean by that last comment?" snapped the seismologist, with the first hint of real dread creeping into his voice. "Are you implying, *commissario*, that I might have known something about this in advance?"

"Your colleague, Romano Di Carlo's body was found this morning up a mountain side. He had a shotgun wound which took away most of his chest cavity," continued Beppe implacably. "We found a suicide note in his car, which was abandoned some half a kilometre away from where his body was found."

Sonia was staggered to see the fleeting hint of a smile on Altadonna's face, quickly replaced by an expression of grave concern. Beppe was not surprised. He interpreted the seismologist's reaction as one of relief. It was, deduced the detective, a sure sign that Altadonna had assumed his colleague had been murdered – which implied that he had had an indirect hand in the killing. Donatello Altadonna was quite unused to being interrogated thought Beppe; he was very inexpert at dissimulation. It was making Beppe's task much easier. Altadonna was, after all, neither as artful nor as ruthless as the average *'ndrangeta 'boss'* back in his native Calabria.

"Poor Romano," said the seismologist. "I had no idea that he was suffering to such a catastrophic extent. We have lost a good friend and colleague. We worked very well together," he added with a degree of hypocrisy which made Beppe cringe, making him even more determined to break him.

"Apart from the blazing row you had with him when you were round at his house the other night," stated Beppe, looking the man fixedly in the eyes. Altadonna turned a bright red – a mixture of embarrassment and anger that he was being unmasked by this deceptively benign police officer.

"Never mind, *professore*. We are not here to dwell on the death of your colleague this afternoon. We can discuss Romano Di Carlo's murder another day..."

Altadonna had turned white with shock.

"But... you said he had committed suicide," he stammered.

Beppe had secretly enjoyed delivering the *coup de grâce*, he had to admit. Altadonna was about to be torn to shreds.

"I am so sorry if I misled you, *professore*. What I said, if you recall, was that we found a suicide note in his car. I apologise if I led you to believe that Romano took his own life. I should have told you the suicide note was a blatant forgery. No, there is not a shadow of doubt that your colleague was brutally murdered sometime early this morning and his body left on a hillside near Sulmona. We shall come back to that matter on a subsequent occasion. Right now, *professore*, we would like to talk to you about the abduction of your niece, Serena Vacri. Where do you suppose she is at this moment in time, *professore?*"

"Why do you keep talking about her abduction, *commissario?* I allowed her to use my flat for a few days. I have no control over her free time. She is well over twenty-one years of age. As to her drug habits..."

Beppe allowed himself to let out a sudden growl of frustration and impatience. The feigned anger on his face was convincing enough to make Altadonna feel physically threatened. Little did the seismologist know that this was a prearranged signal for Sonia Leardi, sitting patiently by Beppe's side, to take over the task of breaking Altadonna's resistence.

"We found your niece in a state of near coma, *professore*," began Sonia. "She had been forcibly injected with a nigh on lethal dose of diazepam and rohypnol – I assume you are sufficiently well-informed about drugs to know just how dangerous they can be."

Sonia spoke non-stop for over fifteen minutes. She managed to instil a tone of bitter anger into her voice, which she maintained throughout her diatribe. She did not omit a single element of the unfolding events of the last few days, including Serena's abduction from the 'safety' of the hospital by the Latin American anaesthetist. But it was being forced to listen to the account of his invasion of Marta's bedroom and his subsequent threatening behaviour towards his niece which seemed to shake the last vestiges of belief in his own immunity from being accused of direct involvement in her fate. But to their amazement, Donatello Altadonna made one last ditch attempt at defending his totally undermined position.

"My lawyer will see to it that none of these accusations stand up in court, *commissario*. It is as ridiculous as trying to blame me for causing an earthquake…"

He had stopped his sentence simply because he had been disorientated and unnerved by the unruffled look of malicious conviction on the face of the usually enigmatic police officer. He feared Beppe's next words simply because he had the instinctive certainty that they would topple his defences like a boy demolishing a sandcastle with one well-aimed kick.

Beppe's voice was relaxed and calm as he delivered the fatal blow.

"Do the words *'little sparrow'* mean anything to you, *professore?*"

The seismologist's face crumpled as he realised the full implication of the words that Beppe had just uttered. It was as if he had grown ten years older within the space of one single second of time.

"Now, *professore,* we shall leave you to contemplate your future in the peace of a police cell," continued Beppe almost kindly. "But remember this – if your niece dies, then you will be complicit in her murder. Oh... and by the way, would you give me your mobile phone, please?"

Alatadonna put a mobile phone down on the table. Beppe had the impression that he had complied with the request too readily. He checked the last number dialled. It was not the number on the piece of paper which Sonia had handed him.

"And the other phone you used to contact... a certain gentleman in Monticchio," he said disarmingly. "I do seriously suggest you make up your mind to cooperate fully before we meet again, *professore.*"

At this juncture, Beppe received a call from Gino, which he brought to a rapid conclusion.

***

Donatello Altadonna spent a restless night in a police cell considering whether he should "cooperate fully" with his inquisitor. By dawn, he had come to the conclusion that he had no choice in the matter. He did not even bother asking if he could talk to his lawyer. During a fitful sleep, he had a strange dream about a cockerel running helplessly round a farmyard amongst the hens – who were clucking gleefully because the bird that was *him* had had all its plumage plucked, ready to be grilled over a hot charcoal brazier standing at the ready.

* * *

Gino, Danilo and Giovanni, were sitting round the kitchen table while Oriana was upstairs peering intermittently through the binoculars at an empty landscape. The desire for action was growing by the hour as was the feeling of frustration that they had not made any more illuminating discoveries since the appearance of Diego Ramirez before lunchtime.

However, they had collectively decided on their next move. Two of them would take a hike down to the bottom of the hill at the far end of Don Alfieri's estate to check out the tunnel and the number plate of the red Audi. This course of action would at least alleviate the tedium for two members of the team – even if the excursion would only account for little more than forty minutes of this long first day of their vigil. There was a fair amount of banter flying about as the three young officers all argued the toss as to who the lucky pair should be. In the end, Giovanni suggested they should see who drew the short straws – literally, as it happened, since they had found a heap of it in the stables by the house. Danilo pointed out that this would not work because they would then have to decide which one of them would hold the straws. That person should automatically be excluded from the excursion down the hillside.

They decided that it would be unwise to make any decision without consulting Oriana first; although the shrew seemed to have become several degrees tamer, a unilateral decision on their part might risk a renewed lashing from her tongue.

"Is it really Oriana you are describing?" asked Giovanni in disbelief. Danilo and Gino regaled their new colleague with samples of Oriana's choicer comments.

Near the end of Oriana's watch, the three men joined her upstairs to explain what they had decided. In true *"spinosa"* fashion, she tartly pointed out that it could only be herself and Giovanni who should make the trip down to the bottom of Don Alfieri's estate since the Latin American anaesthetist would certainly recognise Danilo and Gino from their previous encounter if, by some unlucky chance, he decided to go out in his car while they were lurking about.

"You'd be running the risk of scuppering the whole operation!" she concluded glaring at Gino and Danilo, her expressive mouth turned down at the corners - all her former defiance rekindled. Giovanni was impressed but did not attempt to gloat over his victory.

"By the way, *ragazzi*, there was a local baker's van delivering bread and stuff about ten minutes ago. They had to open the gates," announced Oriana with deliberate coolness.

There was a stunned silence for five seconds before Oriana was greeted by a barrage of protests and questions from the other three.

"Why didn't you call us?"

"What did you see? Who did you see?"

"How long were the gates open for?"

Oriana waited until her colleagues had quietened down before she replied, quite unruffled:

"There was no point in calling you up to have a look, boys; it was all over in a couple of minutes. I saw the woman who we assume is their housekeeper, but I'm not so sure about that. A younger woman in her late forties or very early fifties came out. She was good-looking, dark-skinned – could be Don Alfieri's wife, I suppose. But the way she was talking to the housekeeper reminded me of the way a younger woman would address her mother - you know, in familiar tones. And the older woman was answering her back."

"Could be," said Giovanni. "I imagine a retired *mafioso boss* – assuming he really has retired – would take his family with him."

"They paid the baker in cash," added Oriana, "and that was it."

"But it does give us an idea how we might get in to have a look round. They must have other stuff delivered on an almost daily basis," suggested Gino.

"We'll look into it tomorrow," said Giovanni.

Oriana and Giovanni set off on their mini-trek down the hillside. Having nothing much else to do, Danilo resumed his watch while Gino tried to phone Beppe. Danilo was intrigued to see Giovanni and Oriana briefly holding hands and talking incessantly before they disappeared behind the cover of some trees. Gino got through to his chief, who was, he said, "interviewing a collaborator". Beppe promised to phone him back as soon as possible.

At the bottom of the hill, Giovanni and Oriana were surprised to discover how well concealed the entrance to the tunnel was from the eyes of a casual passer-by. Nobody using the minor road would notice anything untoward.

The entrance to the tunnel itself was overgrown. Only the newness of the metal gates and the substantial padlock would have alerted a sharp-eyed observer to the incongruity of making such a discovery in the middle of the countryside.

"Look at this notice, Oriana," said Giovanni, unconsciously whispering at this sinister discovery hidden in the gloomy shadows of the trees. He was pointing to a yellow metal plaque attached to the gate.

"*Attenti - pericolo vipere,*"[63] read Oriana. "*O dio,* Giovanni. I'm petrified of snakes!"

"Obviously designed to put off the faint-hearted," said Giovanni. "It is rare to die from the bite of a viper," he added enjoying sounding reassuring in the presence of a fearful Oriana. He was secretly relieved to discover that this bright, sparky girl was actually afraid of *something*. It made her more approachable.

"Let's get out of here, Giovanni," said Oriana.

"We'd better check the car number plate first."

The red Audi was parked between two trees, invisible from the road. Another car, a silver-grey Renault Clio was parked nearby. Giovanni made a mental note of the car and its registration number.

"AP 115 CK. That's the anaesthetist's car alright," said Giovanni, checking the number against the one Gino had scribbled down for him before they set out. "Now we can go, Oriana, if you want," suggested Giovanni mindful of her nervousness about poisonous snakes. "Oriana?" he said as he noticed that she was no longer standing by his side. He experienced a moment's panic before he realised that she was round the back of the red Audi, peering through the rear

---

[63] Beware of vipers

window. She moved quickly to the side window, beckoning Giovanni to come nearer.

"Look!" she said excitedly, pointing to something.

A young women's pink cardigan lay where it had been discarded on the back seat. It had the initials S.V. embroidered in blood red cotton on the breast pocket.

"Where a pink cardigan and a red Audi are, the Sleeping Beauty shall not be far away!" intoned Giovanni solemnly as if it had been a quote from the Old Testament. Oriana linked her arm under Giovanni's and they started the twenty-minute hike back towards the house – a tiny ray of hope illuminating the darkness of this sinister case. At least, the discovery indicated that Serena Vacri was still alive.

"They would hardly leave her clothes lying around if they had bumped her off," argued Oriana.

11: *Midnight manoeuvres*

"*Bravi, ragazzi!* Thank you for all your hard work – and patience. If you can just keep going for another couple of days and see what else you can find out. Or I can send some of the Pescara team to relieve you, if you want…"

"No, *capo*, we've got into a good routine," said Danilo, who had looked questioningly at the others, who were listening to the phone call in loudspeaker mode, before answering: "We'll manage."

"As you wish, but I agree with Oriana and Giovanni that you need to put tracking devices on those two cars as soon as possible. I don't believe Donatello Altadonna has told us everything he knows yet. We must face up to the possibility that our Sleeping Beauty is not being kept in Alfieri's house. In any case, I should like to know what Ramirez-Rojas, the anaesthetist, gets up to. I want to make sure we nail him as well."

"Yes, *capo* – so do we!" Danilo added with feeling. "Is there any chance of you sending someone up to L'Aquila with the tracking devices early tomorrow morning? The sooner the better…"

"Tomorrow morning, Danilo? You must be joking!" said Beppe.

"*Mi dispiace, capo.* I just thought…"

"I'm going to get someone – probably Giacomo D'Amico – to bring them up this evening. He knows the area round Monticchio. He'll find you. We need those tracking devices on the cars immediately – just in case the anaesthetist decides to take a midnight trip somewhere. Can you sort that out – even if it's after dark?"

Danilo looked at Giovanni and Oriana again. They both nodded, although Oriana's nod was very half-hearted. She was having visions of treading on a viper in the dark.

"Yes, I think so, *capo,* although Oriana is anxious about stepping on a…"

The three men could not believe the speed with which Oriana closed the intervening space between her and Danilo, wresting the mobile phone from his grasp while she glared at her colleague in fury. She addressed their chief with the words:

"No problem, *capo*. Giovanni and I will do it after dark."

She gave Danilo and Gino a withering look of scorn and avoided looking directly at Giovanni as she realised too late the ambiguity behind the words she had uttered.

"*Giovanotti puerili!*"[64] she hissed under her breath, before realising that Gino and Danilo had maintained a perfectly expressionless look on their faces. She even managed a crooked smile in their direction, adding pointedly: "Not tonight, anyway!" Danilo and Gino laughed good-humouredly, conquering the tinge of envy they both felt. Giovanni, still technically on watch, continued to study the horizon intently. There was a discreet smirk on his face.

All three of the men remembered that their chief was still on the other end of the line.

"*Ci scusi, capo,*" said Dino. "Did you overhear that?"

Beppe feigned ignorance. He had latched on to the innuendo immediately. Nature seems to be taking its course, thought the *commissario*.

---

[64] Oriana's viper tongue at work! Puerile youths!

"By the way, *ragazzi*," he added. "Don't worry too much about gaining access to Don Alfieri's house and grounds. Just make sure you don't run any risk of alerting the household that they are under surveillance. We've just had a talk with Altadonna's brother-in-law, the architect and builder. He's proving to be far less intractable as to what's at stake in this investigation than Altadonna himself. And guess what he did when he finished renovating Alfieri's house?"

Nobody hazarded a guess, so Beppe continued:

"He made a 'virtual reality' DVD of the whole place – including the cellars. He managed to do it all without Don Alfieri realising what he had done."

"Why did he make the video, *capo?* Did he suspect that...?"

"I had the impression he was simply proud of what he had achieved. He seems to be a real craftsman," Beppe replied.

"Che bello!" said Oriana.

"Now we'd better return to Pescara," continued Beppe. "*Agente* Leardi is looking at me accusingly. I think it must be past her lunchtime! *"Ciao, ragazzi. A domani."*

* * *

If Sonia was entertaining the hope of spending some precious time with Beppe that evening, she was to be disappointed. He looked crestfallen but gave her a long list of things he had to do before midnight. All Sonia had eaten that afternoon was a *panino* filled with *salame* and lettuce. Beppe had not given a moment's thought to food. In the end he compromised.

"If I finish by ten o'clock, I'll call you, Sonia, and we could go out for something to eat."

It was the best she could hope for.

"Is there anything I can do to help?" she asked plaintively.

Beppe was tempted to say 'yes' but in the end, he suggested she went home and relaxed. Tomorrow was going to be another long day, he told her.

Reluctantly, she turned her back on him in order to hide the tears which had begun, quite unbidden, to well in the corner of her eyes. She left the police station without looking back. Thus, she could not see the look of sadness on Beppe's face as her determined footsteps increased the physical gap between them.

Commissario Stancato did his best to complete the tasks he had set himself before ten o'clock. Left to himself he might have managed it. But *agente* Remo Mastrodicasa, on duty at the front desk, informed him apologetically that the *Questore* was on the warpath, demanding to see him as soon as he returned.

"He said he would wait until midnight for you if he has to, *capo*," added Remo, looking even more contrite.

Beppe gave his junior officer a rueful smile and asked him to inform the *Questore* that he would be up there in fifteen minutes.

"There is something else I have to do before I see him, Remo. But don't tell him that please! By the way, Remo...tomorrow morning, I want you take this photocopy to the Audi concessionaire and compare the writing to Ramirez-Rojas's signature on his car lease agreement." Beppe handed him a copy of Romano Di Carlo's suicide note.

"Don't believe what it says, Remo," said Beppe, as he saw the look of horror on Remo's face. "It's not what it seems. He was actually murdered in cold blood."

The *commissario* walked off with the intention of allowing his unduly squeamish junior officer to come to terms with the realities of being a policeman. Beppe thought to himself that Remo might never have witnessed anything more blood-curdling during his career than a severely under-cooked steak. Little did Beppe suspect that this former waiter would turn out to be their reluctant hero before the long week was over.

He ran into the senior member of his team, Giacomo d'Amico, who was all ready to set out for L'Aquila to deliver the car tracking devices.

"Thank you, Giacomo for giving up your time – and for holding the fort here during the last couple of days."

"I shan't mind taking a drive up the mountains, *capo*. My wife is not best pleased. She always claims I allow myself to be exploited by my superiors."

"I'm sorry to have given her grief, Giacomo. Please convey my apologies if you think it will help."

"Oh, she's alright, underneath it all. She never holds grudges for long, *capo*."

"So, do you feel confident you'll find the house where our team is?" asked Beppe.

"Yes, *capo*. I've got a satnav in my car and Gino has given me the necessary coordinates. I'm taking my car because we don't want a police car nosing about near Don Alfieri's place. I'll stay there until they've fixed the devices on the cars. That way I shall know that I won't have had a wasted journey."

"*Di nuovo grazie mille,* Giacomo," said Beppe shaking his senior officer by the hand.

Beppe's head told him he should go straight up to the *Questore's* office on the top floor and face the music without procrastinating. But inexplicably, he found that his feet were leading him down to the basement where the two technicians worked. They were both preparing to go home but Pippo was manning the telephone intercept apparatus, one earpiece of a set of headphones held up to his left ear whilst complex green and red lines danced on a couple of screens in front of him.

"We've got all the phones tapped now, *commissario,*" said Bianca Bomba. "How did you obtain Altadonna's new number? You're really quite a smooth operator, aren't you?" she added with an impudent smile on her face. Beppe found it impossible to take umbrage at the two technicians. He suspected it was only a challenge on their part to put him to the test – as well as, possibly, to alleviate the tedium of having to spend so much time in the windowless basement.

"We are assuming you must have confiscated Altadonna's mobiles, *commissario,*" Marco Pollutri chimed in. "He hasn't made any calls for several hours."

Beppe replied that their deduction was correct and told them about the seismologist's attempt to conceal one of his phones.

"Well done, *commissario!*" The compliment sounded sincere.

Bianca handed him a file containing the transcripts of Altadonna's recent conversations.

"You should find some interesting material there," said Bianca as the two technicians headed for the exit.

Procrastinating yet again, Beppe sat down and skimmed through the three or so pages of dialogue. If he could find something incriminating in these conversations, he reasoned, he would be able to convince the *Questore* more easily that he was not squandering police resources – which is what he suspected their *tête-à-tête* would be about. Not that he believed it was really his role in life to mollify his superiors. But experience had taught him that they could only be ignored for a limited period of time. Thus, the interruption to his main purpose in life at this moment in time was to be regarded as a necessary evil.

The telephone call from Altadonna to the person whom he now recognised as the mafioso '*boss*' Don Alfieri was all the ammunition that he needed – despite the covert language used by the latter. The call must have been made almost immediately after they had set up the original phone tap, he calculated. Beppe scanned the transcript rapidly:

Altadonna: Buonasera signore.   Io sono il Professore Alta....
Alfieri: I know who you are. Why are you disturbing me now?
Altadonna: There's a problem with one of my team. He claims to know about our... our project, and about my n... the girl, I mean.
Alfieri: Where can we find your colleague? We shall talk to him man to man – in a way he will be sure to understand.
Altadonna: I don't want anything to happen to him. It will look bad if...
Alfieri: Signor professor![65] *Choose your words with care. Remember we have your "little sparrow".*

Altadonna: *(Stammering)* He'll be in L'Aquila tomorrow, talking to his lawyer.

Alfieri: *Text me the lawyer's address and details of his car – especially the registration plate. Leave the rest to us.*

Altadonna: Where is my… *"little sparrow"*? How is she?

Alfieri; *Buona notte, professor!*

Beppe shuddered instinctively as he read the transcript, hearing the voices in his head. The ruthlessness of people like Don Alfieri struck terror in the heart of normal mortals. It was diabolical in its remorseless single-mindedness. Whereas other people felt fear, Beppe became more resolved to stamp out the evil – even if he was painfully aware that the beast would grow two heads once one was cut off. He made his way upstairs and would have carried on to the top floor to keep his appointment with the *Questore*. He was already more than thirty minutes late.

Remo, manning the phones, called him over urgently.

"*Commissario…* we've just had a call from the police station in Orvieto. Serena Vacri's mother turned up to report she has not been able to contact her daughter for over a week…"

"You didn't tell them anything, did you, Remo?"

"No, *capo*, of course not."

Beppe was pensive for so long that Remo was becoming embarrassed.

"*Capo?*" he asked nervously.

"Phone them back, Remo, and tell them to suggest to Serena's mother that she come down to Pescara – without saying anything about her daughter being missing, naturally.

---

[65] By omitting the final 'e' of the word 'professore', Don Alfieri embues the title with a hint of disrespect. Italian can be very subtle.

By the way, Remo," added Beppe with a mischievous smile on his face. "Talking about missing girls, what have you done with our Marta? I hope *her* mother isn't going to report a missing daughter too!"

Remo blushed to his roots but had a sheepish grin all over his face. How on earth had his chief managed to winkle *that* little secret out of thin air, he wondered.

"No, *capo*. Don't worry. She's told her mother she won't be home for a couple of days."

"*In bocca al lupo,* Remo," said Beppe sincerely. To his horror, Beppe had felt a tinge of envy in respect of his junior colleague's good fortune – a reaction that might well have subconsciously influenced him later on that night.

Remo went to pick up the phone to call the police station in Orvieto when the internal telephone emitted a shrill ring – not to be ignored.

"It's the *Questore* again, *capo*."

"Tell him I'm on my way up," said Beppe hurriedly heading for the stairs.

The *Questore,* Dante Di Pasquale, beneath his severe mask of authority, was a reasonable man, even an understanding one, according to those who knew him. Nevertheless, he felt he should register some form of protest at the late arrival of his Calabrian colleague.

"*Commissario* Stancato," he began sarcastically, "I am aware that clocks in the deep south of our Peninsula work at a totally different rate to official Italian time, but I have been waiting for you to appear for something approaching two hours. I do hope my opposite number in Catanzaro didn't send you up to Pescara simply because he despaired of your time-keeping! You are looking a little weary, by the way," he finished more kindly.

Beppe had to revise his opinion of his chief very rapidly. The trouble with good leaders of men, thought Beppe, is that they succeed in disarming one with just a few well-chosen words.

"I do apologise, *Signor Questore*," he said contritely. "My lateness is inexcusable. It won't happen again, I promise."

The *Questore* listened to his fellow officer talking non-stop for well over an hour, by the end of which time, he too had been forced to revise his opinion of his recently appointed *sostituto-commissario* from the deep south of their country.

"*Bravo, commissario! Bravi a tutti voi!* I cannot believe how much ground you have covered in such a short space of time. I agree entirely with you that solving the disappearance of your Sleeping Beauty – as you call her – must be the priority. I'm backing you all the way."

They parted with a weary but warm handshake.

* * *

It was twenty-five minutes to eleven; too late to call Sonia, he realised. So he called her anyway. A sleep-blurred voice answered the phone:

"*Pronto. Chi è?*" asked the voice.

"It's me, Beppe. I'm sorry. I've woken you up, haven't I? I wanted to say good night, Sonia. I've missed you. I've only just finished here."

The silence was so prolonged that Beppe became anxious. Then he heard a sound. He could not be sure whether she was giggling or sobbing.

"Why don't you come round and say goodnight in person?" whispered Sonia's sleepily seductive voice.

"Alright, yes," he replied after what seemed to Sonia like an eternity. "I'll be there in ten minutes."

Still torn between duty and pleasure, he went back down to wish Pippo goodnight.

"How long have you got to stay here, Pippo?"

"Someone will relieve me at midnight, *capo*. Go home now. Don't worry about me."

Beppe did not go home but headed for Sonia's apartment with a mixture of anticipation tinged with guilt. By morning time, they both knew that the first link in a chain which might bind them together for a lifetime had been forged. Such a prospect must have occasioned dismay in the heart of Sonia's next-door neighbour, who had banged crossly on the adjoining wall just before midnight.

"Next time we'll go out to sea in the boat," Beppe promised Sonia. They fell asleep in each other's arms until six o'clock – at which time Beppe woke up ravenously hungry.

* * *

Round about the same time that Beppe had finished relating the case of The Sleeping Beauty to the *Questore*, Giacomo D'Amico had slipped his car into neutral and was steering the car down the hill to the bottom of Don Alfieri's estate with the engine idling. Oriana and Giovanni had both agreed there was no point in walking. It was pitch dark in the countryside with no street lights to mar the beauty of the night.

Giacomo was steering the car with only the side lights switched on.

"How can you see to drive?" asked an anxious Oriana.

"Good night vision," was all Giacomo answered tersely. He was having to concentrate hard to avoid ending up in a ditch - despite his hitherto undisclosed ocular talent.

On Giovanni's instructions, he pulled up just before they reached the secret clearing where the red Audi and the silver-grey Renault Clio were parked.

Oriana and Giovanni proceeded by torchlight, the beam pointing down on the ground just in front of them. They had to scrape caked mud off the underside of the floor pan with their fingers before attaching the strong magnet on the tracking device, thereby ensuring a sound contact with the metal of the car. They were about to do the same to the red Audi when they heard a noise which at first they could not identify. It sounded like a horse's hooves clip-clopping over cobblestone. Then an eerie blue light dimly lit up the clearing. It was Giovanni who first realised what was happening. He switched off the torch immediately.

"*Merda!* Somebody's coming down through the tunnel," he whispered furiously in Oriana's ears. He led her quickly into the shadow of the trees. They crouched down behind a broad oak tree and peered cautiously round the trunk. Oriana heard a slithering sound in the pitch black of the undergrowth. She nearly screamed out in panic, digging her frightened fingers hard into her companion's arms. He put his arm round her shoulders in a protective gesture.

"If someone takes the red Audi, then we've had it," whispered Giovanni into Oriana's right ear.

But they could just make out a woman wearing high heels, accompanied by a short, skinny man - unbelievably wearing dark glasses despite the time of night - getting into the Renault.

"I pray to the saints they don't spot Giacomo's car," whispered Oriana.

The Renault turned right, not left, and drove off at speed up the hill in the opposite direction. They stayed frozen to the spot for a good thirty seconds before they emerged from behind the tree and lit the torch again.

"Come on, Oriana. Let's get this done and get out of here."

Back at the house, they agreed that the night watch should last three hours instead of one in order to give everyone a chance to sleep. Giacomo bid them 'good night' and drove back to the arms of his wife in Pescara. Giovanni took the first watch and Gino, Danilo and Oriana slumped exhausted on their beds with only the minimum of words exchanged. The three men were sharing one bedroom. Oriana had commandeered the only other bedroom with an old bed in it for herself. She certainly wasn't going to allow Gino and Danilo the satisfaction of knowing about her personal preferences in men at this early stage.

As chance would have it, it was yet again Danilo who happened to be on the final watch, when the only event of that long night took place. He had caught sight of the headlights of a car arriving at the bottom of the hill. He trained the binoculars on the only corner of the house that was visible and waited for what seemed like an eternity. He spotted the figures briefly before they vanished out of sight.

Oriana was up early making coffee for them all. Round the breakfast table, Danilo told them what he had seen.

"So that couple came back from wherever they went," stated Oriana flatly.

"Couple?" said Danilo puzzled. "No, there were three people in the group. There was a woman with high heels – I could just hear her shoes on the paving stones – a skinny little man wearing sunglasses - and there was someone else walking between them. It looked as if... *Mio dio!* I thought they were arm in arm, but now I think about it, they could have been supporting the weight of the third person."

"Was the other person a...? asked Oriana, not wanting to destroy her hopes by being told that the third figure had been male.

Nobody round that kitchen table wanted to put their shared hope into precise words.

"Could it have been...? began Oriana.

"It makes sense," said Gino.

"So the third person *was* a woman, Danilo?" asked Oriana anxiously.

"If I were to go on first impressions, Oriana, then yes – I'm sure it was a young woman."

The revelation was sufficient to add urgency to their second day's long vigil.

12: The die is cast

Later on, that morning, back at the police headquarters in via Pesaro, Beppe had toyed with the idea of announcing his alliance with Sonia publicly at the briefing meeting with the remaining members of the team – if only to diffuse any veiled speculation on their colleagues' part. He was aware that some of the team were covertly eyeing them up – the air of eager surmise on their faces was unmistakable. It had seemed an unnecessary precaution for them to arrive separately at the police station that morning. Beppe had been looking furiously inscrutable but Sonia's softened features must have betrayed signs of the recent release of pent-up passion.

During the short meeting, Beppe brought the team up-to-date with events. He had not yet been told about the mysterious arrival at Don Alfieri's house late the previous evening. The four officers stationed at Monticchio were still debating whether to phone their chief or to wait until they met him in person later that day. In the end, cautious optimism had won the day; they would wait and see if anything happened to lessen the element of guesswork in their discovery.

"So, *ragazzi,* we shouldn't have long to wait before we see some real action. Today is Tuesday. Tomorrow is the first day of the trial in L'Aquila. I am sure we shall be in a position to take action by Friday at the latest."

Any questions the team had wanted to ask about the course of action their *capo* had in mind were interrupted by Beppe's mobile phone ringing. He took one look at the screen, frowned deeply and switched the phone off. Sonia had seen that look of controlled irritation mixed with resignation on his face on previous occasions. She deduced – correctly as it turned out – that it must be his mother, inevitably managing to choose an inopportune moment in which to speak to her beloved but wayward son.

Beppe hurriedly asked the officers present to make sure that the phone tapping was constantly monitored.

"Don't miss *any* details of conversations between Don Alfieri and the outside world – however trivial it seems to you. Be extra alert if you hear the words *"little sparrow"* – because that seems to be their *parola d'ordine*[66] for our Sleeping Beauty. Remo, you're going to go and check the handwriting on that document... I think that's all, *ragazzi*. Thank you again for holding the fort," Beppe concluded.

He headed for the main entrance with Sonia following some distance behind him. A junior officer manning the desk stopped him in his tracks.

"Excuse me, *commissario*. You have a visitor," he said indicating a portly lady sitting waiting on the row of plastic chairs.

Beppe's facial expression changed in an instant, expressing the conflicting feelings of surprise, annoyance... and a hint of guilt.

"Mamma!" he said, in a voice that betrayed all the feelings that his face had so eloquently but inadvertently expressed. *"Che diavolo stai facendo qui?"*[67]

"What a charming way to greet your own mother, Giuseppe! A mother who has been sitting on a crowded coach all day and night to come and visit her only son! The son who never shows his face in the town where he was

---

[66] Code name
[67] What the devil are you doing here?

born and raised! The son who doesn't even look pleased to see..."

Beppe went over and embraced his mother as warmly as circumstances allowed.

"*Mamma*," he said, with a note of scolding in his voice. "You should have told me you were coming up..."

"You think that would have helped?" she replied tartly. "You would have made some feeble excuse..."

"You shouldn't have travelled all that way on your own, *mamma*. There are too many bad people..."

"I didn't travel on my own, did I?" she replied defiantly. "Laura came with me! She has something very important to tell you."

Beppe was blushing with embarrassment - or guilt - as Sonia drew level with them.

She had patently overheard Beppe's mother's last words and had instantly cottoned on to what was happening. The words had registered an inner shock to her system, which she had under control in seconds. This crisis needed immediate intervention on her part.

"Laura?" Beppe had said alarmed. *"Mamma*, you have no right to bring Laura up here like this – all unannounced. I can't possibly take care of you today. Where is Laura, anyway?"

"She's waiting in our hotel, near the station. We're not going back home until you have spent time with us. What case is so important to you that you can't spend a few hours with your own mother?" continued the determined lady, undaunted.

"It's too complicated to explain, *mamma*," Beppe said, desperately racking his brain for inspiration. "It's all to do with a concert pianist who lost his finger in his hotel room. We need to find it before he plays in a concert this evening."

Beppe knew that his mother never listened to his explanations – rational or otherwise. He had resorted ages ago to inventing fantastic tales – just to relieve his own frustrations.

"That's absolutely no excuse whatsoever, as you well know, Giuseppe," she continued unabated.

Sonia had once again had to stifle her mirth at the preposterous story he had just concocted on the spur of the moment. She tapped Beppe on the arm. *"Capo,"* she said urgently. "Can we have a word together? It will only take a minute, *signora,*" she added smiling at Beppe's mother.

"Who's this woman?" asked Beppe's mother bluntly, defending her right to her son's undivided attention at all times.

"My deputy, *mamma,*" said Beppe.

Beppe and Sonia walked a few metres away. Beppe was looking guiltily at Sonia.

"I'm so sorry, Sonia," he began. "I had no idea..."

Sonia cut in without hesitation.

"Listen, Beppe. Why don't you let me take care of this today – until you get back? You go to L'Aquila and do what you have to. I'll stay with your mum – and Laura. She's like any Italian mum I've ever met who loves her son. She'll be fine with me. *Dai!* It's the simplest solution."

Beppe heaved a sigh of something resembling relief. He could not find any solid objections to Sonia's proposal. It might even make the difficult task of telling Laura that he was not coming back to her much easier. With luck, she might even work it out for herself, thus avoiding the necessity for him to break the hurtful news to her himself.

"*Grazie,* Sonia. I don't know how to thank you..."

"Yes, you do, Beppe," she said simply.

It was settled.

"I'll look after you today, *signora.* You and Laura will see your Giuseppe later on today. I shall so much enjoy getting to know you both," said Sonia smilingly and with total conviction.

* * *

"Come on, Pippo," said Beppe. "You're coming with me to L'Aquila, today. It's time you had a change of scenery. I'd like you to make the acquaintance of our devious seismologist."

"What's happened to Sonia?" asked Pippo.

"She's...how can I put it? ... performing some essential community police work."

Beppe agreed with Bianca Bomba and Marco Pollutri that they should carry out the eaves-dropping on Don Alfieri's phone calls - if only to give Pippo a break. The two technicians were under strict orders to phone Beppe immediately if they gleaned any vital information on the *mafioso 'boss'*.

"What about the car tracking devices?" asked Beppe. "Are they up and running?"

"Oh yes, *commissario.* Last night, one of the cars drove all the way to a place just outside Penne called Vestea. It's a village perched half way up the Gran Sasso mountain range. You know, *commissario,* the one we call *La Bella Addormentata* – you must have noticed how it looks just like a sleeping girl," explained Marco.

"Oh yes," said Pippo. "Our *commissario* knows all about The Sleeping Beauty, don't you, *capo?*"

"The strange thing is, *commissario*," said Bianca, "the closer you get to the mountain range, the more the shape of the girl turns into an ordinary mountain."

"That seems to sum up this case admirably, Bianca!" said Beppe wistfully, as he and Pippo made as if to leave.

"You might like to hear this before you go, *commissario*," added Bianca quietly.

Beppe and Pippo left the room five minutes later with a feeling of outrage and indignation against Don Alfieri and the callous world of mafia *bosses*. They had heard Don Alfieri talking to his counterpart in Naples – his son in all probability. They were laughing and joking at the number of deaths that had taken place in L'Aquila and the extent of the destruction as a result of the earthquake.

"Victims and collapsed buildings mean a lot more money for us, Gianluca."

"You're right, Stefano. I understand they want to build hundreds of houses outside the old city to house the homeless. It will be a goldmine for us! And my little seismologist is still dancing beautifully to our tune..."

"Too bad you had to waste time dealing with that Civil Protection guy..."

"*Bo!* He would have squealed during the trial tomorrow. It was a bit messy but..."

The phone call came to an end with a callous snigger from each of the men.

"Come on, Pippo. Let's go and cause some death and destruction of our own," said Beppe with controlled anger. "Thank you, Bianca, Marco. You're a couple of stars!"

"He's alright, that one," opined Bianca as soon as Beppe was out of earshot.

"*Eh sì*," agreed Marco simply, "even for a Calabrian!"

* * *

Beppe and his most trusted young male officer were sitting facing an apparently submissive Donatello Altadonna in the interview room of the police station in L'Aquila. Beppe was aware that the seismologist's apparent desire to cooperate was only superficial. The *commissario* had deliberately avoided any mention of Altadonna's suspected collusion with Don Alfieri over the setting up of the illicit construction tender. The priority was to rescue Serena Vacri, who, Beppe believed, would probably turn out to be a key witness. Thus he had decided in advance to play the role of the solicitous policeman.

"I hardly dare ask you if you slept well, last night, *professore*. I'm sure you must have had too much on your mind to be able to relax."

Altadonna merely looked at Beppe with an expression of mild disbelief at his adversary's opening words.

"Where's the young police woman who was with you yesterday, *commissario*?" he ventured to ask. The change of one familiar face on the opposition bench to an officer whom he did not recognise was evidently mildly unsettling, Beppe observed to himself.

"She's working on another case, *professore*. Would you like me to convey your regards?"

Altadonna blushed and looked cross.

"No, but I would prefer my lawyer to be present," he stated with the first hint of antagonism returning.

"Of course, *professore*! Give us his mobile number and we'll contact him for you, if that will make you any happier.

But since you are only helping us with our enquiries at present..."

"*Her* mobile number," snapped Altadonna defiantly.

Beppe did not press the point. In the end, the seismologist shrugged his shoulders and did not repeat his request – as Beppe had predicted would be the case.

"Now, *professore*, you must take the first step towards redeeming yourself by helping us rescue your niece. We need to know where she is – and we need to know immediately. Giving us this information is - I have to point out to you - the *only* way in which you can expect to extricate yourself from a very precarious position *vis-à-vis* the law. Aiding and abetting abduction is bad enough, but should any harm come to Serena, I hardly need to tell you..."

Beppe's voice was calm, almost reassuring, but Altadonna had the feeling his flesh was being caressed by a razor blade. He sighed and began talking:

"I don't know for sure where she is," he stuttered. He was embarrassed and humiliated, Beppe understood, because by uttering these words, Altadonna knew it must be obvious to what extent he was under the *mafioso's* heel. "But, there was a hint that they have taken her to a private clinic just outside a village called Vestea. I don't know much about it, *commissario*," concluded Altadonna lamely.

Pippo had heard about this place and its notoriety.

"It's called *Il Clinico della Santa Croce, capo.*[68] Everybody round here knows about it."

Pippo looked at Beppe to see if he wanted him to continue speaking. Beppe gave Pippo a covert signal which

---

[68] The Holy Cross Clinic

implied that he would like Pippo to lay it on as thickly as possible.

Pippo rose to the challenge.

"Yeah, rich and influential people from as far away as Rome pay a whole heap of money to this clinic to take their kids off their hands when they've got serious drug problems. The clinic claims it can wean their young patients off drugs within days. The inhabitants of Vestea say that the cries of the young patients often can't be told apart from the wolves howling on the mountain slopes..."

Altadonna's blood had drained from his face. Beppe began speaking to the seismologist in the same quiet voice as before.

"Well, *professore,* now we know! Let's just hope that she has survived her stay in this place. That's all I want to know for now. We'll keep you posted, of course. We'll see you tomorrow – at the trial."

Altadonna winced at these words – a cruel reminder of the ordeal that was ahead of him.

Beppe signalled to the officer outside the door to take Altadonna back to his cell.

Left alone, Beppe patted Pippo amicably on the shoulder.

"Nice work, Pippo. You wax quite eloquent when it comes to it, don't you!"

"So what do we do next, *capo?*" asked Pippo.

"I think we might go and see if *Ispettore* De Sanctis will run us up to this clinic – for a quick visit. It would be almost too good to be true if Serena Vacri is being hidden there – but I guess it would be a mistake not to check it out. Then we must go and see how Oriana and company are faring. Can you give them a call and say we'll be there after lunchtime? No need to tell them where we're going – in case it's a wild goose chase."

Pippo had not yet had the privilege of discovering for himself that "after lunchtime" in Beppe's language did not necessarily imply the intervention of food at any stage.

* * *

On the hillside opposite Don Alfieri's estate, Gino had been on watch at the upstairs window. As he was raising the binoculars to eye level - a reflex action by now - he caught sight of a glint of reflected light from the top corner window in the house opposite. In a split second of time, he realised that he was looking at somebody who had a pair of binoculars trained on the window where he was standing. By Oriana and Giovanni's description, it must be the short man who had worn sunglasses the previous night. The fact that he was still wearing them whilst looking through the binoculars might just have saved the situation. Gino had lowered his binoculars hastily. He went through the act of opening the windows wide and stretching his arms out as if he had been greeting the morning sunlight after just waking up. He hoped it would be enough to alleviate any suspicions.

He ran downstairs to warn the others.

"We had better go outside and pretend we're working on the house," suggested Giovanni. They found some old tools in the outhouse next to the house and set about chipping away at the loose mortar between the rough-cut stone of the walls, no doubt shaken by the earthquake. Gino continued his watch until the hour was up, standing well back from the window without using the binoculars.

His vigilance just saved them all from being caught out by the rapidity of the next event. Gino watched as the big black wrought iron gates of the house opposite swung open. The unmistakable figure of the Latin American anaesthetist came into view. He was striding athletically towards their house.

Gino lent out of the window and hissed a warning to the three figures working below him. Giovanni turned round just as the anaesthetist walked into view. He stopped what he was doing and waved a friendly hand as he and Oriana walked down to head Ramirez-Rojas off. Danilo continued to chip away methodically with his face turned to the wall. There was a risk that the anaesthetist might recognise him from their previous encounter. From his upper window, Gino looked on anxiously. There was a lot of shaking of hands and nodding of heads over the next few minutes, until the anaesthetist turned round and walked back to the house opposite without looking back.

"That was too close for comfort, *ragazzi!*" warned Danilo.

"He's a real nasty piece of work!" exclaimed Oriana. "It's as if there's a coiled spring inside him - just one touch of the hairspring trigger and he'll go for anyone who's near him!"

"That sums him up perfectly!" agreed Gino.

"Never mind," said Giovanni. "I think I managed to reassure him that we are just some young family members out to help their uncle put his house to rights."

"You were very convincing, Giovanni," said Oriana beaming at him. "But do you know what the man had the audacity to say? That he wouldn't have to call the police after all!" added Oriana. "It was intended to sound like a joke. But he managed to make it sound like a threat."

They noticed that the gates had not shut behind the anaesthetist. They were wondering why until the older woman who was the housekeeper or Don Alfieri's relative came out of the house with the *mafioso,* still wearing his dressing gown. He was short and stocky and looked like a pugnacious bull dog. It was, for Oriana at least, her first sighting of a truly malevolent criminal. She shuddered instinctively. The older woman, empty shopping bags in her hand, got into a dark blue FIAT Brava and drove out of the gates in the direction of the town.

"I'm going to see where she goes," stated Oriana. There was no point in arguing with her. "Besides which, I can buy us some lunch if nothing else comes of it," she added convincingly. Nobody there would argue with her decision if food was involved, she reckoned.

An hour later, they noticed the gates of the house opening again and the blue FIAT returned. The older woman got out carrying two full shopping bags.

The three police officers waited anxiously for Oriana's return. It was a full hour later before she drove up to the house with one supermarket bag full of cold meats, cheese and bread rolls, as well as six two-litre-sized bottles of mineral water wrapped together in plastic film. But she had an unmistakable gleam in her eye, which told the waiting men that she had not had a wasted journey. She seemed to delight in arranging every item she had purchased in its proper place before she was willing to impart what she had learnt. In the end, Danilo and Gino could no longer contain their impatience.

"Come on, Oriana! Tell us what you're looking so smug about!"

"It's very little really, *ragazzi*. But added to what you said about a young woman arriving last night, it just might mean something."

"WHAT?" Gino and Danilo called out in chorus.

"Well, first of all she went to a big wine merchant's warehouse and ordered about €2000 of drinks - soft drinks too. It was like they intend to have a party. I had to go back and check it out after I followed her to the supermarket where I got our lunch stuff and she headed back here. The wine merchant was very reluctant to give me any details. I had to threaten him with a visit from your *capo*, Giovi," she said, accidently using the affectionate abbreviation of Giovanni's name for the first time. "I even got my mobile out and pretended to call the police station. He showed me the till receipt after that. She had paid cash for it all. He told me they're delivering the stuff tomorrow morning."

"And that's it?" asked Gino, disappointed.

"No, not quite," said Oriana, the smugness back in her voice again. "She went to a chemist shop. I had to go through the same rigmarole again to get anything out of the chemist..."

"Well?" said Gino and Danilo together. Giovanni remained impassive, realising Oriana was enjoying keeping them on a string.

"She purchased prescription sleeping pills – strong ones – and, guess what? A packet of tampons!" she proclaimed triumphantly.

Giovanni looked immediately enlightened. It took Gino and Danilo a few seconds to register the significance of what she was saying.

"You mean, they could only realistically have been bought for one person," said Danilo.

"Exactly!" said Oriana. "She's there. I'm sure of it."

It was, admitted Giovanni, another positive indication that there was a young woman in the house – and very probably one whom they wished to keep sedated.

"Well done, Oriana," said Giovanni. "It was well worth the trip."

"Yeah, especially as we've got something to eat for lunch!" added Gino irreverently.

He was rewarded by one of Oriana's most contemptuous looks. He almost made the mistake of winking at her. "Well done, Oriana!" he added rapidly, thereby sparing himself from some acerbic comment.

* * *

To the surprise of the whole group, Beppe Stancato arrived just after lunch with Pippo in a police car driven by Giovanni's boss, Fabrizio De Sanctis.

The four of them looked horrified at the arrival of a police car at this delicate moment.

"Excuse our reaction, *capo,* but don't you think it is very unwise arriving in a police car? I thought we weren't supposed to be drawing attention to ourselves!" It was, of course, Oriana who had spoken these words reprovingly.

Beppe merely smiled and looked at the uniformed inspector.

"It seems that it is *you* four that have been drawing attention to yourselves," said the inspector smiling. "We had a phone call from one of my team on our way back to L'Aquila. Someone in Don Alfieri's house called the police station."

"That bastard actually had the nerve to call out the police!" said Giovanni in total shock.

"We had a visit from the Latin American anaesthetist this morning, *capo*," explained Gino.

Pippo was looking longingly at the remains of his colleagues' lunch. It was Oriana who understood his hungry glance.

"Sorry, Pippo. Help yourself to anything you want."

"And what have you been up to this morning, *capo*?" asked Danilo.

Beppe told them all about the tip-off from Altadonna about the clinic outside Vestea.

"We established one important fact, *ragazzi*. We had to threaten the director of the clinic with more than a visitation from the Holy Spirit. But in the end, he told us that a patient known to them simply as Serena was removed late last night by two individuals..."

Danilo interrupted his chief quietly.

"By a woman in her forties and a diminutive thug wearing dark glasses, *vero capo*?"

"How the hell did you...?" began Beppe in total disbelief.

Beppe and the inspector from L'Aquila then had to put up with the sight of four young officers doing a kind of jig in a tight circle in front of his eyes, chanting *"We've found the Sleeping Beauty! We know where she is!"*

They stopped as suddenly as they had begun and explained all that had happened since the previous evening. Beppe was grinning broadly for the first time since his move to Pescara.

They were all talking animatedly when Beppe's phone rang. He put his finger to his lips to ask for quiet.

"It's Bianca Bomba," he said. He listened intently to what she was saying, the look of surprise giving way yet again to the broad grin of pleasure.

"You'll never guess what, *ragazzi*," he said when the conversation with Bianca had come to an end. "Don Gianluca Alfieri is seventy years old this week. He's having a party this Thursday for all his family. I reckon we shall be paying him a surprise visit. It'll make his day!"

13: *A turn in the tide of events*

"You drive us back, Pippo," said Beppe handing the keys to his companion. "I want time to think about what I shall have to do when I get back to Pescara."

Pippo assumed that his chief was talking about the steps he would have to take before they descended upon Don Alfieri's house. In point of fact, he was dreading having to face Laura and his mother as soon as they returned.

"No need to drive too fast, Pippo. There's no hurry this time."

He was painfully aware that he was being a coward. He could face down any mafia *boss,* but he found the prospect of dealing with his mother and his neglected *fidanzata* far more daunting. What he secretly feared most was that Laura was going to tell him she was expecting his child. This would put him in a position which he knew he could not turn his back on. He wanted to phone Sonia but such a step would instantly reveal to Pippo that his relationship with their colleague had moved on a pace. It was second nature to him to be obsessively reserved about his intimate personal life.

Beppe had intended to call Sonia on his arrival back at the Pescara police headquarters, but he was immediately assailed by Remo telling him that Romano's handwritten 'suicide note' was certainly not the work of the Latin American anaesthetist.

"Ramirez-Rojas, whatever his name is, writes with big, bold letters," explained Remo.

"Well, he couldn't have been on his own when Romano Di Carlo was murdered," stated Beppe. "Besides which, we have another possible candidate now, living in the same house as Ramirez. Thanks Remo – it was worth the try."

There had been an urgent call from the *colonnello* from the *carabinieri* station in Pescara who wished to meet him 'at his very earliest convenience'.

"The *colonnello* was most insistent, *capo*," Remo informed him.

"Phone him, Remo, and tell him I'll be over to see him now."

Beppe had already met – and liked – the high-ranking *carabiniere* officer, Riccardo Grimaldi. The colonel had suggested to him that he should come back and see him if somebody got murdered.

Beppe and the colonel shook hands.

"I've just had the forensic report back on the death of a gentleman called Romano Di Carlo, the Civil Protection agent who was involved in the High-Risk Commission's assessment of the earthquake. It appears that you agreed with my colleague in Sulmona that Di Carlo committed suicide. Well, I have to inform you, *commissario*, that..."

"... he was brutally murdered, *colonnello*. I know."

Beppe then had to spend half an hour explaining the complexities of the case to his colleague, finishing up with an appeal for help from the Pescara *carabinieri* when it came to raiding Don Alfieri's home.

"That means we only have two days to organise things. We had better meet tomorrow and clarify the details, *commissario*..."

"Please call me Beppe, *colonnello*."

"And I'm Riccardo," replied the colonel, extending the invitation. "By the way, don't you want to know what our forensic team found out?"

Beppe nodded.

"The suicide thing was just a clumsy attempt to dress up a mafia-style 'elimination' killing. I don't know why they bothered. Forensics found recent finger prints both on the shotgun and on the door handle of the white Alfa Romeo which did not belong to Di Carlo. By what you say, we might have a couple of candidates for those finger prints by Thursday night..."

The two officers agreed to meet up at 17.00 hours the following day.

"Thank you for your help *colonnello*."

"It will be a pleasure and a privilege working with you," added the *carabiniere* colonel as they shook hands.

He simply had to phone Sonia before he became involved in something else. When he got through to her, she sounded suspiciously chirpy, he thought.

"Don't worry, Beppe," she told him gaily. "I'm quite happy to stay with your mother... and Laura. We had a long and very interesting chat while your *mamma* was having her *pisolino*[69] – she was exhausted by this afternoon and slept for three hours. I don't think you have too much to worry about, Beppe. But, *per l'amor di Dio*,[70] when you talk to Laura later on, please don't say that I told you..."

"You haven't told me *anything*, Sonia," protested Beppe. But Sonia refused to be drawn any further.

"I'll be at the hotel as soon as possible, Sonia. There's so much to tell you about today."

Beppe contemplated taking his revenge by not even dropping a hint – but he relented at the last moment.

"We know where Serena Vacri is, Sonia," he revealed.

---

[69] A little snooze : a siesta
[70] Lit: For the love of God

Sonia let out a cry of joy.

"I'll fill you in later when I see you," said Beppe. "It'll take too long to explain now." This was as close as he could get to paying back her reticence in kind, he thought without any real malice. To do events justice, he really would need an hour at least to enlighten his new partner.

Beppe returned to the police station in Via Pesaro, feeling relieved, even if he did not quite know why he should feel relieved. Whatpisolino had Laura told Sonia? What, he wondered, might Sonia have said to Laura? Certainly, he concluded, Sonia would never have divulged their personal secret to *anyone*, let alone to his official *fidanzata*. He would just have to wait on tenterhooks for another few hours. He must give up speculating and contain his frustration.

As soon as he stepped inside the police headquarters, he was told by the officer on the desk that he was needed 'down in the basement'. Marco Pollutri and Bianca Bomba took one look at Beppe's stress-worn features and decided it was not the moment to tantalise him with their latest discovery.

"*Ciao, commissario.* We've just intercepted a call from Don Alfieri's landline – made by a woman. She was phoning a catering company here in Pescara called *Dinner Time* – funny how Italians always like to adopt an English name for their business enterprises! As if the English name bestows some prestige and quality on the product!" said Marco.

"Especially strange when it's a business in the catering sector. The idea of English cooking being superior to Italian *cuisine* is stretching credibility to its limits!" Bianca contributed.

Beppe smiled. "I couldn't agree more," he said, remembering the inedible food he had been obliged to consume on his one and only visit to London.

"Anyway, it's this company – it's got a good reputation locally – which is going to supply and serve the food at Don Alfieri's birthday party on Thursday," said Marco.

"Here are the catering company's contact details, *commissario*. We just wondered if this information might be of help to you in some way," added Bianca.

Beppe was looking thoughtful. He had just had an interesting, if risky, idea. One member of his team would be able to blend in perfectly in such an environment. He would then have a man on the inside. He would go and have a private talk with Remo straight away.

Fifteen minutes later, Remo, looking as white as a sheet, was nodding obligingly at every word Beppe was saying to him.

"I can only ask you to volunteer, Remo. But having someone on the inside might turn out to be crucial. Think about it, please."

With a degree of courage – or rashness – that Remo did not know he possessed, he turned to his chief and said: "I don't need to think about it, *capo*. I'll do it!"

Beppe just stopped himself hugging his junior colleague.

"We'll sort it out first thing tomorrow, Remo. We can hardly tell the caterers that there's going to be a police raid – or they might decide to cancel the whole thing. Or, more likely, they would be so edgy that they would give the game away as soon as they arrived. Leave it to me – I'll think of something. By the way, Remo, how did you leave things with Marta?"

Remo looked at his chief quite sternly, Beppe thought - to the extent that he felt he should add that, of course, he would be very happy for Remo if he had found himself a girlfriend.

"We shall be seeing each other this weekend, *capo*," replied Remo with dignity.

"I had no business to ask, Remo," Beppe added lamely. "Forgive me."

Remo smiled and shrugged his shoulders to indicate an apology was not necessary. Beppe thought how significant it was that the existence of another person in one's life could transform insecurity into self-composure. He touched his junior colleague on the arm and left him looking secretly pleased.

Beppe spent the next thirty minutes on the phone with the surveillance team in Monticchio. "I want you back for a briefing meeting tomorrow afternoon at 3 o'clock, *ragazzi*."

He could hear Gino discussing this with the other three with his hand partially cupped over his phone.

"*Capo*, we were just thinking that Giovanni should stay here in the house to keep an eye on things. We are a bit worried that the occupants in the house opposite have grown suspicious of our presence here. We feel that if the house is suddenly abandoned, they might put two and two together. What do you think, *capo*?"

His colleagues were right, of course.

"I agree with you, Gino. But I need you, Danilo and Oriana back here. And thank you all again for what you've achieved."

It was agreed. The four police officers were almost sorry to break up the team, but the prospect of some real action at last gave them a sense of achievement.

Beppe phoned Altadonna's brother-in-law – but it was his wife, the seismologist's sister, who answered the phone.

"Oh, *commissario*," she said anxiously. "Is my husband in trouble?"

"Not at all, *signora!*" he reassured her. "He is being a great help to us at the moment."

"But my brother's got himself into big trouble, hasn't he, *commissario*? I'm convinced of that. I know my brother all too well."

"He, too, is helping us with our enquiries, *signora*. Don't be anxious. Now, may I talk to your husband?"

"Can I get him to call you back? He's out with the kids at the moment. They've got dancing and fencing lessons," she added, as if to reinforce a sense of normality in a situation which, she suspected, was very far from normal. Beppe found her words strangely reassuring. Had it aroused some latent sense of paternity in his subconscious mind?

"Tell him it is vital that I talk to him tomorrow morning, *signora*. I shall be at your house at nine o'clock. And thank you, *signora*. You must be very proud of your children."

"We are, *commissario!* And thank you," she said, disarmed and reassured by his gracious manner.

He could no longer procrastinate. He phoned Sonia to tell her he was on his way, just remembering in time to ask her the name of the hotel.

"The Hotel Adriatico," she said. "It's just opposite the big *piazza* in front of the station."

***

"You're expecting a child, aren't you, Laura?" were Beppe's nervous opening words, as soon as the two were on their own. Sonia had left as soon as Beppe had arrived. She had looked business-like and given him a quick, professional smile as she left him alone with Laura. Beppe found Sonia's reaction mildly disturbing.

"Is *that* what you thought I came all this way to tell you, Beppe?" she asked, her mouth open in astonishment.

As Beppe did not reply, she continued talking for nearly fifteen minutes about how her father was finally in a nursing home. He was losing his memory and was slipping away into his own world as the days went by.

"I'm sorry, Laura...truly I am."

"It's time I got on with my own life, Beppe," Laura continued. Tears were filling the corner of her eyes as she spoke these words. "I'm just sorry it's not going to be with you," she blurted out as she began crying properly. "I met someone else and I've started going out with him. His name's..."

Beppe held up a finger and placed it on her lips.

"Please don't tell me, Laura. I didn't realise... I should have understood..."

Beppe was feeling a mixture of emotions which ranged from relief to a sense of nostalgia for the life he had lost and left behind in his home town. They walked out arm in arm and went in search of his mother.

During a supper in a local restaurant, his mother complained that the food was not the same as in Catanzaro, told him that Valentina, his sister, was going to get married, supposed that her son might just deign to make the journey down to Calabria on the day of her wedding. It mattered little that neither he nor Laura found much to say. Beppe's mother managed to fill the vacuum of silence without too much difficulty.

"I suppose you think you are going to remain single all your life?" she accused her son at one point. "You could do worse than asking that nice colleague of yours to marry you," she added.

"Let's have a dessert and a coffee, shall we?" suggested Beppe to cover up his mother's insensitive suggestion.

Laura placed a hand on Beppe's arm to indicate that she was not offended.

"We're going home tomorrow, Giuseppe. I don't suppose I shall see you again for an eternity. You seem to have spurned your real home and your old mother..."

Beppe tried to remind her of the reason why he had had to leave in the first place, but he could not be sure that his explanation had registered.

He and Laura embraced warmly before they parted company.

"Be happy, Laura," he said sadly.

"And you too, Beppe. I'm sorry things didn't..."

Beppe left, feeling in some strange way that it was *him* who was the loser on that decisive night. He suddenly felt he belonged nowhere.

He spent the night on his boat, waiting for Sonia to call. But she didn't. He finally fell asleep in the small hours as the undulating boat soothed his mind enough to allow his brain to welcome the oblivion of sleep.

Sonia lay alone in the bed that she had shared with Beppe so recently. She was perturbed and felt betrayed because he had not come round – or even phoned her.

14: *Four seismologists on shaky ground*

When Beppe woke up, feeling groggy from the poor quality of his sleep and suffering from the acute feeling of isolation which he had experienced the night before, he had to force himself to stand up and open the cabin door. His depression turned to elation and something close to pure joy when he was greeted, not only by the warm sunshine, but by the sight of a uniformed Sonia sitting plaintively on the padded seat at the stern of the boat.

"Thank God," she said smiling broadly. "I was afraid I had climbed on to the wrong boat."

Did her glance dart rapidly towards the interior of the cabin? Beppe had noticed the fleeting movement of her eyes. A thought struck him in a flash of revelation as he hugged Sonia warmly and kissed her.

"Not only am I a shallow man, but a totally insensitive one as well!" he accused himself roundly. "It should have been *me* that phoned *you*, yesterday evening, Sonia. I'm sorry."

"I waited until past midnight for you to call me. I didn't want to call you because I thought...well, I was afraid you might have been with... I know it was silly, but..."

"I left Laura with my mother at the hotel as soon as we had finished eating, Sonia. I felt like a lost soul in no man's land. But when I saw you sitting patiently out here, I understood at once how *you* must have felt. I'm sorry..." he said again.

"Never mind, Beppe - now we understand each other better, don't we? Come on, *capo!* It's going to be a long day for you, I imagine. Let's go and get a cup of coffee."

"I'd better get dressed, I suppose," said Beppe reluctantly.

* * *

Officer Giacomo D'Amico had been drafted into service to attend the first day of the "earthquake" trial. He had travelled up to L'Aquila with Beppe and Sonia in a police car.

"I'm just curious to know how the opening of the trial goes, Giacomo. I suspect it will be a brief affair today - when the judge discovers that one of the defendants is no longer with us and another is in police custody."

"I'll let you both know what transpires. I find court procedures quite fascinating," said Giacomo. "It's so remote from what we have to deal with on a day-to day basis – the atmosphere in a court room is so *rarefied*."

Beppe and Sonia left Giacomo outside the improvised courtroom and went to keep the *rendez-vous* with Altadonna's brother-in-law, Antonio Breda.

"See you here at about 11.30, Giacomo?" suggested Beppe.

* * *

Usciere: All rise for His Honour – *Giudice* Ruggero San Buono.

(The judge sat down and very meticulously arranged a pile of documents on the solid oak table in front of him before he deigned to look round the makeshift courtroom. He looked pointedly in the direction of the table where three of the

scientists were seated. Corrado Viola, Raimondo Leonti and Salvatore Manca were looking very subdued.)

Giudice: I was under the impression that there were five people on trial today. I see only three. I do hope that this trial in my court is not going to be as shambolic as the events surrounding your seismic occurrence seem to have been. Can anyone throw a little light as to the reason why there should be such a dearth of defendants? I hope my journey from Rome won't prove to have been wasted.

(An elegant woman in her early forties coughed politely as she stood up to face the judge.)

Malandra: Avvocato Fiorella Malandra, *vostro onore*, counsel for the defence.

Giudice: Yes, counsellor, I think I had managed to work out your title for myself.

("Why," thought Giacomo D'Amico, "do some judges take such perverse delight in snubbing as many people as possible in the courtroom? I feel sorry for those scientists already.")

Giudice: Well, counsellor?
Malandra: I have only just been informed of this myself, *vostro onore,* but I understand that *Il Professore* Altadonna will be arriving in the next few minutes – under police escort. It appears he has been assisting the police with their enquiries. I'm afraid I have as little information about this as your honour..."

Giudice: Do you mean to imply, counsellor, your client is under arrest?

Malandra: I believe he has been detained over a matter that may or may not be related to this trial, *vostro onore*.

Giudice: None of this sounds as if it is going to assist you in the difficult task ahead of you, does it counsellor?

(The judge's words should have sounded sympathetic, considered Giacomo. But his tone of voice managed to imply that the lady counsellor had little hope of success. Obviously, the lady advocate for the defence felt the same way, since she decided there and then that this judge needed to be reminded that his role was to remain impartial.)

Malandra: With respect, *vostro onore*, I believe the difficult task of deciding whether my clients' involvement in the tragic events of this city amount to a crime - or not - will fall equally on *your* shoulders.

(She sat down in a dignified manner to the admiration of the selected dignitaries – including the mayor - alongside a cross-section of solemn looking citizens from the stricken city of L'Aquila – plus one police officer from Pescara. Giacomo had to stop himself from leading a round of applause for the lady advocate. He looked round at the fifty or more persons forming the "spectators" of this drama. Had he been part of the team of officers in the house at Monticchio, he might well have recognised a smartly-dressed lady, probably in her fifties, who was following the legal proceedings with rapt attention.

She did not seem to "belong" to the general mass of people present that day.)

Giudice: Aren't you forgetting something, counsellor? And please stand up again before you address me.
Malandra: *Vostro onore?*

Giudice: There is the small matter of the other absentee defendant, is there not, counsellor?

(Before the besieged lady lawyer could answer, the door opened and Donatello Altadonna was ushered in between two uniformed police officers. He was not handcuffed and looked sprucely dressed and freshly shaven, Giacomo D'Amico observed. At the same time, Fiorella Malandra's junior counsel slipped in and handed her a note, which she had time to read since Giudice San Buono had transferred his attentions to the newcomer. Fiorella Malandra's face turned pale as she read the note. She asked her assistant counsellor a question, but the young lawyer shrugged his shoulders and spread his hands in a gesture which clearly said that the content of the note left him equally puzzled. Giacomo switched his attention back to the judge, who was studying the chief seismologist intently.)

Giudice: Good morning, *professore*. I am so glad that you felt able to attend proceedings this morning – despite the vital role I am told you are fulfilling in helping the local police with their enquiries. I must say, *professore*, you do not look like a man who has spent the night in a police cell.

Altadonna: No, indeed, *vostro onore*. I insisted on being taken home to make myself ready for such an important business as the one in hand. I trust that I have not inconvenienced your honour by...

(The judge waved a dismissive hand in the direction of the chief seismologist and turned his attention back to Fiorella Malandra.)

Giudice: Well, *Avvocato* Malandra... It appears that we only have to account for one missing defendant now. Can you shed any light on the matter? You seem to be looking rather distressed, counsellor.

Malandra: Indeed, your honour, I have just learnt that the fifth defendant is ... no longer with us.
Giudice: Do you mean he has fled the country?

Malandra: No, *vostro onore,* I mean he is dead. The police suspect a suicide, but the results of the autopsy are currently in the hands of the forensic team in Pescara. It is a most distressing affair. His body was discovered in the mountains outside Sulmona. I don't know what to say...

(Three of the four scientists' faces had turned pale as they absorbed this shocking news. The judge turned his attention to the lawyer for the prosecution. Giacomo D'Amico noted privately that the truth about Romano Di Carlo's death had been successfully stifled for the time being. Commissario Stancato had particularly wanted to be reassured on this point.)

Giudice: Did you know about this distressing affair, counsellor...?

Torrebruna: Ludano Torrebruna, *vostro onore.* No, frankly, I am as surprised and disturbed by this turn of events as my learned colleague for the defence appears to be.

Giudice: *(Once again addressing the counsel for the defence)* I hope, counsellor, that this desperate gesture on the part of your former client will not be construed by anyone else as an admission of guilt. Do we know of any other circumstances in his life which might have induced this defendant to take such a tragically desperate step?

(Counsellor Fiorella Malandra was on her feet in an instant, glowering in the direction of this judge.)

Malandra: I would be most grateful, your honour, if – in the complete absence of any authority other than yourself and in the absence of a jury in this trial – you would be so good as to refrain from making assumptions of guilt on behalf of the defendants, be they living or dead!

Giudice: *(Replying in a matter-of-fact tone of voice that smacked little of remorse)* I apologise if I have conveyed to the court a negative impression of the defendants, counsellor. It was unintentional. Now, in the light of this unfortunate event, we shall restrict ourselves today to hearing the opening arguments from the prosecution and the defence – which I imagine will not have changed in principle. I shall need a day or so in which to bring myself up-to-date as to the legal implications – if any - following this singular tragedy. So, *Avvocato* Torrebruna, if you are ready...?

Torrebruna: Yes, *vostro onore.* Thank you. I am quite ready to begin.

Giudice: We are all ears, counsellor!

Torrebruna: I am privileged to represent the people of L'Aquila – headed by our mayor of fifteen years' standing. The grounds for litigation are simply that the group of four scientists, plus, I'm sorry to say, the late *Dottore* Di Carlo, the representative of the Civil Protection Agency, who constituted the High-Risk Commission, signally and tragically failed to inform the people of this city of an impending major earthquake. Their criminal oversight led inevitably to a catastrophic loss of...

Giudice: Your learned friend from the opposite bench, *avvocato,* is, I feel, on the point of protesting that it is the judge's role to decide whether a criminal act has been committed.

Torrebruna: I apologise to the court, *vostro onore.* I have been too deeply affected by the anger felt by the people of this town. I must have got carried away. I shall be calling on a series of witnesses – including a young laboratory technician who alerted the High-Risk Commission of an unprecedented escape of radon gas from the ground only two weeks before the earthquake. It was this technician's warning which led to the first emergency meeting of the High-Risk Commission team on 30th March.

    I shall maintain that, despite obvious signs that a major earthquake was about to occur, not only was no cogent warning given beforehand, but rather the message conveyed to the mayor of this city – not by the official Civil Protection agent, but by the chief scientist *Professore*

Altadonna – was that there was no call to evacuate the city. The absence of a clear warning of an impending earthquake led many citizens to remain in L'Aquila on that night in April with the consequent loss of human life that we shall all have to live with for the rest of our time on Earth. One of my witnesses, a father of two teenage children, lost both of them as a direct result of acting upon the erroneous assurance that there was but a minimal risk of a major seismic event taking place. We will further maintain that their failure to act must be construed as a clear case of criminal negligence and manslaughter.

(There was a short burst of applause from the "gallery" – many of whom were families who had lost loved ones. Judge Ruggero San Buono looked severe and raised a hand to signal that their reaction was not welcome in his court)

Giudice: This is not, I need hardly remind you, a theatrical spectacle where you may applaud your favourite actor, ladies and gentlemen. I would urge restraint from now on. Thank you. *Avvocato Malandra?* I trust you will be able to emulate the brevity of your colleague.

Malandra: Whether I am able or not to emulate my learned colleague's brevity in respect of the length of time I am allowed to expound on my clients' case, *vostro onore*, depends rather more on the complexity of this case than a need to bring proceedings to a premature close. I trust your honour will respect this need – all in the cause of justice, of course!

("This lady really does deserve a round of applause!" thought Giacomo D'Amico, whose hands had quite spontaneously begun to clap. The gesture was not taken up by anyone else, however, and earned him a scowl from the bench. He had drawn unwanted attention to himself. Judge Ruggero San Buono had not really noticed the presence of a single police officer among the gathered assembly until that point. He gave Giacomo a kind of "see-you-later" look of disapproval.)

Giudice: (uttering an irritated sigh and adding sarcastically) Please continue, counsellor. Take as long as you please!

Malandra: Before I offer any arguments in defence of this team of scientists, I would like to convey the sentiment expressed by Professor Salvatore Manca, on behalf of all four defendants. He wishes to say that he feels no resentment towards those who have brought him to trial.

(Mutterings of angry protests from many present)

The professor states that, in your position, he would have felt the same anger and would have reacted exactly as you have done. I make no further comment.

(The only man to show any further reaction to these words was Donatello Altadonna, who shifted in his seat. A brief look of irritation passed fleetingly across his face. Only Giacomo D'Amico and the judge appeared to notice. The judge raised a quizzical eyebrow but said nothing.)

During the course of this trial, the defence will base its argument on one principle contention. To wit: despite gigantic strides being made in the science of seismology, it is still absolutely impossible to predict with any accuracy when a major earthquake will occur. Terrible though this tragedy might be, the fault – excuse the geological reference – lies deep beneath our feet. The massive forces involved are quite unpredictable and well beyond the abilities of mankind to control them.

(The counsel for the defence fell silent for so long that the judge was obliged to fill the hiatus)

Giudice: Is that all you have to say, *avvocato* Malandra?

Malandra: You implied that you would welcome brevity, your honour. You will be hearing at a later stage that an analogous event occurred in Umbria very recently – where a series of earth tremors were thought to be the precursor to a major quake. In the event, the minor tremors dispersed the pent up energy deep below the surface and no major quake took place. Two of the present High-Risk Commission team on trial now formed part of the investigating team in Umbria. Your honour, you might just as well blame God in his heaven for his failure to warn the dinosaurs of the arrival of the meteor that wiped them out. Some events just cannot be foreseen…

Giudice: Not even by God, counsellor? I am not entirely convinced that your analogy applies to the present circumstances.

Malandra; I only wish to make the point that certain events are nigh on impossible to predict and quite beyond our power to influence, your honour. Besides which, I too am anxious to ascertain details of Romano Di Carlo's death before the trial proceeds. Knowing the gentleman concerned as well as I do, I very much doubt whether he is capable of...

Giudice: Are you implying, counsellor, that you don't believe that he took his own life?

(Giacomo Di Amico was on the alert. He was a naturally reserved man who would hesitate to draw attention to himself publicly. But he could not stand by and watch the necessary secrecy behind their own mission to rescue Serena Vacri being compromised by a few chance words from a lawyer. He coughed loudly and stood up in the silence of the improvised courtroom)

D'Amico: *Vostro onore,* I wonder if I may see you privately? I may be able to clarify the situation for you.

Giudice: *(After a pause in which he considered whether this interruption by a relatively low-ranking police officer was acceptable, he said:)* Very well, ladies and gentlemen, we will halt proceedings here and reconvene for the full trial at a later date. The court will inform you as to the time and date. I too, would like to have time to clarify certain matters that have arisen before we proceed.

(The judge had looked very hard in Donatello Altadonna's direction as he spoke these words. The chief scientist was being led out by the two officers who had accompanied him to the courtroom less than half an hour previously.)

One thoughtful and distinguished-looking lady in her mid-forties to early fifties headed for the exit and drove a silver-grey Renault Clio back in the direction of Monticchio. Later that day, the technicians were able to confirm that somebody from Don Alfieri's household had been present at the opening of the trial.

*   *   *

"The judge turned out to be really easy-going when I got him on his own, *capo*. He even told me confidentially that he always puts on an act of severity whenever he opens up a new trial. 'It stops the main parties from trying to gain an unfair advantage by currying favour with me,' he told me. But I'm glad it was you, *capo*, who filled him in with the details over the phone."

"You did well, Giacomo. Someone could easily have let slip more than they intended. In any case, the judge certainly did not need to know precisely what we intend to do tomorrow."

"He opened up to me when you had finished talking to him, *capo*. He even told me that he was under serious political pressure from Rome to come down heavily on the scientists – just to placate the citizens of L'Aquila."

"Yes, I don't suppose they will get off scot free," said Sonia.

"My guess is they will be found guilty but not be sent to prison – pending an appeal. "But we'll make sure we settle our score with Altadonna," he added.

The three of them drove back to Pescara at top speed. Beppe had a DVD which the builder brother-in-law had given him. They would all have a chance to become familiar with the layout of Don Alfieri's spacious dwelling before the end of their final briefing. Beppe was mindful that he had an appointment with the *carabiniere* colonel, Riccardo Grimaldi, at five o'clock. Not even Sonia attempted to bring up the matter of lunch. She had recognised the expression of deep concentration on Beppe's face and knew that he would never agree to interrupt the journey for something as trivial as food.

"Sonia, I could do with some moral support when I go to see the *colonnello*. Will you accompany me? You might think of something that I have omitted. We just cannot afford to make a single mistake tomorrow."

It was Sonia who had thought to ask the *carabiniere* officer about the Rottweilers and opening the main gates to Don Alfieri's estate.

"We may be able to get officer Remo smuggled in a bit later than the other caterers," said Beppe, who had concocted a half-formed plan along these lines.

"No, that might look odd," the *colonnello* pointed out. "In any case, don't worry if that doesn't work. We *carabinieri* have got a new-fangled device that can work out entry-phone codes in less than fifteen seconds. We are quite sophisticated these days," he added with self-deprecating humour. "And we'll take care of tranquilizing the dogs."

This senior *carabiniere* police officer then made a suggestion which left Sonia open-mouthed with amazement and her future partner laughing out loud at the sheer audacity of the idea.

A few minutes later, Beppe and Sonia stood up to take their leave. There were fervent handshakes all round. Beppe had a persistent grin on his face as he mulled over the *colonnello's* subterfuge.

"You're a genius, Riccardo!" said Beppe to the *colonnello,* dropping all formality between them.

"*A domani, ragazzi!*" said the Riccardo Grimaldi.

* * *

By seven o'clock, the atmosphere in the police headquarters in *via Pesaro* was electrically charged. Beppe's mental preparation had been meticulous. Everybody wondered when he had had the time to think things through in such detail. He had decided not to tell his team about the colonel's idea. But he added a covert warning.

"Things rarely go according to plan with this kind of raid," Beppe told his team before closing the meeting. "Be prepared for *anything* unexpected. In the end, it will be your initiative which counts. Above all, remember that the most dangerous character – physically speaking – is probably the Latin-American anaesthetist. What do we know about him?"

"He's left-handed," they chorused.

"And as rapid in his reactions as a striking cobra," added Gino.

"Any final questions?" asked Beppe.

"Do we know how many people will be sitting round the table, *capo?*" asked Oriana.

"Remo? Over to you," said Beppe.

"Yes, *capo,* more or less; we've been told to cater for around thirty people in all. I gather that nine of them will be children or young teenagers."

"Doesn't that add to our problems, *capo?*" asked Pippo.

Beppe paused for a good ten seconds before replying.

"I think it will work in our favour, Pippo. Even members of the *'ndrangheta* are very reluctant to let off firearms when their own children are present. I doubt whether the *Camorra* are different in that respect."

The chilling sound of the names of the mafia clans of Calabria and Campania caused a silence to fall in the briefing room. They were suddenly aware of the full significance of the operation that they were about to undertake – in less than twenty-four hours. It was a sobering thought.

"Sleep and eat well, *ragazzi,*" said Beppe ironically.

He caught up with Sonia who had dawdled in her office waiting for Beppe to finish.

They walked out together before going their separate ways.

"It will soon be over now, Sonia," said Beppe quietly as they briefly linked arms. "In one way or another," he added wistfully.

"Are you sure the *carabiniere* colonel's idea was really that good, Beppe?"

"Oh yes, Sonia. It will be a quite unforgettable and unique experience for our *mafioso* friend. A lovely touch!"

15: Don Alfieri's birthday party

Another night spent on the boat, but *Commissario* Stancato managed to fall into a deep sleep from which he awoke to discover that it was already seven o'clock on a bright, warm summer's day. He was irrationally disappointed not to find Sonia sitting in the stern of the boat. It took him a quarter of a minute to dismiss the thought that he could sail out of the harbour and spend the day fishing. No, today was Don Alfieri's birthday! Today was the day when they would rescue the Sleeping Beauty. A wave of grim premonition that they would not find her alive swept over him – only to be resolutely dismissed as he began the process of getting ready for the day ahead. It made little difference how many times he had had to face similar operations in the past; he always had to smother his negative fears. The fear was never for himself but for the victims of crimes and that of letting down his team. This time, a twenty-two-year-old girl was involved, not to mention another woman to whom he was increasingly drawn. Letting them *both* down would be unbearable. He shook himself to free his mind from the shadowy dread of failure. He put on his oldest clothes, knowing that he would have to don the full regalia of his official uniform later on in the day. It was gathering dust in some cupboard in his office.

* * *

"There's a lady to see you, *commissario*," said the officer on the front desk. He felt an illogical spasm of annoyance on hearing these words, imagining that his mother or Laura had returned unexpectedly. But the lady in question was in her mid-forties, tall, raven-haired and striking looking. She had obviously passed on her good looks to her daughter.

"Ah," he said walking towards her and holding out his hand in greeting. "You must be Serena Vacri's mother. Please come with me. Send *Agente* Leardi up to my office as soon as she arrives," he asked the officer on desk duty.

Seated in his modest office, the *commissario* stalled until Sonia arrived. He feared a hysterical – even if totally understandable – outburst of grief as soon as he told the mother what had happened. Sonia would deal with tears better than he could.

"What can you tell me about Serena's uncle, *signora?* Is the professor your brother, by the way?"

"No way!" she denied vehemently. "He's my ex-husband's first cousin – or something like that," she continued as if such a tenuous genetic link explained everything undesirable about the seismologist. "Serena calls him *uncle* merely to be polite. This is all to do with Donatello, isn't it? What's he done to my daughter, *commissario?*"

Beppe took a deep breath and looked at his watch, willing Sonia to appear. He wished he hadn't given his team an extra couple of hours off that morning – knowing that it was likely to be a very long day – and night - ahead of them.

"Come on, *commissario!* Don't keep me in suspense. I know something bad has happened to my daughter. I've been trying to phone her for a week."

Beppe Stancato told her what had happened and about the rescue attempt that evening.

When Sonia appeared breathless in his office fifteen minutes later, she found a very pale faced but silently angry mother. "I'll kill him myself, when I set eyes on him," she muttered. Beppe realised that the anticipated outburst of hysterical grief was not going to happen.

"Then, it's probably a good thing that he is locked up a in a police cell, *signora!*" Beppe added.

"I'm coming with you tonight," announced Serena's mother quietly. Sonia began to explain to her that the mission could be dangerous, but Beppe looked at Sonia and shook his head imperceptibly.

"It's a good idea, Sonia. Serena will be in shock when we find her. Seeing her mum will be just what she needs." Sonia realised that her *capo* was talking the situation up so as not to deprive Serena's mother of hope. Perhaps he too needed to feel optimistic about the outcome.

"Don't worry, officers. I won't get in your way," she said. "Now I shall go to my hotel and sleep – which I didn't manage to do on the train."

Sonia drove Serena's mother to her hotel and said she would pick her up at five that afternoon.

"Thank you, Sonia. My name is Valeria, by the way – Valeria Prosperini."

Beppe was heading back towards his office when he was hailed by the officer at the reception desk.

"Ah, *commissario!* The *Questore* would like to see you. Immediately, he said."

* * *

Don Alfieri was feeling irascible and ready to lash out at anyone who crossed his path that morning - despite it being a supposedly significant day for him. He did not feel in festive mood. His brothers and sisters, plus his nine grandchildren, were already on the road out of Naples heading for L'Aquila. Cancelling the festivities was out of the question. Ones family could never be let down; it was the glue that held the rough fabric of his life together.

He was secretly weary of wielding power, of ordering executions, of protecting his reputation as a ruthless *boss*. Even the one and only priest, back in his native Campania, still willing to hear his bi-annual confession – via Skype since he had moved to Abruzzo – was becoming increasingly critical of his way of life. "Sometimes you shake my faith in a man's ability to truly repent, Gianluca," the elderly priest had declared during his latest confession. "This really cannot continue. I shall be forced to refuse you absolution. You are going to turn seventy in a few weeks' time. In the not-too-distant future it will be God who decides whether you deserve absolution – or eternal damnation."

In common with many of his kind, Don Alfieri remained convinced that a deathbed confession – as long as it was sincere – would be enough to open the doors of paradise. The Catholic Church had always encouraged him in the belief that God forgave sinners, however many times they transgressed. It was the only moral straw left for Don Alfieri to cling to these days.

It was the incompetence of the two remaining henchmen in his immediate entourage which had really annoyed him over the last few days. They were just hangers-on, blood-sucking minor players who had no idea about how to deal with murder in a professional manner. Then there was the disturbing news from his wife that someone at the trial had questioned whether that Civil Protection agent had really committed suicide – the result of the bungled attempt by his two cronies. And now that spineless scientist had allowed himself to be arrested. Who knows what he was telling the police! The Latin American doctor – who should at least be a competent killer with his background in Colombia – had intimated that there might be police officers, disguised as civilians, spying on him from the house opposite. He would have dismissed the notion as fanciful had it not been for the fact that most of the young people had disappeared as furtively as they had arrived a few days previously - immediately after Ramirez – or whatever he called himself - had paid them a visit. But it did not make sense; the police car which had visited the house opposite had been summoned by *him*. They would never have given the game away like that had the three men and the woman really been police officers. Surely, that Ramirez was being paranoid?

Don Alfieri had to concede that Ramirez had dealt with the scientist's niece quite effectively. Obviously, his specialist field was drugs – which made sense, him being a doctor. But with the way events were turning out, Don Alfieri was beginning to wonder whether it was worth the trouble keeping the girl alive. He had the scientist, Altadonna, quite effectively under his thumb, with or without his troublesome niece.

"I want that girl kept out of sight all day," he snarled at Ramirez and Paride.

'Paride' indeed! What an inapt name for a member of *his* clan! And why does he always walk round with sunglasses on – even after dark? The discomforting aspect of Paride's sunglasses was, thought Don Alfieri, that he was obliged to look at his own face reflected in his undersized henchman's lenses on the rare occasions when he deigned to address him. At least he could visually judge whether he was looking sufficiently disdainful.

"If anyone finds that girl here under my roof, we've all had it!" he added menacingly.

"Don't worry, Don Alfieri. I can take care of her – whenever you want," Ramirez replied with an animalistic leer on his face. He had worked out some time ago how he envisaged her last few moments on Earth would be spent.

Don Alfieri had endured the daylight hours stoically. The twenty-six members of his clan arrived late in the afternoon in two Lancia Deltas[71] and a sophisticated minibus. The caterers were the next to arrive from Pescara and busied themselves in the vast kitchen. By seven o'clock, a man and a woman were organising the dining room, preparing the places round trestle tables pushed together to form a large rectangle and covered with immaculately white table-clothes. A nervous-looking man was in charge of arranging the cutlery, glasses and, as ordered by Don Alfieri's wife, a whole range of white candles equally spaced around the table. Don Alfieri looked intensely at the man who looked like a waiter. He could swear he had something plugged into his ear.

"How many candles are there?" he asked the timid-looking man from somewhere behind where Remo was arranging the wine-glasses. Remo was so nervous that he almost turned round instinctively to answer the question which Don Alfieri had barked at him. He remembered just in time the drill which Beppe had told him to follow.

"How many candles are there, *signore?*" repeated Don Alfieri coming into Remo's line of vision. Remo visibly

---

[71] A luxury car that was favoured by politicians.

jumped as if startled at being addressed by the *mafioso boss*. This was not difficult to achieve since Remo's legs had been shaky as soon as he saw Don Alfieri come into the vast reception room. Of the Latin American anaesthetist there had been, mercifully, no obvious sign.

"Exactly seventy, as you ordered, *signore*," replied Remo, raising his voice just as a deaf man might do. Don Alfieri nodded in silence in Remo's direction and walked off without a word. His paranoia that his house was being invaded by police officers disguised as caterers was set aside. As the daylight began to fade and nothing untoward happened, Don Alfieri felt he could begin to relax.

At twenty past eight, his guests filed into the vast dining area. The French windows were opened wide on to the Abruzzo countryside. The family began to settle down at the tables. By half past eight, everyone was seated, with glasses filled with *Prosecco* in front of them. The tiny bubbles sparkled in the candlelight. The room was lit by subdued wall-lighting. Outside, dusk was falling as the sun sank behind the mountains. Remo had spoken a few words into the concealed microphone tucked under his waiter's collar.

Don Alfieri's eldest sibling stood up and formally raised his glass. "A toast to Gianluca - our head of family!" he stated. Everybody, including a little six-year-old girl followed suit. The younger children's glasses had been filled with something non-alcoholic, which might have been Fanta lemonade.

Choruses of "To Gianluca" or "To *nonno*"[72] echoed round the room and out through the French windows into

---

[72] Granddad

the countryside. Five shadowy figures had materialised, unobserved, on the patio outside the French windows in the gathering darkness, silhouetted by the half-moon that was rising over the treetops. They were holding trumpets, cornets and a trombone. They began playing "Happy Birthday" with consummate musical skill. The dinner guests applauded as the *antipasti* dishes were brought in and placed on the tables by the caterers while the musicians played another chorus.

Only Don Alfieri, his wife and his mother-in-law, who had organised everything down to the last detail, were looking alarmed at this unscheduled item of entertainment. Don Alfieri looked briefly over his shoulder without turning right round. His worst fears were realised; the five musicians were all wearing *carabinieri* uniforms. He was being serenaded by the police! He had been out-manoeuvred and the sensation left him feeling impotent with inner rage. Why weren't the bastards being attacked by the dogs? Paride was supposed to be making sure the animals were patrolling the grounds after dark. Don Alfieri came to the conclusion that his seventieth birthday was going to prove memorable in only the most negative sense. How fortunate, he thought, that he had had the foresight to make provisions for such an unexpected contingency. Self-preservation was a long-standing habit.

*   *   *

"Good evening, Don Alfieri. I would wish you a happy birthday but I somehow think you might feel I was being sarcastic in the circumstances. I am *Commissario* Stancato from Pescara and these are two of my colleagues," said

Beppe, indicating officers Giacomo D'Amico and Giovanni Palena.

Don Alfieri was looking thunderously at Beppe, standing at the opposite end of the long tables. All Don Alfieri's dinner guests had their heads skewed round at an angle and were staring with varying degrees of astonishment and resentment at the row of police officers. Here were three fully armed police officers standing calmly in *his* house! The *commissario* was completely unruffled – just as if it was a social call. None of them were pointing weapons at him. Their nonchalance was totally disconcerting. He had never experienced such behaviour from the forces of law and order in all of his fifty-five years as a mobster.

"*Che cazzo volete?*"[73] snarled Don Alfieri, finally and crudely breaking the silence.

Beppe tutted disapprovingly.

"Such language in front of the children, Don Alfieri! You'll get them into bad habits!"

The gentle sarcasm was more than Don Alfieri could tolerate. He stood up and shouted at Beppe:

"State your business now and leave my family in peace or I'll..."

"...call the police?" smiled this irritating cop.

"It's outrageous!" These words were spoken by Don Alfieri's wife.

"As outrageous as holding a twenty-two-year-old girl prisoner and plying her with dangerous drugs?" asked Beppe with the first hint of anger in his voice. "We have come to take the girl away, Don Alfieri. If you cooperate with

---

[73] What the f... do you want? (says the mafia boss)

us, we shall be out of here – at least temporarily – within five minutes. It's up to you."

"I don't know what you are talking about," growled the *mafioso boss,* whose natural instinct was to deny all accusations whenever he was in the presence of the police.

"Our colleagues are searching the whole house as we speak, Don Alfieri," said Beppe, praying silently that this scenario could be brought to a rapid conclusion. He knew this was too much to hope for.

Beppe missed the hidden, prearranged signal that either Don Alfieri or, more likely, his wife or the older relative had given. All that was needed would be a simple touch of a key on a smartphone to one of his henchmen not present at the dinner party. He was not surprised, therefore, when all the lights went out. He had even anticipated this eventuality, based on his experiences of similar house raids in Calabria. In no time at all, his team had their torches out of their pouches or lights fitted to a headband shining in the darkness of the house. Some of Don Alfieri's brothers began to extinguish candles round the tables, but out of fear of being left in total darkness, a lot of the younger children left their candles burning. They hadn't had their slice of birthday cake yet. That was the moment when you blew out the candles!

Even though Beppe had expected such a ploy, by the time he pointed his torch down the room to where Don Alfieri should have been, he could see that his place at the table was vacant. He would have slipped surreptitiously out of the French windows, so recently vacated by the *carabinieri* musicians. Beppe momentarily enjoyed the image of the mafia *boss* creeping down his escape tunnel and ending up in the arms of the waiting *carabiniere* colonel and his men.

"I must insist that *nobody* else leave this room," stated Beppe with a voice of authority. "I cannot take responsibility for anyone's safety if you do!" As Beppe had correctly surmised, in this respect at least, the presence of the children made their task easier. Nobody moved from their seats despite rebellious mutterings from some of the Alfieri clan.

In the rest of the vast house, there was a great deal of frenetic activity.

Following a rapid instruction from Beppe, Pippo headed for the cupboard where the electric lighting board was installed; its location had been one of the more precise questions that Beppe had asked Altadonna's architect-cum-builder brother-in-law.

Others were searching the upstairs rooms. Most of them were occupied by Don Alfieri's family's belongings sitting in opened suit-cases on the tops of the beds. On the second floor, under the sloping roof, they discovered the rooms permanently occupied by Rojas-Ramirez and Paride – 'the-gnome-with-sunglasses' as he had been nicknamed by the team. They were all aware that Paride was, as they searched his room, squatting hand-cuffed inside the dogs' cage, under the watchful eye of the patrolling *carabinieri*. The two Rottweilers were lying tranquilized at Paride's feet, their yellow-stained teeth grinning grotesquely in the moonlight.

Sonia, Gino and Danilo were making a rapid check of Paride's room.

"Look, he was writing a postcard to his mother, would you believe," said Danilo. "Just look at the handwriting, *ragazzi*. Haven't we seen that handwriting before?"

"Yes, we have," replied Sonia. "That's one positive thing we've achieved."

There were two more "servants' quarters" rooms along the top corridor. One was completely empty and the second room revealed an unmade-up mattress on a single bed. There were a few items of female clothing neatly folded in the drawer of a dressing-table.

Sonia's sharp sense of smell detected the faint hint of *"Eau d'Issey"* – a distinctive perfume typically favoured by young women, Sonia remembered from her younger days.

"This is where they have been holding our Sleeping Beauty – until quite recently," said Sonia in a subdued voice to her two male companions.

"So, the bastards have moved her somewhere else!" said Gino.

"Let's hope and pray it's in some other part of this house," added Danilo as Sonia relayed this vital piece of information to Beppe, patiently standing guard in the dining hall.

In the big darkened kitchen, the catering staff were looking nonplussed. It seemed pointless to dish out the pasta course while most of the diners were sitting in front of piles of uneaten *antipasti*. Only the hungry children had picked at the food – almost guiltily - as the adults sat in angry silence. Remo took hold of the last tray of *antipasti* and walked towards the dining hall. He spotted Oriana in the hallway on guard near the front door.

A fleeting figure appeared from a room leading off the hallway and headed towards the stairwell leading to the cellar under the house. Oriana recognised the tall figure of the Latin American anaesthetist immediately. It was astonishing how such a tall man could move so stealthily, she thought. He was carrying something in his raised left hand. The object briefly glinted by the light of the torchlight fitted round her head; too thin to be a knife. To her horror she realised it was a hypodermic syringe.

"Remo!" she whispered furiously at his retreating back. He had obviously not noticed the anaesthetist crossing the hall. All Remo saw was the diminutive figure of Oriana beginning her descent down to the cellar. His waiter's instinct to take the tray of food into the dining room almost got the better of him. Fortunately for the fate of Oriana Salvati, Remo succeeded in overcoming his instinctive need to carry food to the nearest table. He remembered to speak into the microphone hidden under his starched collar and say to Beppe:

"Just following Oriana down to the cellar, *capo*," he said, dumping the tray on a table in the hallway.

Beppe noted the comment, but since there seemed to be no urgency in Remo's voice, the significance of the message did not register for another vital forty-five seconds. Only then did he query why Oriana should be going down to the cellar on her own initiative. His senses were immediately alerted to potential danger. He was already striding into the hallway when he heard her voice in the earpiece.

Oriana had begun her descent of the marble staircase, trying to keep her prey in view by the beam of the torch attached to its headband. The Latin American moved with incredible speed, even though there was little light to see by. Ramirez stopped and turned round suddenly. Oriana was only six paces behind him. She came abruptly to a halt. She could plainly see the leer on his face. He was holding the hypodermic syringe in his raised right hand. He took three steps towards her. She felt terrified but managed to speak out loud into the small microphone attached to the headset.

"Quick, someone. The cellar!"

By that time, Ramirez was almost on top of her. The words of the chorus they had all chanted back during the meeting the previous evening came back to her in that split second. As his left hand struck out at her head, Ramirez was perplexed to discover that the girl was no longer visible. The rigid middle and index fingers that were aimed at her eyes struck empty space. He felt momentarily perplexed and the light from the torch attached to her headband was dazzling him. He felt a foot placed behind his leg followed simultaneously by a vicious kick below his kneecap. He knew he was losing his balance and there was nothing he could do to prevent himself falling heavily backwards onto the marble floor.

At that point, the house lights came on again. Pippo had finally managed to locate the main's switch. Ramirez cursed loudly from his prone position on the floor. He had reckoned that his prompt response to *la signora's* covert signal would allow him to move about freely in the gloom. How the hell had those fucking cops got the lights on again so quickly? As soon as the lights were on, the anaesthetist saw the diminutive figure of this police woman standing at his feet with a gun held in two hands pointing the barrel at his nether regions. He would need to be very deft if he was to disarm her. Surely, he had seen this police woman somewhere before?

To her surprise, Oriana noticed that the man was still clutching the syringe in his right hand. But it was his left arm that she should be wary off. She spoke once again into the microphone. "The cellar, PLEASE someone come and help me!"

Her sense of relief on hearing footsteps coming down the stairs was enormous, but short-lived. Her heart sank as she saw in one brief glance behind her that it was Remo. In the next instance she felt the violent blow from the kick aimed at the hands that were clutching the pistol. It scuttered across the floor and in seconds Ramirez was towering over her, the hypodermic needle in his left hand now. He was leering at her again, toying with her as he made jabbing gestures at various parts of her body.

"This little dose was intended for that *girl!*" he was snarling. "But she can wait. You'll be dead before anyone can rescue her, little police woman!"

Ramirez was enjoying himself. He had spotted Remo – but did not recognise him from their previous encounter in the hospital, seeing only a waiter edging nervously towards him. Nothing to worry about! He could relish the expression of terror on the police woman's face as the needle plunged into her body.

Remo had retrieved Oriana's pistol from the floor. He realised that Oriana had only seconds of her life left. Fortunately, he had no time to suffer from any moral dilemma. He could hear several of his colleagues coming down the stairs. Ramirez had heard them too - the time for games was over.

Remo, who had only fired a revolver at the cardboard outline of a human figure on the police firing range, raised the gun and saw only the hated figure of the Latin American doctor. The noise of the shot in the enclosed space of the cellar was deafening as it echoed off the stone walls. But Remo had hit the mark with unfailing accuracy. A bullet in the anaesthetist's left flank had penetrated his heart. Oriana, a deathly white, had passed out on the floor where she had fallen.

Outside, the *carabinieri* heard the shot and a couple of them came indoors. Thinking the sound had emanated from the dining hall, they headed in that direction. Giacomo and Giovanni were relieved to have the support of their colleagues. The sound of the shot had caused panic among the children who had begun to wail. The adult guests were on the move.

Giacomo told everybody to remain seated in a calm voice – although his hands had instinctively gone to his revolver in its sheath.

"I need to go to the toilet!" wailed a distressed ten-year old. Giacomo nodded to the mother and she was allowed to take the girl out of the room.

Back in the cellar, Sonia was bending over the figure of Oriana.

"She's alright. She's only fainted. Pippo, could you go upstairs and take over from Giovanni please? I think Oriana might appreciate seeing him when she comes round."

Beppe just had the time to think yet again what a store of sympathy and understanding Sonia possessed. Sonia was thinking more or less the same about Beppe as he put an arm round Remo's shoulder. Remo's whole body was trembling violently as the inevitable reaction set in. He had just taken the life of another human being.

"You saved Oriana's life, Remo," he was saying quietly. "She will be eternally grateful to you. You did the right thing. Bravo, Remo! You and Oriana are tonight's true heroes!"

"I don't feel like a hero, *capo*," he replied between chattering teeth.

After a few minutes, the medics arrived to deal with the Latin American doctor's body.

"Just a minute, *ragazzi*," said Beppe. "He should have a set of keys on his belt. We need them right now. And be careful of that hypodermic syringe. It probably contains a lethal dose of something."

The keys were retrieved and the syringe put in a rigid plastic sleeve as evidence.

"Now, *ragazzi* - search everywhere down here. She's got to be *somewhere* nearby."

"She is, *capo*," said a shaky voice from the floor. Giovanni was holding Oriana in the crook of his arms. "He was going to use that hypodermic needle on *her*. *He* told me that... Remo... Thank you. You're wonderful - and so very brave!" And she passed out again in Giovanni's arms. Oriana Salvati's outlook on the world had just changed for ever.

16: But where can she be?

"I'm sorry, *capo*," said a downcast Pippo on behalf of the team of police officers some thirty minutes later. "She's just nowhere to be seen. We've looked everywhere down here. There are one or two tiny rooms at the far end of the cellars. We unlocked them with keys from the bunch which Ramirez was carrying, but there were no signs of life in any of them."

"We've even looked upstairs again, *capo*," said Giacomo D'Amico. "The guests are getting impatient and the catering staff are wondering whether to serve the remaining food or just go home to Pescara."

The shadow of failure and despair was hovering like a black raven with flapping wings inside Beppe's head. His morning fears were being horribly realised.

"Nobody leaves this house," said Beppe harshly. "We *must* be overlooking somewhere really obvious!"

Beppe made a by now partly recovered Oriana repeat the words of the Latin American anaesthetist while he was threatening to stab her with the hypodermic needle.

Beppe Stancato was feeling weary for the first time since the investigation began. He could not focus his thoughts even though he had the nagging sensation that he had missed some patently obvious aspect of the search.

"There's this single long key on this key ring, *capo*," said Pippo. "It must belong to *some* keyhole we haven't found yet. Otherwise…"

"WASHING!" exclaimed Danilo and Gino almost simultaneously. "We saw that older woman with a whole basket-load of washing the other day."

"That's right Beppe," said Sonia, forgetting to call him *capo*. Where are the washing machines?"

"And the central heating boiler…" added Giacomo.

Beppe clapped a hand to his forehead, angry with himself for being so obtuse. Antonio Breda had obviously not thought to make a video recording of the boiler room.

"Of course! We haven't looked outside! There must be a door along this corridor that leads out on to the patio which runs round the house. The entrance to the laundry-boiler room must be on the outside of the house. Go to it, *ragazzi!* I shall nip upstairs and reassure our *carabinieri* colleagues that we are not just wasting our time. Sonia, you had better go and see if Serena's mum is alright. She's been sitting in that car for over an hour. She must be nearly out of her mind with anxiety by now."

Upstairs, a false sense of normality was re-establishing itself amongst the seated guests, under the watchful eye of the *carabinieri* officers. The children, and even some of the adults, had begun picking at the copious quantities of food on the table, hunger getting the better of them. The caterers decided to serve the pasta course, which remained largely untouched. Remo had been given a glass of grappa, which he normally would never drink. He was sitting at the kitchen table trying to regain his composure and come to terms with the brutal reality that he had taken a man's life away from him. What alarmed him more than anything else was the secret feeling of satisfaction that he had avenged the act of humiliation which that man had inflicted on him in the hospital. Such feelings had been quite alien to him up until that moment in his life.

The caterers, on the other hand, were simply relieved at having something meaningful to do. Some of Don Alfieri's relatives were taunting the police officers with offers of food.

While Beppe was still upstairs, the *carabiniere* colonel drove through the entrance with Don Alfieri sitting handcuffed in the back seat of the police car. He looked in ugly mood.

"We've left a couple of officers down the hill – just in case. We thought we might be more needed up here, Beppe," said the *colonnello*, Riccardo Grimaldi. "Where can we put our prisoner?"

"Put him in the dog compound with his henchman for now," suggested Beppe coldly. "They must have got quite a lot to talk about."

Paride, sitting uncomfortably in the dog compound with his sunglasses still in place, looked as petrified as a rabbit in the presence of a cobra, as the *carabinieri* politely ushered Don Alfieri into the spacious cage. The dogs were groggily beginning to stir again.

Sonia was sitting in her car with Serena Vacri's mother. She was talking earnestly, obviously at great pains to reassure the anxious mother.

Then, the whole atmosphere changed in a trice. Gino came running round the side of the house looking for Beppe.

"*Capo*, we've found her!" he said excitedly.

"Alive, I take it," said Beppe hopefully.

"Oh yes, *capo*. Very much so! But there's a slight problem. She's barricaded herself inside the boiler room. She doesn't believe we're policemen. She keeps saying that she would rather die than be injected with any more drugs or have to see that '*bastardo maligno*'[74] again – I guess she means Ramirez. She sounds as if she's bordering on the hysterical."

---

[74] Evil bastard

Beppe ran over to the car where Sonia and Serena's mother were sitting.

"Come on you two. We've found her. *Signora*...?"

"Prosperini... but please call me Valeria."

"We need your help, Valeria," said Beppe. "Serena has locked herself in the boiler room and is refusing to open the door. She doesn't believe we're police officers here to rescue her." Beppe was almost smiling as a huge wave of relief was already beginning to flood over him after days of pent up tension.

A strong sheet metal door was the only obstacle between Serena Vacri - on the wrong side of it – her would-be rescuers and her anxious mother.

"Serena, *amore... apri la porta. Sono tua mamma.*"[75]

There was a prolonged silence from inside the boiler-cum-laundry room. Then a thin little voice cried out plaintively: *"Mamma?* Is it really *you?"*

Serena's tears of relief turned to frustration as she tried to dislodge the metal wedge she had jammed underneath the door. Beppe spoke to her through the metal shield.

"Don't worry, Serena. We'll have you out of there in no time."

The police officers, gathered outside the door, tried to shoulder the door open, but to no avail.

"We're making matters worse, *ragazzi,*" said Giacomo D'Amico despondently.

"Hurry up, *PLEASE,*" said Serena desperately. "That monster will be down here again soon."

---

[75] Open the door, darling. It's your mum

"Serena, listen to me," said Sonia. "That man will never bother you again, I promise. Your ordeal is over."

Beppe secretly thought that this was not quite the case. Certainly, she could be protected from physical harm. He was not so sure about the psychological damage. The other problem was that she was almost certainly going to be their key witness. Beppe himself went in search of Colonel Riccardo Grimaldi. The *carabinieri* must have something at their disposal to open doors.

After another ten minutes had elapsed, a flat plate attached to a hydraulic jack was inserted under the door. It lifted the creaking, buckling metal of the laundry room door a couple of millimetres and Serena was able to remove the obstacle to her freedom.

There was a gasp of horror from everyone present as a considerably skinnier version of their Sleeping Beauty emerged from captivity and fell into her mother's arms. After the initial shock at the amount of weight she had lost, the police officers cheered and applauded as Serena Vacri smiled briefly at them before bursting into a flood of unrestrained tears. The party climbed up the few stairs and emerged into the warm, moonlit Abruzzo night. The police officers embraced each other and applauded their *capo* with enthusiasm. Beppe Stancato shook his head modestly. Sonia threw caution to the winds and hugged Beppe, who did not resist on this occasion. There were one or two sage nods exchanged between the team as if to say: "There, I told you so!"

* * *

Upstairs, Don Alfieri's house guests were becoming restless. The children were unable to stay in their seats any longer and their parents were showing signs of mounting antagonism.

"Where's my father?" one of the senior Alfieri clan members was demanding to know. "What exactly are you accusing him of? I want to see him immediately." The man spoke with such a pronounced Neapolitan accent that the *carabiniere* colonel was pretending to ignore him rather than try and decipher what he was saying. Beppe made a brief appearance in the dining room to tell the colonel, Riccardo Grimaldi, that they had found the girl. They held a brief consultation amidst the growing unrest in the dining room. Beppe turned to face the rebellious Alfieri clan. There was something about this policeman's expression that defied definition. He showed none of the signs of fear or respect that their presence usually provoked. The elder son repeated his previous questions – deliberately exaggerating the Neapolitan dialect in order to muddy the waters. But this police inspector merely looked straight at him without reacting to the provocation.

"Your father is under arrest for abducting and imprisoning a twenty-two-year-old woman – to which we shall be adding the charge of attempted murder. Not to mention a charge of complicity in the full-blown murder of a public official, whose family have been cruelly deprived of a beloved husband and father. Is that enough for you to be going on with, *signore?* You may go and talk to him if you wish – but under police escort. He is outside right now – keeping his Rottweilers company, I believe. Now, we must apologise to you all – especially the younger ones – but this house is a crime scene. We must ask you to collect your things from upstairs and leave the premises within thirty minutes. If you don't want to face the drive back to Naples tonight, there are one or two hotels in town which will be delighted to accommodate you. That is all, ladies and gentleman."

Beppe detained the two women who belonged to the household and informed them that they could stay until the following morning – on condition that they surrendered their mobile phone devices. "There is to be no contact with the outside world," he said with quiet menace in his voice. "If I find out that you have tried to get in touch with *anyone,* I shall have you arrested for obstructing police business," he added with malicious glee. Despite herself, Don Alfieri's wife felt a grudging respect for this police officer.

"May I say goodnight to my husband, *commissario?*" she asked almost humbly.

Beppe escorted her personally outside, walking past Serena, her mother and Sonia sitting in armchairs in the atrium. Serena looked nonplussed – still unable to grasp the fact that the nightmare was over. Her mother was holding her hand and talking to her quietly. Sonia was grinning at Beppe – as if to say: "We've done it!"

Inside the dog compound, a wordless comedy was being played out. As the dogs slowly regained consciousness, it was apparent that Don Alfieri was growing increasingly anxious about being eaten alive. Paride, who had finally taken off his sunglasses, was enjoying the temporary sensation of feeling superior to his boss when he realised that he was the only one who could exercise any control over the hounds - who looked as if they were getting ready to take their aggression out on the nearest living creatures.

The *Carabiniere* colonel took pity on him and had Don Alfieri removed from the dog compound to talk briefly with his wife before he was escorted to Pescara and a police prison cell. Paride, sunglasses firmly back on his face again since the night was now dark enough to justify wearing them, joked Gino, was taken off in a separate *carabiniere* police car.

It was half past ten before the Alfieri clan had departed, revving their car engines noisily as a final gesture of impotent defiance against the forces of the law. Don Alfieri's elder son had endured the added indignity of having his driving license and ID card confiscated by that *commissario,* who showed insufficient respect for his lofty status within the clan.

"I am sure we shall have the pleasure of seeing you again soon, *signore,*" the enigmatic *commissario* had said to him, with an air of affability which conveyed the serene conviction that he knew far more about the *mafioso's* son than he was letting on.

"You've got nothing on me!" Don Alfieri's son had proclaimed defiantly to Beppe's face. He had been totally disconcerted by Beppe's simple gesture of taking out his smartphone and waving it from side to side in a knowing manner. The *commissario* had then turned round and walked away as if the matter was settled. The *mafioso* spat on the ground behind Beppe's departing figure. The *commissario* simply ignored him. An unmarked ambulance arrived and discreetly removed the corpse of the anaesthetist in a green body bag on a trolley. It had taken three of them to get him upstairs.

Back inside the house, Beppe was expecting to find his team standing around, relaxed but as mentally drained as he himself was suddenly feeling. To his astonishment, Serena Vacri, her mother, officer Sonia Leardi, Fabrizio De Sanctis, the inspector from L'Aquila, and the rest of the team were all sitting round the big work table in the centre of the kitchen being served copious quantities of the uneaten food by the willing catering team. Remo had obviously not moved from his seat at the table where he had been previously downing reviving grappas. The others seemed merely to have filled in the spaces round the table where he was sitting. Remo looked as if he belonged to the group for the first time in his career, thought Beppe. Oriana had told everyone how Remo had saved her life. His status had been transformed dramatically by his one act of impetuous courage. He kept his true thoughts to himself, promising himself that he would never tell Marta what had happened that evening.

The whole team stood up and cheered and applauded Beppe as he entered the kitchen.

"Come on *capo*. Even *you* must be hungry by now," said Oriana. Her comment was greeted by general laughter and a rueful smile from Beppe. It was true – he was starving and dying for a glass of red wine. By unspoken consent, the team had left a space for him to sit next to Sonia, who patted the vacant place next to her. Beppe tried to put out of his mind thoughts of how many complicated manoeuvres still lay ahead of him over the next few days.

"Come on, *ragazzi!* Let's have a glass or two of wine with this excellent food. "You all deserve it," he said raising his glass in a heartfelt *brindisi*.[76]

---

[76] A toast

Beppe looked at Serena Vacri – their Sleeping Beauty. She was devouring food enthusiastically – as soon as she realised that Don Alfieri's mother-in-law had had no hand in its preparation.

"She could have poisoned me without the help of that Latin American bastard!" she said to everybody's amazement and amusement.

Beppe was astonished that, despite her loss of weight, her pallid features and occasional involuntary nervous glances towards the door, there were already signs of the spirit and courage that had enabled her to survive the last ten days' ordeal returning. Beppe already harboured feelings of regret that he would shortly have to interrogate her – and even hide her away from the eyes of the world yet again. He just hoped she had the strength and determination to see this affair through to the end.

Beppe was aware that Sonia was trying - and probably managing - to read his thoughts. Her reaction was simply to close the physical gap between them until he could feel her thighs pressed against his under the cover of the tablecloth. He sighed imperceptibly at the double pleasure of savouring the full-bodied *Montepulciano d'Abruzzo*[77] and the promise of intimacy to come. Even Beppe felt his perseverance deserved some small measure of reward.

He held his glass up in the air and said: "You're a great team. *Grazie mille ragazzi!*"

"It was all thanks to you, *capo*," said Giacomo D'Amico, expressing the sentiment of the group, who raised their glasses in silent acknowledgement of the truth of their senior colleague's words.

---

[77] Abruzzo's best known variety of grape for its famous red wine

Only then did Beppe consciously realise that they were all eating at the mafia's expense. In the circumstances, it seemed thoroughly justified, he reckoned.

17: *About Serena Vacri*

Serena Vacri was sitting opposite Beppe and Sonia back at the police headquarters. She was looking composed – almost as serene as her name implied. Only the remaining shadow of the dark circles under her eyes hinted at the ordeal that she had had to endure. Her thin bare arms were resting on the desk in the interview room as she looked expectantly at Beppe, wondering where she should begin – or what questions he would like answered first.

Serena had spent the night in the safety of Sonia's flat, sharing the double bed with her mother. She had slept more soundly than her mother, who told her daughter the following morning that she had moaned in her sleep and had cried out once in anguish. Serena had only vague recollections of her shadowy dreams as she gratefully devoured two jam-filled croissants, whilst sipping her first real cup of morning coffee since her abduction.

Beppe and Sonia had spent the night on his boat, rocked by the gentle waves in the harbour. They had gone through the preliminary moves of love-making but had mutually and wordlessly surrendered to the overwhelming desire for sleep.

"When all this is finally over..." Beppe had murmured in Sonia's ear before he had fallen asleep in her embrace.

"Are you sure you don't want your mother to be present, Serena?" Sonia was enquiring, interrupting her attempts to assemble the nightmare sequence of events into some logical order.

"No, it might inhibit what I have to say about...my so-called uncle," she explained with a note of suppressed disdain in her voice. "After all, he *is* related to my mum."

"Do you remember talking to someone when you briefly regained consciousness in the hospital, Serena?" asked Sonia. She had agreed beforehand with Beppe to put this question to Serena to ascertain just how accurate her recollection of events was likely to be. It was vital that everything she said should be recorded. Beppe was all too aware that presenting a convincing case against Don Alfieri might depend heavily on Serena's testimony. Beppe felt guilty that he was exploiting Serena for his own ends. But it had been his superior officer, the *Questore* himself, who had insisted that any action brought in front of the law courts must be watertight; "irrefutable" had been the word his chief had used. Thus, Beppe had formulated a very precise plan in his head as to how his interrogation of Serena should proceed. He was grateful for Sonia's assurance that he was only doing what was essential – and that it should be carried out while Serena Vacri's memory of events was still fresh in her mind – allowing for the fact that she had been drugged or unconscious for a lot of the time.

On hearing this unexpected question, Serena looked worried. A puzzled frown furrowed her brow as she battled with her memory. Beppe's heart sank a little.

"But it was *you*, wasn't it, Sonia?" Serena asked after a tense lapse of time. The way the question had been put to her had led her to believe that her memory of that moment must have been clouded by the drugs. Then Serena understood the purpose of the question.

"Please, officers, you must ask me whatever questions you need to. I am as anxious as you are to see justice done. My uncle is a bad man. And remember too that I am studying to be a lawyer," she added, seemingly without relevance. But the two police officers understood that it was an indication of how personal the matter was to her.

"Thank you, Serena," said Beppe. "I was feeling callous about putting you through yet another ordeal so soon after you found your freedom again. But we need to be certain your waking memories are lucid."

"Let's get started, then," said Serena determinedly as Beppe switched the recorder on. A little red light glowed on the machine.

The *Questore,* Dante Di Pasquale, had breathed a sigh of relief as he watched the beginning of Serena Vacri's interview on the TV monitor in his upstairs office.

"Do you remember writing this letter before you were captured, Serena?" began Beppe handing the sheet of paper to her. It was the letter she had scribbled hastily and handed over to Marta in her bedroom that night – before she had had to take refuge in the bathroom to avoid her uncle.

Serena smiled radiantly. "That's amazing! I was so worried that Marta might be too anxious about losing her job as *his* house-slave to give it to the police. Or that she might even show it to my uncle. Where is Marta, by the way? Is she safe?"

"We assume so, Serena," replied Beppe with a touch of irony which caused Serena to look quizzically, first at the *commissario* and, receiving no enlightenment from that direction, at Sonia.

"When we last had any information, she was safely in the hands of one of our young police officers," Sonia told her.

"Well, that *is* a pleasant surprise," said Serena, who had caught on to the innuendo. "I was concerned that she would never have the opportunity to meet a man. But is she still working in my uncle's house? I hope not, I don't trust him at all."

Once again, Serena Vacri intercepted a covert glance between the two police officers. Beppe nodded at Sonia, inviting her to fill in the gaps in Serena's knowledge.

"Your uncle is safely locked up in a police cell, Serena. He is... assisting us with our enquiries."

The look of unrestrained delight on Serena's face was unmistakable.

"You've arrested him!" she said with gleeful relief. "It's no more than he deserves."

"Now, Serena, we would like you to help us keep him under lock and key. But before you say *anything,* we have to ask you if you are willing to testify in court against him, even if..."

"Don't worry, officers. I can't wait to face him in court. The answer is 'yes'," she stated unequivocally.

Il Commissario Stancato took a deep breath before saying the next words.

"I feel bound to point out to you, Serena, that you may be needed to testify at Don Alfieri's trial too. In fact, that will be far more important – and possibly with more sinister consequences."

Beppe hated himself for having to be so blunt. But he was apparently underestimating the perspicacity of the young woman sitting opposite him.

Serena sighed and a brief wave of tiredness spread over her features, quickly overcome.

"I am aware of what is involved, *commissario,*" she stated quietly. In point of fact, she was only just beginning to realise the implications of her miraculous rescue the previous night. "I'm just happy to be alive," she added with a wan smile.

"Thank you. You are a very courageous young woman!" said Beppe with quiet sincerity.

Serena Vacri shrugged off the compliment, looking at Beppe as if inviting him to give her a lead. There was so much she wanted to say that she was not sure where to begin.

Beppe held up the letter again.

"You make two serious accusations against your uncle in this letter, Serena. First of all, you say he deliberately and publicly played down the likelihood of L'Aquila being struck by a major earthquake; that is already a damning indictment in itself. Then you go on to state that he is involved with "a local criminal" in setting up illegal reconstruction contracts even before the earthquake occurred. Can you explain to us how you came to these conclusions? After all, at the outset, your uncle couldn't have known for certain when an earthquake would occur. Am I right?"

Serena sighed audibly as she tried to order her thoughts into a logical sequence. Beppe and Sonia tried to remain impassive during the silence that seemed to last minutes rather than seconds. Serena's opening words, therefore, took them both by surprise.

"My uncle is an arrogant man who assumes that he is extremely clever at concealing his true motives from the rest of the world. He believes he is immune from suspicion. This is particularly the case when he finds himself in the presence of some flighty young woman – such as me! I was just a pretty decoration that he was quite happy to have around the house at the time."

Serena paused as she saw the look of mild astonishment on the faces of the two police officers.

"I'm only telling you this to explain to you how careless he was about talking openly on the phone or with the team of scientists who met at his house to discuss the likelihood of an earthquake. It was almost as if he imagined that my presence in the room added to his self-importance. I'm not conceited about my physical appearance, officers, but it was as if he was telling the world: "Look, I've got a pretty young woman in tow. I bet you can't match that!"

Beppe and Sonia just looked at Serena slightly open-mouthed. They had not been expecting this degree of self-awareness from their interviewee.

"Go on, Serena," said Beppe in the end.

"I was in the room when his brother-in-law, the architect came round to see him one morning. You know, the man who had renovated the house belonging to Gianluca Alfieri. I knew little about Alfieri's mafia connections at that stage. But after over-hearing what was said that day, I was alerted to the fact that my uncle was involved in something shady and I made it my business to find out as much as I could."

"Do you mean that your uncle discussed business with his brother-in-law while you were present?" asked Beppe in astonishment.

"Exactly, *commissario.* You understand, at that stage, it was nothing specific. The brother-in-law made a gesture to my uncle as if to query my presence in the room. My uncle just waved a dismissive hand in the air as if to say: *'She's not a problem.'* I pretended to be scribbling notes down and flicking through pages of my law text book. I must have looked very convincing."

Serena paused long enough to sip some water from a bottle. Beppe was thinking hard. He had quite taken to the brother-in-law, Antonio Breda, who had been really helpful before the police had raided Don Alfieri's house. The virtual reality video had been invaluable in their hunt for the young woman sitting expectantly opposite them. Could he have been mistaken about Antonio Breda, the architect brother-in-law? He hoped this was not the case. He decided to reserve his judgement about Breda's involvement until Serena had finished talking. There was no point in sending out conflicting signals. It would be wiser to allow her to speak freely, unfettered by any preconceived notions of what she should say. Nevertheless, he would remain alert as to any nuances in her narrative.

"They were talking about the reconstruction job Antonio Breda had carried out on Alfieri's house in Monticchio." Serena continued. "Antonio was obviously very pleased with what he had achieved. Did you know that he even fitted state-of-the art anti-seismic material to the house? Apparently, it's a Japanese invention. You embed long carbon nanotubes into the outside walls; they're tougher than steel and a hundred times more flexible. It was plain that Antonio Breda was also very pleased about the amount of money he had earned; he couldn't believe how well he had been 'rewarded' – as he put it. *'There's plenty more where that came from, Antonio,'* my uncle said. Then they talked at great length about setting up what he called 'anticipatory' renovation tenders with the authorities – in case there was an earthquake. *'Gianluca Alfieri seems to know all about that side of things,'* my uncle said."

"I imagine your ears pricked up when you heard that!" interjected Sonia.

"Oh yes, I did some very noisy page turning and even more energetic scribbling. *'But is there really going to be a big earthquake, Donatello?'* asked the brother-in-law. *'Sooner or later, there will be a major seismic occurrence, yes. And I suspect it will be sooner rather than later,'* my uncle said. *'There's a team of scientists coming here this week. We'll be discussing it here in my house.'* After that, my uncle said he would keep his brother-in-law informed. And that was the end of that particular meeting."

Serena paused to drink another mouthful of water.

"But there was no mention of Alfieri being part of a mafia clan?" Beppe asked her.

"No, nothing specific, but everybody here knows what he is, although nothing is ever stated openly, of course. Antonio Breda must have had more than an inkling as to the real status of the man he had been working for – even at the outset."

"Now we come to the important part, Serena," continued Beppe after a thoughtful pause. "Your uncle appears to have deliberately suppressed the fact that a major quake was expected. Can you shed any light on this aspect of the case?"

A look of suppressed anger passed across Serena's face in that instant - provoked by the memory of what she had been asked to recall.

"You're not going to believe this…" she began looking at Beppe and Sonia in turn with eyes wide-open in theatrical horror.

"I hope the judge will," said Beppe with the first hint of a smile on his face. This girl had the capacity to take him by surprise at every turn.

"Oh, he or she will believe it alright! There's a witness," was her terse reply.

After a pause, while she searched for the words which would make the memory concrete reality, she continued:

"I walked into the main sitting room where the telephone is. My uncle had just picked up the phone. He was looking nervous. I could just make out a voice which I later came to recognise as Don Alfieri's. For the first time ever, my uncle made a gesture for me to leave the room. Now, you're going to understand why I told you he underestimated me. There's a second, interconnected landline in the house – in Marta's bedroom, of all places. Marta told me that her room used to belong to *la signora,* my uncle's wife…"

"Before she went on her "world cruise," interjected Sonia in order to save Serena the need to relate something they had already gleaned. Serena smiled in recognition of their advanced background knowledge.

"Which is unlikely to come to an end," added Serena sarcastically. "I flew upstairs to Marta's room praying that she had not locked the door. I was astonished to find her standing by the phone with the receiver pressed to her ear. She beckoned me over with a "hurry up" gesture and passed me the phone. I still can't believe the words I heard. It was one of those old-fashioned telephones which had an extra earpiece attached to it. I gestured to Marta to listen in too – thus my "witness". The conversation went like this:

My uncle was saying: "But why is it so important to you Don…"

"No names, I told you. I know who I am! When will you understand the basic rules of this game, professore?"

"Sorry, *signore*. Why should I minimise the chances of an earthquake occurring? It's my brief to warn people about earthquakes. It will be very difficult to persuade my colleagues to..."

"You'll find a way, professore. You have no choice in the matter from now on. I can implicate you in this affair in such a way that you will have no career left and none of the financial rewards that you can expect from our business venture."

My uncle was sounding very nervous by now. He pressed the point home to Don Alfieri – wanting to know why he should suppress the truth about an imminent quake. The next words left us both chilled to the bone. Don Alfieri said as cold as ice: *"Because an earthquake is an earthquake, professore. But a few deaths arouse public sympathy and will create a flood of donations through all the banks in Italy. It's in our interest - it's good for business. I wouldn't worry. It will only be a couple of dozen people at most – people who would have lost their lives, whatever you told them. Just think it over, professore!"*

Don Alfieri hung up without another word. I could tell my uncle was shaken to the core. It must have been from that point onwards that he realised he was in this business up to his neck," Serena finished off.

"We overheard a similar sentiment being expressed when Don Alfieri was speaking to his son over the phone – just a few days ago," added Beppe bitterly. "He was actually gloating over the number of deaths in L'Aquila."

"Che bastardo!" said Serena with a vehemence that shook the two police officers.

"I suppose I should have been more aware of a potential risk to myself at that stage, shouldn't I?" she added. "I was more concerned about Marta's safety. *Not a word of this to ANYONE,* I told her. I swore her to silence."

"Maybe that's why Marta never told us about this overheard phone call," thought Sonia to herself. "Or the incident just didn't seem important enough in her eyes."

"Would being aware of the risk to yourself have made any difference to the way you acted, Serena?" Beppe was asking Serena.

"I doubt it, *commissario.*"

"Don't you want a break, Serena?" asked Sonia. She shook her head. Another sip of water and she continued under her own steam.

"After that, everything happened very quickly. I overheard the discussion the High-Risk Commission held at my uncle's house. It was blatantly obvious that there was a serious rift between the members of the team. The earthquake took us all by surprise – somehow we imagined that it really wasn't going to be quite so imminent. The Civil Protection agent, Romano Di Carlo, was my uncle's most vociferous opponent. He's a good man. I met up with him after the public demonstration which the university students organised. I think he was plucking up courage to talk to me. I saw him watching me from the crowd, so after I had spoken to the local TV team, *TV-Tavo,* I approached him and swapped information about my uncle. He turned white as a sheet when I told him about the mafia connection. I hope Romano is not going to be prosecuted at the trial, by the way. He was vehement in his condemnation of my uncle's failure to warn the people about the earthquake..."

Yet again, Serena had intercepted a meaningful glance between the two police officers, which made her pause in her narrative.

"Has something happened to Romano?" asked Serena anxiously.

"There's no point in shielding you from the truth of what has happened," said Beppe, looking at Sonia in invitation.

"Serena, I'm so sorry. We managed to save your life, but we were not aware of the complexity of this case until it was too late for Romano Di Carlo. He was brutally murdered by Don Alfieri's mobsters – with your uncle's compliance, we suspect," explained Sonia. "They staged his death to make it look like a suicide. I'm so sorry, Serena."

Their witness looked completely shattered by the news. Two tears appeared in the corner of her eyes and trickled sadly down her cheeks.

"We should take a break at this point," said Beppe, switching off the recording machine. "Besides which, I think you've already told us enough to make our task much easier. You've been brilliant, Serena. I'm just so sorry to have to put you through all this, so soon after…"

Serena managed to wave a hand to indicate that his apology was not necessary.

"Give me thirty minutes with my mum, officers. I want to tell you what happened afterwards just to get it off my chest."

* * *

"It's remarkable how lucid Serena's mind is after being drugged for days," observed Sonia to Beppe when they were on their own.

"If I remember correctly what Doctor Esposito told me last week, he seemed to think that the effects of the drugs would wear off rapidly enough. I'm guessing that after Serena was brought back to Don Alfieri's house from the clinic, they didn't fill her up with anything stronger than sedatives."

"Saving her up for a worse fate, I suppose," concluded Sonia.

Some of Serena's crusading spirit had been broken when they reconvened in the interview room just before midday. Serena had stayed with her mother for almost two hours. Sonia was about to point out to her chief that they really would have to take a proper lunch break – preferably at the conventional time - when, to her surprise, he confessed almost guiltily that he was beginning to feel hungry.

"I'll take us all out to lunch – somewhere nice, along the coast, I think. Serena needs a treat after what she's been through this morning, don't you think?"

"Yes, she deserves it - and so do we come to that! Lunch will be lovely - and I know just the place to go."

"I thought you might, Sonia."

Serena came in to the interview room accompanied by her mother. Serena began haltingly to pick up the thread of her narrative, but she seemed despondent; learning about Romano's death had left its mark more than her own acute suffering.

"*He* should have been my uncle," she explained simply. She took a very deep breath and continued talking quickly so as to bring the subsequent events to as rapid a conclusion as possible.

"The night after the demonstration in L'Aquila when I left that letter with Marta, I had already arranged to take a few things and escape from that house. I sensed danger in the air. I had already agreed to go and stay with my friend Gabriele – he's a fellow law student at the uni…"

"Gabriele Rapino, yes, Serena – we know about him," added Sonia.

It was Serena's turn to look mildly surprised. She realised that she knew nothing about how these two police officers had actually succeeded in tracking her down and rescuing her.

"I want you to tell me all about my rescue later," she said brightly, as if it was a treat to look forward to, after she had furnished them with the grim details of her abduction. "I realised I should have been more cautious about leaving my uncle's house that night. Gabriele would have come round on his scooter to pick me up but I insisted on doing everything myself…"

"They would have caught up with you sooner or later, Serena. Maybe Gabriele would have become implicated too. They certainly would not have spared his life as they did yours," Beppe reassured her.

"My uncle must already have tipped off those two thugs. I was walking through the streets of L'Aquila towards the students' camp site – as I called it. It all happened so rapidly. They were waiting for me in a big black Audi. The door swung open to block my path. I heard the driver – that little crook who always wore sunglasses at night time – hissing: "Are you sure this is her?" Then that foreign doctor got hold of me and twisted my arm up until I thought it was going to snap. I felt the needle going into my neck and… I blacked out. I can't really remember much else until I was in Don Alfieri's house. I believe they took me to some sinister clinic – full of the saddest cases of drug addiction I've ever seen. You probably know more about that than than I do.

When they locked me up in the laundry room, I felt instinctively that my days were numbered. I caught a look on that brute's face. I knew what he had got planned for me by the lascivious look in his eyes. That's when I realised they had little further use for me alive... And then you people turned up and saved my life," she said before the flood gates opened and the hot tears gushed down her cheeks.

"That's all we need to know for now, Serena," said Beppe quietly. Serena had composed herself with remarkable speed and had begun smiling through her sobs as if she found her own uncontrollable emotions amusing.

In the car, on their way to lunch, Beppe felt compelled to ask one more question. It sounded so trivial but it had been bothering him for days. "How come we found a photo of you in L'Aquila before the earthquake on that Latin American anaesthetist's smart phone, Serena?"

She looked puzzled.

"Did you?" she asked. She fell silent for several minutes before it came to her. *"That's* why my uncle took all those pictures of me on his smart phone! I was wondering why he suddenly became all avuncular that day. I assumed he was going to send them to you, *mamma,* to reassure you that I was happy. The bastard must have sent pictures of me to that ..."

"... other bastard," said Beppe completing the sentence for her.

Sonia had driven them a long way down the coast in the direction of Vasto before she pulled up at a little restaurant overlooking a stretch of unspoilt beach. "This is the place I wanted to take you to last time, Beppe," she said, no longer caring about the consequences of using his first name in company. Neither Serena nor her mother appeared to notice.

Over lunch, which consisted almost entirely of copious sea-food *antipasti* and sea bream baked on a bed of potatoes flavoured with parsley and pecorino cheese, Serena plied Beppe and Sonia with questions about the case, fascinated by the skilful manner in which Beppe had conducted the investigation with so little to go on and overwhelmed with gratitude when she discovered how many officers had been involved in her rescue. The only aspect of the story which amused her was the description of the *carabinieri* brass band playing "Happy Birthday" to her jailer.

"I thought I heard a brass band playing," she said. "While I was looking for something to jam that door shut."

Over desserts and coffees, Beppe tentatively suggested to Serena that she should go into hiding pending her court appearance. He was not surprised, however, when she refused categorically to do any such thing.

"I have to catch up on my university course," she stated firmly. "Now, even more than ever, I want to become a lawyer and prosecute people like Gianluca Alfieri and...my uncle. Don't worry. I'll keep a low profile. I'll make sure I'm always in company day and night. And I'll never accept lifts from strange men again, I promise."

Beppe knew that it would be pointless insisting at this juncture. He would leave it to Valeria, her mother, to talk her round.

"Well, you have given us so much information today, Serena – for which we are immeasurably grateful." Beppe was about to signal for the bill to be brought over when Serena, speaking with calculated coolness, said:

"By the way, *commissario,* I nearly forgot to tell you. I have a copy of the contract which my uncle drew up with Don Alfieri. It's got lots of interesting things on it – like bank account details and so on…"

Beppe and Sonia just stared at Serena with their mouths agape.

"How did you…?" asked Sonia finally.

"I downloaded it from his computer while he was out of the house. It's on a pink USB memory stick. Gabriele Rapino's looking after it."

Beppe signalled the waiter over and ordered more coffees and four glasses of the local liqueur, which he had been dying to try again. He had to ask Sonia what it was called.

"*Genziana,* Beppe. But I can't…"

"Yes, you can, Sonia. You're with a *commissario,* don't forget."

Serena had an impudent grin on her face when, to her mother's embarrassment, her daughter asked out of the blue:

"Are you two an item, by any chance?"

Sonia smiled radiantly but Beppe looked hard at Serena, his solemn countenance firmly back in place.

"Well, Serena," said Beppe reprovingly, "we probably would have been by now - had you given us half a chance, that is."

The meal – indeed the whole episode in their collective lives – came to a genial conclusion. Apparently, Serena Vacri had caught a glint of humour behind the *commissario's* mask of severity.

What Beppe did not reveal to Serena, and even less to Oriana later on, was that the analysis of the substance in the hypodermic syringe which the Latin American anaesthetist was carrying contained a lethal dose of curare. If it had not been for Remo Mastrodicasa's timely act of unpremeditated courage, either or both of the women would have been dead within minutes.

18: Face to face with Don Alfieri

It was Saturday morning. To Sonia's dismay, but not to her great surprise, Beppe decided that he would press on with his interrogation of the main protagonists of this case – finishing up with Don Alfieri himself. The *mafioso boss* was being detained in the local penitentiary. He had a cell entirely to himself as befitted his status as a *"signore di onore"* – or so he had been told by the *carabiniere* Colonel, Riccardo Grimaldi, who had graciously conceded to the *mafioso's* request that his lawyer should be summoned from Naples. Don Alfieri had been unsettled by the ease with which this request had been granted. In his experience of previous arrests in his native Naples, the police always procrastinated for as long as they could before conceding he had a right to a lawyer being present. This departure from the norm left Don Alfieri with the uncomfortable sensation that *that* police inspector with the disconcerting stare already had sufficient evidence to put him away for good. For once, Don Alfieri was feeling vulnerable and wished his wife was nearby. He must really be getting too old for this way of life.

Beppe had consoled his fledgling partner with the absolute promise that they would take the boat out to sea – come rain or shine – before the week was out. "For our fishing trip," he had stated euphemistically.

"My mind will be free from this investigation by then," he had optimistically declared to Sonia.

She headed back to her flat to talk to Serena Vacri and her mother, Valeria. Despite Sonia's assurances that they could stay on for as long as they felt necessary, Serena and her mother announced they would be heading for L'Aquila.

"It's the last place anyone will look for me, Sonia," Serena said. "We won't be there for more than a week, but I have an exam next week. After that, we'll disappear back home to Orvieto."

"She's very determined to carry on as if nothing had happened," her mother sighed in resignation. "She has always been very stubborn."

"Stubbornness and determination usually go hand in hand, Valeria," said Sonia philosophically.

Despite being faced with Serena's determination to waltz off to L'Aquila, Sonia insisted that she consult with her *capo* before allowing them to leave.

"We can't detain them. They've done nothing wrong, after all," Beppe said. "But what you must insist on is that you take them back to L'Aquila in a police car. Take Oriana with you. My guess is she'll be delighted to have an excuse to see Officer Giovanni Palena again. Then you can all take them to find Serena's friend, Gabriele Rapino. I want that pink memory stick in our safe keeping."

"Anything else, *capo?*" added Sonia pointedly.

"Yes, if I'm not back, take the memory stick to our two technicians and get them to make copies of the USB – plus printed copies of any documents. I want to be able to impress on Altadonna that there is no point in him attempting to conceal anything else from us…"

"*Chiaro, capo,*" said Sonia, impressed with his thoroughness. "And I thought it was all nearly over," she thought wistfully as she brought the phone call to an end.

"Come on you two!" she said to Serena and her mother. "Your wish is granted, but you have to let us escort you to L'Aquila – *Commissario* Stancato's orders!"

* * *

Beppe, with Pippo in tow, headed for the *carabinieri* headquarters in Pescara. He had decided to interrogate – or rather soften up – the skinny little mobster with the sunglasses before tackling Don Alfieri. If he could get Paride to confess to even one of the crimes he must have committed at Don Alfieri's bidding, it would make his task easier. Paride was likely to be the weakest link, he reasoned.

Il Colonnello, Riccardo Grimaldi, greeted Beppe and Pippo like old comrades-in-arms.

"I would like to be present when you talk to our little *mafioso* friend, Beppe – if you have no objection, that is. I've heard all about your interrogation techniques. I feel sure it will be an instructive experience for me."

Knowing full well that this senior State police officer had every right to be present at the interview, Beppe merely grinned at him.

"What's his surname, by the way?" Beppe asked the *colonnello*.

"One of the most common surnames in Naples – in contrast to his first name; it's Russo," replied Riccardo Grimaldi. "By the way, if you can persuade him to take off his sunglasses, you will already have achieved more than anyone else in this police station has done. They seem to be grafted on to his face."

"I think we shall discover there's a good reason for the sunglasses, *colonnello*," said Beppe enigmatically.

Riccardo Grimaldi looked quizzically at Pippo but received nothing more informative than a shrug of the shoulders in reply.

Beppe took one look at Paride Russo as the three of them entered the interview room. Their prisoner inspired pity in almost equal measure to any other emotion. Here was a man whose sole purpose in life was to carry out the wishes of some heartless mafia boss. If Paride had ever slept with a woman, it would be because his overlords had dragooned some local girl into an act of sex under threat of some dire consequence if she refused. Beppe's condemnation of the likes of Paride was always tempered by pity – whatever heinous acts they might have committed in the service of their masters. It was the reason why he instantly treated the man in front of him with a semblance of respect. His attitude to their prisoner caught Pippo and the colonel off their guard - whereas the prisoner himself looked totally bemused at Beppe's opening words.

"Good morning, Paride. I'm sorry to have to detain you like this. You must be missing your two dogs quite badly by now."

The reaction from the little man was instantaneous. His face lit up and, without thinking, he removed the sunglasses to reveal a very pronounced squint in his left eye.

Pippo and the colonel exchanged glances with eyebrows raised, as if to say: "How on earth did he know?"

"Are the dogs alright, *commissario?*" asked Paride.

"At the moment, they are safe in a police dog compound," replied Beppe. "I'm hoping you'll be able to take charge of them again before long."

Paride was not that gullible. His face clouded over again. He understood the direction in which this unusual policeman was heading. His instinctive reaction of self-preservation was to put his sunglasses back on again.

"Paride," resumed the disconcerting *commissario* in a soft, persuasive voice, "we have you linked to the cold-blooded killing of an innocent man whose body you left on a mountain slope outside Sulmona last week."

"*I* didn't kill him, *commissario*," protested Paride too quickly. "I wasn't even there…"

Beppe frowned at the little man and stared fixedly at Paride's sunglasses. He couldn't help wondering which of his victim's eyes was focussed on his face. Beppe made an impatient sound with his tongue and raised his voice just fractionally as he showed him the post card he had been writing to his family at the time of his arrest - side by side with the fake suicide note.

"Well, you are not going to deny you wrote *this*, I hope. And I somehow doubt that even your partner-in-crime, Ramirez, carried out the killing all by himself. And, if that is not enough to satisfy you, you certainly aided him kidnapping the girl just outside the university. We've already identified your finger prints on the steering wheel," the *commissario* lied smoothly. They had found identical prints to Paride's on the driver's side door handle, as Beppe knew well.

"Impossible, *commissario*," said the gullible Paride without reflecting. "I was wearing gloves while I was driving…" He stopped in mid-sentence, looking crestfallen.

"I thank you for your candour, Paride. I think you would do well to tell me the truth about everything else, too."

"What have you done with Ramirez?" asked Paride, fear in his eyes.

Beppe realised with an element of shock that it was unlikely that either Paride or Don Alfieri, for that matter, would realise that Ramirez had been killed. They must have heard a shot but would have no idea who was involved. Beppe decided he would leave things that way.

"We're taking care of him, Paride. He can't get at you now," he replied ambiguously.

Paride Russo continued to look petrified, however. The idea of spending ten years in an Italian jail, where his failure in the eyes of his clan would almost certainly be rewarded by a razor cut across his throat while he slept, was a terrifyingly real probability.

"I couldn't do anything to stop him... We were just carrying out orders..." stuttered the diminutive *mafioso.*

"Whose orders?" barked Beppe so suddenly that it made Paride jump out of his skin.

Paride did not answer the question. Beppe instantly reverted to his quiet, respectful voice:

"I was just thinking, Paride... You have such a talent and an affinity with dogs. There's no way I can spare you at least a ten-year sentence for what you have done – even just taking into account your two most recent crimes as an accomplice to murder and the brutal abduction of an innocent young woman – not to mention slugging one of my police officers from behind. But I could make sure you spend your time helping to train police dogs instead of going to jail. And you might even get to keep your own animals. That, Paride, is a promise I am making to you in front of two other police officers. Now what do you say?"

Beppe allowed the ensuing silence to continue for almost three minutes, while the diminutive little man considered his alternatives.

"Now whose orders were you carrying out?" Beppe asked again when it was obvious that Paride was unable to resolve his conflicting loyalties.

"Don Alfieri's," muttered Paride so quietly that *Colonnello* Grimaldi asked him to repeat the words for the sake of the recording.

The three officers visibly relaxed. The recording machine was switched off.

"You meant what you said, didn't you, *commissario?*" stammered Paride, now dreading the consequences of his irrevocable betrayal.

"Yes, I did. You'll be sent to somewhere near Vicenza – in the north of Italy. A long way from Naples," he was assured. "None of your friends will ever guess where you are hiding."

Beppe prayed fervently that his prediction would turn out to be well-founded.

* * *

"That was very impressive, *commissario!*" stated Riccardo Grimaldi.

"But can you really be so certain about Paride working with dogs, *capo?* Surely, you wouldn't just say such things merely to make him confess to..." began Pippo, who left the sentence unfinished because it would have been impertinent to have cast doubts on his senior officer's rectitude.

Beppe grinned at his colleagues, tapping the side of his nose with his index finger to signify that he was privy to information that they were unaware of.

"I have a cousin up north who trains police dogs. There have been a couple of minor criminals who my cousin, Santino, has helped me out with in the past – in exchange for their cooperation, of course."

The colonel chuckled. *"Viva l'Italia!* We'd never survive as a country if it wasn't for *the people we know,"* he said. "But how could you be so sure that Paride – squint and all – was good at handling dogs?"

"Didn't you see him when he and Don Alfieri were shut in the cage with the Rottweilers the other night?" asked Beppe.

"Yes, I could see Don Alfieri was becoming increasingly nervous as the dogs began to wake up. That's why I had him removed from the cage."

"But didn't you notice that Paride looked more relaxed at that point?" asked Beppe. "He even took his sunglasses off – a sure sign that he is feeling marginally more secure in any given situation."

Pippo merely sighed in response to this minor revelation. *"Bravo, capo!"* he said quietly, storing away in his mind yet another facet of his chief's ability to see beneath the surface of things.

Beppe was shaking hands with Riccardo Grimaldi.

"I would like to go and interview Don Alfieri tomorrow, *colonnello*. I know it's Sunday but..."

"I'll drive you out to the prison myself," offered the *carabiniere* officer. "You are right - we must strike while the iron is hot."

"I'll meet you there, *colonnello*. I've got a little charade worked out for tomorrow," said Beppe with the now familiar grin on his face whenever he had hatched some devious plot which smacked of the unconventional.

"Can I come too, *capo?*" requested Pippo. "Unless of course, you want S…. someone else to accompany you," he added quickly covering his tracks.

"The more the merrier," replied his chief sarcastically. "Although I suspect *Agente* Leardi will be otherwise engaged – for your information, *Agente* Cafarelli."

Pippo blushed at being picked up on his minor *faux pas.* "Sorry, *capo!*"

* * *

Back at police headquarters, Beppe waited for the return of Sonia and Oriana – assuming that she had managed to prise her younger colleague from Giovanni Palena's arms. They both arrived soon afterwards, looking smug, and held out the pink USB memory stick.

"Go and have some lunch, *ragazze*. And then I'd like you to go back to L'Aquila again, Sonia. You too, Oriana, if you're up to it. Otherwise, I can ask someone else."

The request was put very kindly. Sonia sighed as the prospect of time spent with Beppe that evening receded once again. Oriana looked as if she was about to make some cutting comment about wasting a policewoman's time. Beppe thought it would be wise to forestall such an eventuality.

"I'm sorry – truly. We're nearly there now, *ragazze*. I just want all the loose ends tied up. After tomorrow, I suspect the technical details of the case will be in the hands of the *Guardia di Finanza* – or the DIA." *(The financial police and the Direzione Investigativa Antimafia, the antimafia police – author's note)*

"But what do you want us to do precisely, *capo?*" asked Sonia, resigned to the idea of driving all the way back to L'Aquila.

He told them. The two officers stood looking at him with mouths agape.

"But we don't have the same experience in interviewing people as you do," protested Oriana. "The whole case could unravel if we mess up."

"Oh, *Professore* Altadonna will be putty in your hands, *ragazze!* I have complete confidence in you both. You'll tear him to shreds. The important thing is to record everything – Giovanni's chief will set that up for you. I'll tell him you're coming. Just get Altadonna to agree to testify against Don Alfieri. You have *carte blanche* as to how you achieve this. I'm going to ask Giovanni's *Ispettore* De Sanctis to pay Antonio Breda a visit, too. I can't bring myself to believe that he is really part of this illegal contract conspiracy."

"And what, may one enquire, are you going to do, Beppe – having relegated the responsibilities for this investigation to us?" asked Sonia sounding mildly sardonic.

Beppe wore an elusive expression, thought Sonia. He grinned but proffered no explanation

Sonia and Oriana went away to have lunch. They felt a mixture of annoyance at the thought of driving all the way back to L'Aquila for a second time in one day. But they were secretly pleased that their chief had sufficient faith in the two female members of his team to entrust them with the vital task of breaking the last vestiges of the seismologist's resistance. They both agreed over a simple lunch that they would rise to the challenge. They set out on the long drive back to L'Aquila armed with a brown envelope containing a slim sheaf of documents, which had been downloaded from a pink USB memory stick.

* * *

It was Sunday morning. Beppe woke up on his boat knowing that, if this day panned out in the way he envisaged, his first major case on Abruzzo soil would be virtually out of his hands. One of the first things he had done the previous afternoon was to hand in his notice on the cramped little apartment on the outskirts of Pescara. The thought made him feel instantly more optimistic about everything else.

Another thing he had done was to pay a visit to the archbishop of Pescara, a man with piercing grey eyes and a nearly bald head. His tearful, almost wordless sermon in the immediate aftermath of the earthquake had endeared him to the whole population of Pescara - to churchgoers and agnostics alike. He was in his sixties and looked like a medieval abbot. Beppe had made a very extraordinary request, to which the holy man had immediately agreed as soon as Beppe assured him he might well be saving a man's soul from perdition.

"Mille grazie, monsignore,"[78] Beppe said as he left the archbishop.

"For heaven's sake, just call me Don Emanuele. I'm happy to help you, *commissario*."

On Sunday morning, he was up at seven o'clock. He went into the almost deserted police station in *Via Pesaro*. He headed for his office, donned his uniform and left, waving a greeting to Gino who was sleepily on duty.

---

[78] The correct courtesy title for cardinals and archbishops

"Busy night?" asked Beppe.

"Nothing, *capo!* We all miss the excitement of the last few days."

"Something else is bound to materialise sooner or later," he added consolingly. "By the way, could you apologise to Pippo for me, please, Gino? Tell him it would be better if he wasn't present at Don Alfieri's interview – I'll explain when I see him."

"D'accordo, capo. In bocca al lupo!" replied Gino.

Beppe headed for the Cathedral – built in the 1930s and dedicated to San Cetteo, the patron saint of Pescara. It was entirely due to the intervention of San Cetteo, Beppe had once been told by Sonia, that the recently built church had escaped the fate, inflicted on much of the city, of being bombed by the Americans during the Second World War. The area of Pescara near the railway station still looked as if it had merely been patched up.

The archbishop had agreed to meet Beppe after mass. Beppe drove them both to the out-of-town jail where Don Alfieri was being held. The colonel, Riccardo Grimaldi, was already there waiting for Beppe to arrive. He raised a quizzical eyebrow as the familiar figure of the archbishop got out of the police car.

"Good morning, *monsignore*," he said quietly to the distinguished looking cleric, bowing his head slightly.

"Don Emanuele has kindly agreed to be present when we talk to our friend, Don Alfieri."

Riccardo Grimaldi had cottoned on to Beppe's strategy – as well as to the archbishop's preferred form of address. He also realised why his colleague had wanted to interrogate the *mafioso* on Sunday – a day on which Don Alfieri's lawyer was very unlikely to arrive at an early hour, coming all the way from Naples to Pescara at short notice. The presence of the archbishop was designed to impress on their prisoner the seriousness of his fate in the eyes of God and his Church. It would be fascinating to discover how such an encounter would affect Don Alfieri. It was, thought Riccardo Grimaldi irreverently, like having a spiritual trump card up one's sleeve.

* * *

The effect on Don Alfieri, when he was ushered into the interview room, was immediate. The oft-practised stony face, the hard mouth, the tightly pursed lips, coupled with the studied swagger that he adopted – in so far as his short stature allowed him to swagger - were transformed into an expression of bewilderment. His shifty eyes travelled in rapid succession from the two uniformed police officers to the tall, dignified clergyman standing behind them, with a stole resting on his shoulders and a holy book clasped in his hands.

Then Don Alfieri noticed to his horror that there was a photo of Pope Francis on the table - looking at him with that gentle smile of inner sanctity which he exuded.

"Where's my lawyer?" he managed to snarl, in an attempt to regain control of the situation.

"He'll be here later on today, *signore*," stated the *Colonnello* convivially "Don't worry - we shall conduct the official interview in his presence. Right now, we would just like an informal talk with you."

"I'm not saying *anything* until my lawyer is present," snapped Don Alfieri.

"Very well, Don Alfieri, no problem at all! You can just listen to what we have to say to *you*" said Beppe in a totally unruffled manner.

Don Alfieri looked again at the *commissario* with the unperturbed eyes and then at the high-ranking *carabiniere* officer by his side. They both looked sublimely unconcerned. It was this single fact that Don Alfieri found more disturbing than anything else. He disguised his discomfort by sneering at them both. "Why don't you light up a couple of candles and we can say mass while we're waiting for *Avvocato*[79] Brunello to arrive," he said disrespectfully.

"You are so very far away from the state of grace necessary to find yourself in the presence of Jesus Christ, my son. You carry Satan inside you. I sense nothing but evil in you. You would do well not to mock holy things."

Don Alfieri froze at the sound of these simple, damning words from the mouth of the archbishop – of whose lofty ecclesiastic status he was blissfully unaware. He glanced at the photo of Pope Francis, half expecting to see a fearful change of expression on the Pontiff's face.

Beppe had visibly started at the unexpected – and unrehearsed - interruption by the archbishop. He saw the brief look of fear on Don Alfieri's face. Beppe had read the earlier signs correctly. The archbishop's words had acted like an admonition from beyond the grave on the already sensitised nerves of the ageing *mafioso*. Beppe began to talk quietly.

"This is the end of the road for you, Gianluca Alfieri. You would be a happier man if you just accepted that this is the end game. We have all the evidence we need to put you

---

[79] Lawyer

away for the remainder of your days. You should make your peace with God today. If you cooperate with us, we shall endeavour to make sure your prison sentence is short enough to allow you to enjoy the rest of your life in freedom, with your wife and family around you – under house arrest, needless to say.

The hypnotic voice of the *commissario*, offering him an escape route, fell silent.

From experience, Beppe knew he had struck a chord deep in the elderly gangster's soul. He knew equally well that Gianluca Alfieri would not give up without the semblance of resistance; his whole psyche had been programmed to oppose the forces of law and order under all circumstances.

"If you like, Don Alfieri, you can make your peace with God right now." It was that "priest" again, uttering the words of temptation which were so hard to resist. The priest's steely grey eyes seemed to drill into his very soul. It was even more disquieting than being stared at by the policeman. Alfieri did not answer. The archbishop was gesturing to the two policemen to leave them alone.

"There's a chapel in the prison, father," said Riccardo Grimaldi. "Maybe you and Gianluca would prefer to go there – while we are waiting for his lawyer to arrive?"

Now the other policeman was using his first name! What was happening to him? He nodded brusquely at the prelate and allowed himself to be led to the chapel without a police escort.

After what seemed an eternity, Beppe looked at his watch and smiled knowingly at the *colonnello*. Nearly an hour and a half had elapsed since Don Alfieri had left with the archbishop.

"What a pity priests are bound by the secret of the confessional!" exclaimed the *colonnello* wistfully.

"Yeah, just think how much police time would be saved!" added Beppe.

* * *

As soon as *Avvocato* Brunello stepped out of his brand new silver-grey BMW, Beppe recognised instantly the kind of lawyer he had to deal with: in his late thirties, pushy, smart, without scruples, D&G sunglasses in place, employed solely by the mafia to get them out of tight corners. Lawyers like Brunello sprang up all over the place like garden weeds.

"*Avvocato* Luigi Brunello," said the man brusquely, holding out the hand which was not clutching the five hundred euros' worth of leather brief-case.

Commissario Stancato simply ignored the proffered hand.

"This way, *avvocato*, please," said Beppe in a studiedly neutral voice. He led the way back inside, leaving the lawyer to follow him some paces behind.

"I trust you have not been interrogating my client in my absence, *commissario*?" said the lawyer for the sake of form. The question lost some of its force since the lawyer was having to trot behind Beppe in order to keep up with him. Beppe noticed the man was slightly out of breath. "A smoker," he thought.

"Certainly not, *avvocato!*" replied Beppe coolly. "We didn't need to."

The unexpected reply caught the lawyer off his guard for a few seconds.

"I hope you are not about to claim my client has already confessed, *commissario?*" The lawyer could not understand why the police officer openly laughed at the question.

"In a manner of speaking, yes, *signore*," replied Beppe, downgrading the lawyer's title to "mister" to put the man in his place. It was water off a duck's back to this hardened individual. After all, why should he care what this policeman thought of him?

In the interview room, the lawyer was invited to sit down at the table with a vacant chair next to him for his client. The two police officers sat opposite him and stared at him as he went through the ritual of taking papers out of his briefcase. The lawyer was not one to be easily intimidated.

The expression of surprise on Luigi Brunello's face when his client was ushered into the room by a priest was quickly replaced by one of indignation as he understood in that instant the reason why the *commissario* had previously laughed at the mention of confession. The photo of Pope Francis had been moved and placed on a window-sill.

"It is duly noted, gentlemen, that you have taken steps to negatively influence my client prior to my arrival. The attempt to prejudice my client's case will certainly be mentioned in court."

Meanwhile, the archbishop, Don Emanuele, had taken up a position behind Gianluca Alfieri and his lawyer. He remained standing, towering above them like a terrestrial guardian angel.

Neither of the two police officers deigned to react to the lawyer's words.

Luigi Brunello looked over his shoulder at the archbishop with something close to a sneer on his face.

"In fact, I see the feeble attempt at intimidation of my client is continuing."

Unexpectedly, the lawyer turned to Don Alfieri and pointedly began talking to him very rapidly in Neapolitan dialect. Beppe realised what an effective ploy this was. He knew full well that the dialect which he spoke in Calabria stretched across from Puglia to Sicily. The dialect in Naples was virtually a different language. The *colonnello* was equally in the dark.

Don Alfieri was listening to his lawyer, but Beppe detected just a hint of embarrassment on the *mafioso's* face. Don Alfieri was being castigated for his weakness. After a minute, Riccardo Grimaldi intervened and insisted that the lawyer conduct the rest of the interview in Italian.

"I was merely advising my client that he should not allow himself to be adversely influenced by outsiders at this stage," replied the lawyer tartly. "Now, officers, if you would like to proceed, my client is ready to cooperate."

Beppe drew a deep breath. He spoke for nearly an hour without asking Don Alfieri a single question. He began with the discovery of Serena Vacri in the apartment and continued through to the moment of Don Alfieri's arrest. He played recordings of the conversations between Alfieri and the seismologist in addition to the conversation with his own son. The clinching moment came when, to the lawyer's dismay, the police officer produced printed evidence of the complex contract that had been signed by Altadonna – and apparently his brother-in-law – and the authorities responsible for the reconstruction of L'Aquila. It even had the IBAN number of a bank account in Lugano, into which funds could be channelled.

"So you see, Don Alfieri, the case against you is watertight," he concluded. The mafia boss looked almost serene at the end of Beppe's account, as if he was relieved that he had no further room for manoeuvre. He felt like a boxer at the end of a long bout of being punched all over his body, who was listening with relief as the referee finished counting up to ten.

The lawyer, however, was not prepared to give up so easily.

"It strikes me that you are very short on people who will corroborate your account of events, *commissario*. For instance, the Latin American doctor - who seems to be the main instigator of the Vacri girl's misfortunes and the death of the Civil Protection agent - clearly acted entirely on his own initiative throughout. You have only circumstantial evidence to support my client's direct involvement in the matter of the drugging and abduction of the girl. As for the building contract, I see little direct evidence of my client's role in this aspect of your flimsy case. It appears to me that the seismologist bears a far heavier responsibility for these crimes than my client."

Beppe Stancato had very much wanted to minimise the role of Serena Vacri and Paride Russo as potential first-hand witnesses. He knew that their lives could be at risk if their involvement was known by Don Alfieri's clan members. He thought carefully before replying.

"The Latin American doctor was on the point of injecting "the Vacri girl"- as you dismissively refer to her – with a lethal dose of curare, under the direct orders of your client. I have not mentioned the full extent to which other people involved are willing to act as witnesses – notably Daniel Rojas."

"Who...?" queried the lawyer without stopping to think. Beppe had taken a risk and established that the dual name used by the Latin American was unknown to the lawyer. Beppe felt sure that Alfieri too was unaware of the death of his main henchman.

"Yes... Don Alfieri," continued Beppe, holding his breath. "*You* know how deeply involved you are, don't you!"

Don Alfieri was about to open his mouth and end all the turmoil in his brain. His lawyer sensed this and leapt in before his client could admit defeat. He had to worry far more about the reaction of Don Alfieri's elder son if he was forced to admit his total failure to avert a public scandal on his return to Naples. His livelihood as well as his life would no longer be assured. He understood the price of failure only too well.

Luigi Brunello turned to a weary Don Alfieri and began talking to him in dialect again. Beppe could guess only from the words "Paride Russo", "Altadonna" and "Serena Vacri" that he was telling Don Alfieri that the clan would take care of the witnesses. Beppe cursed himself for not foreseeing the problem of the lawyer communicating in dialect.

What happened next was positively surreal. It was akin to the twelve apostles suddenly being able to speak in tongues after the visitation of the Holy Spirit at Pentecost.

The archbishop, Don Emanuele, was thundering out words of warning to Don Alfieri and dire threats of hell and damnation to his lawyer. But he appeared to be speaking in fluent Neapolitan dialect. Beppe could just understand enough to know that the lawyer was being informed that he was about to be accountable directly to God for the evil deed he was intending to commit.

The lawyer looked shocked for all of ten seconds before the arrogant sneer reappeared on his face. He picked up his briefcase and headed nonchalantly for the exit.

"*Forza, Gianluca!*" he said to his client over his shoulder. His first act as he reached the door of the interview room was to light a cigarette with a pearl-studded lighter whose flame sprang to life at the click of a button.

* * *

In the police car going back to Pescara, Beppe turned to the archbishop, who was sitting next to him with a beatific smile on his face, fully aware of the effect he had created.

"Don Emanuele...? May one be let into the secret? Do you really possess the gift of tongues?"

"Sorry to disappoint you, *commissario!* Not many people know that I grew up in the backstreets of Naples."

Beppe laughed. But he felt a sense of disappointment that the archbishop's gift had been demystified.

"But what did you say to them, might I ask?"

"I warned Don Alfieri not to go back on his promise to Jesus Christ to leave his former life behind him. As for the lawyer – who was threatening to get the clan to eliminate your witnesses – I warned him that his life was in danger and that he is about to be accountable to God for his actions."

"And is he? In danger I mean?"

"That side of things is in God's hands now, *commissario*," replied Don Emanuele.

Beppe's disappointment at the demystification of the archbishop's talents, was soon to be transformed into a sense of wonder at the workings of the invisible world which envelopes us all.

* * *

The lawyer was driving back at 150 kilometres an hour towards Naples. He had the names of the potential witnesses to be eliminated firmly in his mind. He was in need of a smoke and was lighting a cigarette when his mobile phone rang. It was Don Alfieri's son – he had a special ringing tone to let him know that the call was urgent. He let go of the steering wheel for a brief second. His car swerved off the carriageway. When he woke up two days later, he was in a hospital with so many bits of his body broken that he feared his brilliant career was in shreds. The final words of that terrifying priest rang in his ears like the prophecy of an Old Testament Jehovah. The problem was, he could no longer recall the names of the three people who... In fact, he was very vague as to why he had gone to Pescara in the first place.

The account that appeared on *TV-Tavo* that evening stated that the victim was suffering from partial amnesia. Luigi Brunello, according to the reporter, stated that he had been blinded by a bright light when he lost control of his vehicle.

Beppe Stancato, when he had recovered from the shock of hearing the account of the lawyer's accident, felt a sense of gratitude that his witnesses might remain anonymous for a while longer. He couldn't resist phoning the archbishop immediately to express his wonderment at the quasi-supernatural nature of their stroke of good fortune.

"But what about the blinding light, Don Emanuele?" he asked, when the archbishop had modestly rejected the notion that he had played a part in the lawyer's fortuitous accident.

"Probably dazzled by the flame from his own cigarette lighter," chuckled Don Emanuele in delight.

19: The Verdict of Judge San Buono

Back in his flat that Sunday evening, Beppe was feeling neglected by Sonia – even if he admitted to himself that there was no justification for feeling that way. It disturbed him that her apparent independence could affect him so deeply. It really was a bad sign! Or was it a good sign? He had phoned her on Saturday evening expecting her to be back in Pescara. But she and Oriana had stayed on in L'Aquila, quite rightly he had admitted to her, because they simply could not face the return journey for a second time on the same day. When he had asked her how the two of them had fared with their interview with Donatello Altadonna, she had replied:

"Oh, you'll be very pleased with us, Beppe. We made a brilliant team!"

But Sonia had refused to go into details over the phone. He had grudgingly told her that she deserved a rest on Sunday. What he had not intended was for her to stay on in L'Aquila. She was, she told him on Sunday, with Oriana and Giovanni Palena, trekking across the mountainside and heading for a hilltop *osteria* where they would be having lunch.

"I just wish you could be here too, Beppe!" she had added tantalisingly. "I feel like the odd one out. Can I come and see you early on Monday morning?"

He had managed to say: "Of course you can, Sonia," without sounding too peeved.

And that was it. He could not wholly escape the irrational feeling he was being 'punished' for his neglect of her. He sighed. The only consolation he could offer himself was a shower, a change of clothes and a solitary afternoon and evening spent on his boat. He fell asleep mentally exhausted just before midnight.

It was technically Monday morning when Sonia tapped increasingly loudly on the cabin door, calling out "Beppe, are you asleep?" in a ferocious whisper. She gave up being polite and pulled at the door fearing it would be locked from the inside, but it swung open as she tugged it towards her. What an incredible lack of security, she thought, as she groped around in the semi-darkness. She could hear his quiet, regular breathing. He was a very deep sleeper. She snuggled up to him and he stirred but did not wake up until the sun rose above the distant mountain tops of Croatia and Montenegro. He discovered her curled up fast asleep on the very edge of the bed, one shapely bare leg invitingly exposed outside the bed cover. He began caressing her foot gently, his hands travelling ever upwards until, after what seemed like a timeless voyage of discovery, he reached the soft, warm flesh of her thighs. He looked to see if she was awake and found two sleepy eyes smiling her morning welcome between two strands of tousled hair.

"*Buongiorno, amore,*" said Beppe. "I'm sorry to take advantage of you like this."

"*I'm* not," she murmured. "Please don't stop..."

* * *

Beppe and Sonia were sound asleep. It was a telephone call from Riccardo Grimaldi which woke them up. The *carabiniere* officer had just found out about the lawyer's car accident and wanted to share the seemingly supernatural event with his colleague.

Beppe and Sonia lingered on for another hour in bed. An enthralled Sonia listened to the tale of Don Alfieri's "conversion", his act of contrition and the extraordinary role played by the archbishop.

"He's got an awesome reputation in Pescara," said Sonia. "He is a truly spiritual man of unbelievable insight. People who've met him never forget him."

Beppe was dying to hear about Sonia and Oriana's encounter with Donatello Altadonna on Saturday afternoon but time was pressing and they needed to get to the police station because Beppe had convened a meeting at 11 o'clock to bring the team up to date. He also had an appointment with the *Questore* before their meeting.

"Let's take the boat out to sea on Friday," said Beppe. "I'll make sure we get time off."

"Come rain or shine?" said Sonia reminding him of his earlier words.

"Or even an earthquake."

* * *

"*Bravissimo, commissario! Veramente bravissimo!*" the *Questore*, Dante di Pasquale, had said, showering his (substitute) inspector with compliments. "Now you must let me relieve you of the burden of contacting the *Guardia di Finanza* and the DIA – and all the other matters that need sorting out. I'll leave you to sort out your cousin, the dog-handler in Vicenza – an idea of pure genius, Beppe!"

"I couldn't have done any of it without the team, *Signor Questore*," said Beppe.

"Especially not *Agente* Leardi, I understand," said the *questore* pointedly.

Beppe did not flinch.

"Especially every member of the team," he corrected.

"Just be careful, Beppe! Romantic involvement in the work place can be tricky. I shall never mention it again. But I am hoping you will become a permanent fixture here in Pescara. Nothing would please me more than to be able to drop the *"sostituto"* bit of your title." concluded his singularly perceptive *capo*.

Beppe decided to trust his chief.

"This investigation seems to have brought everybody together, *capo*. A number of romantic attachments seem to have been formed."

"So I believe. I am wondering whether it will be *Agente* Salvati who requests a transfer to L'Aquila or *Agente* Palena wanting to transfer to Pescara," said the *questore* smiling.

"You are very well informed, *capo*," said Beppe in quiet admiration. "It might work out better for both of them if they were to stay where they are."

"I agree with you, Beppe. By the way I should mention to you that *Agente* Remo Mastrodicasa came to see me earlier. He doesn't seem to think police work is for him. I hope I've reassured him that he is mistaken. Apparently, his new *fidanzata,* Marta, doesn't think she can marry a man whose life is in constant danger. Remo tells me she's of a nervous disposition."

"But Remo was the hero of the day last Thursday – as I am sure you aware by now, *capo*. It would be a pity to lose him from the team. The others treat him like one of them now. Indeed, there's a touch of envy that he was the one who saved Oriana Salvati's life."

"We'll see. Give Remo a few weeks to put the shooting behind him. I've suggested that you'll keep him on light duties for the time being."

The two men shook hands warmly and Beppe went to his meeting with the team.

He was greeted with a standing ovation from everybody as he walked – ten minutes late – into the operations room.

He filled them in on everything that had happened since their invasion of Don Alfieri's home the previous Thursday. The whole team were spellbound by their leader's account of the interviews with Paride Russo and, even more fascinated when he gave the account of the interview with Don Alfieri and his encounter with the archbishop.

"If any of you are ever tempted to disbelieve in the power of the spiritual world, I would recommend that you go and see the archbishop first," concluded Beppe to his rapt audience.

"Now, before we break up, Sonia and Oriana are going to bring us up-to-date on the fate of the seismologist, Donatello Altadonna. Incidentally, the judge is going to give his verdict on Wednesday morning. I need to pay one more visit to L'Aquila and would welcome some company. Giacomo, I wonder if you would like to attend the trial again?"

Giacomo D'Amico nodded.

"Now, Sonia, Oriana... tell us all."

"Thank you for making us drive all the way back to L'Aquila for the second time in one day, *capo*," began Oriana to the horror of all those present. There were gasps of surprise at her temerity from most of the men.

"Oh no... sorry, *capo*, I didn't mean it to sound that way. I meant, Sonia and I were really pleased that you sent us back," she corrected herself to subdued laughter from her audience. "We felt really nervous about interviewing Altadonna without your support. But you were absolutely right, *capo*. When two women walked into the interview room, he thought his luck had changed..."

"He had the gall to say to us that he was glad that two such attractive young ladies would be keeping an eye on him when he was put under house arrest," continued Sonia. "Oriana was brilliant. She just looked witheringly at him and said: *'Well, professore, I'm glad you have so much faith that two sweet young things like us are sufficient to protect you from the wrath of Don Alfieri.'*

"You should have seen how his face collapsed, *capo*," said Oriana. "He began to stutter and he asked us what we meant. *'I thought Don Alfieri was under arrest,'* he said."

"I told him it wasn't Don Alfieri he needed to worry about, but his whole family who would come looking for him as soon as his trial was over..."

"Then we showed him the contract he had set up with Don Alfieri and the bank account in Switzerland..." said Oriana. *"How did you get hold of that?"* he asked. He was totally perplexed and completely deflated."

"We said the *Guardia di Finanza* had downloaded it from his computer, *capo*," said Sonia. "We didn't want him to know that it was Serena who had done it."

"And then I said to him: *After the trial on Wednesday, we'll be happy to drive you home and leave you on the pavement, professore. After that you'll have to fend for yourself.*" This comment was from Oriana.

"He just collapsed after that. *'I want witness protection from the police,"* he said. *Good, I said, so you are happy to testify against Don Alfieri? But don't worry, we shall look after you, professore, if only to make sure you are safe and sound to attend your* own *trial."*

"He won't be any more trouble from now on, *capo,"* concluded Oriana.

"Congratulations, you two," said Beppe, leading a round of applause.

"Just one more thing, *capo,"* said Giacomo D'Amico. "We want to suggest that we take you out to dinner in Pescara on Friday night. Our two technicians from downstairs insist on being included. The *questore* said that would be fine."

"Ah, just one problem, Giacomo... It's a great idea but can we make it another evening? I've got some urgent family business to attend to on Friday."

There were ribald cheers from the team. "We understand, *capo*..." said Gino ironically – or was it Danilo? "We don't want to interfere with your family life!" Remo Mastrodicasa was smiling too but did not join in the cheering. Sonia was blushing. It was Giacomo who saved the situation. He held up his hands to ask for silence.

"I apologise for my colleagues' rudeness, *capo.* I just want to say that we are all delighted that you and Sonia are together and we hope you will always be so."

This time, the applause was sincere. Beppe was glad it was out in the open at last.

The meeting broke up at midday, the dinner date having been rescheduled for the following week.

* * *

Tuesday could have been a quiet day but Beppe and Sonia drove out to Sulmona to attend the funeral of Romano Di Carlo. They both believed it was their solemn duty to give official moral support to Mariangela Abate and her daughter Tiziana. They were pleased to notice that the two young *carabinieri* officers from Sulmona were present as well. Sonia was reduced to tears when the ten-year-old Tiziana stood up during the ceremony with the other mourners and courageously paid a tearful tribute to her missing *papà*. Beppe held Sonia's hand tightly as he attempted to suppress his own welling tears. Children can be so much more poignantly aware of reality than one gives them credit for, thought Beppe. Sonia squeezed Beppe's hand. He looked at her and nodded. It didn't need too much telepathy this time to understand the drift of their respective thoughts.

* * *

The Trial: Wednesday
Judge Ruggero San Buono had assumed his severest expression as he sat behind his makeshift podium. He eyed the court with a frown and would not utter a word until the members of the public had settled down. He knew all too well that the majority of his fellow-countrymen – and especially countrywomen – held the firm belief that the rule of respectful silence in such a situation as this applied to all other Italians except themselves. There were some angry *Shhhh* sounds from the more restrained members of the public, impatient to hear the judge's verdict.

Judge San Buono eyed the two lawyers and finally turned his attention to the three scientists, who quite instinctively, it seemed, had left an appreciable gap between themselves and the 'other' scientist, Altadonna, as if they fervently wished to distance themselves from their senior colleague; with good reason, considered the judge.

I shall be brief, ladies and gentlemen. There is little point in making a drama out of the inevitable conclusion to this trial. I thank the two lawyers for the defence and prosecution for their clearly expressed and, quite obviously, heartfelt convictions as regards the two sides to this tragic case. I am quite clear as to the stance that I have to take in respect of the various parties. Professors Viola, Leonti and Manca – I shall address your role in this affair first of all.

The three men looked tense and white-faced.

Whereas I accept your lawyer's defence of your position, I can only deplore your lack of courage in allowing your senior colleague to minimise the risk of the likelihood of an imminent seismic event. If you had had the courage of your own convictions, you would have overruled your group leader's conclusions and the tragic loss of life in this city could have been avoided. However unintentionally, you have contributed to this loss of life by your unprofessional silence. This is most clearly a case where Silence has not been golden! I am obliged, therefore, to pass a severe sentence on the three of you. That is, you are each to serve a five- year jail sentence for your grave act of omission in the cause of public safety.

The general public rose to cheer this verdict with unseemly joy. The three scientists sat like white marble statues, too shocked to react. Judge Ruggero held up a hand for silence.

Before your natural desire to rejoice reaches excessive proportions, I am obliged to say to you all that the five-year sentence is suspended until such time as your lawyer can arrange an appeal – as I assume that is the course of action that you will wish to pursue, Avvocato Malandra?

"Yes, your honour - without a shadow of doubt," replied the lady lawyer for the defence.

"Vostro onore," said Ludano Torrebruna, the counsel for the prosecution, "on behalf of the people of the city of L'Aquila, I must protest at the leniency of this sentence. I would have expected..."

What you, or anyone else might have expected, Avvocato Torrebruna, is a matter you will all have to come to terms with in your own way. A sentence of five years in jail cannot be considered lenient by any stretch of the imagination. If their appeal fails – as might well be the case – these three men will serve the sentence they probably deserve. Indeed, I suspect that at least one of these three scientists is convinced he deserves a severer punishment than the one I have just meted out.

The judge turned to the group of three and said:

Professors Viola, Leonti and Manca, you are, for now at least, free to return to your universities and your families. Whatever sentence the law imposes on you, I consider that you are guilty only of great cowardice in the face of another party who has clearly used and totally abused his position of authority.

All eyes were now turned on Donatello Altadonna, who was staring at some point above the judge's head. He was trying hard to retain his image of public dignity.

Professore Altadonna, now I come to you. If it were left to me, I would give you a sentence of fifteen years in prison merely for taking it upon yourself to overrule the wishes of your four colleagues, with the tragic consequences of which we are all too painfully aware. I should remind those of you who may have forgotten from our last session that the fifth member of the team, the Civil Protection Agent is no longer with us. I understood at the time that Romano Di Carlo had taken his own life. I have since learnt that this gentleman, a father and loyal husband, was brutally murdered by men belonging to that sinister sector of Italian society which we darkly call "la malavita". [80]

There were gasps of horror from the members of the public. Judge San Buono continued without a pause. The many reporters and journalists present were alerted to the smell of a scandal about to be revealed. They suspected that a big story of national significance was in the offing.

Your involvement with the forces of evil, not to mention your role in the abduction of a twenty-two-year-old girl, a law student at this university – and, bewilderingly, your niece, I believe – are - or soon will be - common knowledge. Is this not the case, professore?

"I am helping the forces of law and order with certain issues, yes, *vostro onore,*" said Donatello Altadonna feebly.

If by 'helping the forces of law and order' you mean you are no longer obstructing the course of justice or in a state of denial about your personal involvement, then, yes, I suppose it could be said that you are assisting the police. As you are going to be retried for your part in the abduction of your niece and being complicit in the murder of your colleague, you will remain in police custody, pending your trial. That is the end of these proceedings, ladies and gentlemen.

---

[80] The underworld : Lit: The bad life

Judge Ruggero San Buono stood up abruptly and left the courtroom, leaving behind him a fever of confused activity and wild conjecture.

"Now the cat is out of the bag and no mistake!" said Giacomo D'Amico to himself. "The *commissario* won't be too pleased."

* * *

"It was inevitable, Giacomo," said Beppe when they met up in a prearranged bar near the improvised courtroom. Beppe turned to Sonia and added: "Inevitable or not, we should go and find Serena and her mother to make sure they understand the urgency of returning to Orvieto – just in case."

"The judge never mentioned her by name, *capo*," Giacomo said hopefully.

"Yes, we have at least managed to keep her name a secret - so far. I shall get the *questore* to make sure that her identity is withheld – for an indefinite period of time. We need to persuade Serena and her mother to go and stay somewhere obscure for as long as possible. I may be worried about nothing but I would resign from being *commissario* and become a missionary in Africa if that girl ever disappeared again."

Sonia put a reassuring hand on Beppe's arm, but did not try to express any false sentiments. Serena Vacri was – and would always remain – a subject for concern.

"I'm not sure she realises the true nature of her enemy just yet," said Beppe fearfully. He was thinking of Roberto Saviano, a journalist from Naples, who was tireless in his condemnation of the mafia. He would require a police escort for the rest of his time on earth.

"Sonia, can you give Serena a quick ring to see if she has finished her exam yet, please? It might be a bit too soon."

"No reply – her *cellulare* is switched off, Beppe. I could try her mother!"

Valeria Prosperini answered after three rings. She was outside the examination room waiting for Serena to come out at 12.30.

"Don't worry, Sonia," she said. "I'm not letting her out of my sight. She'll be finished at 12.30 and then we'll take a bus to Pescara. We've got our suitcases here with us."

Beppe gestured to Sonia to convey to Valeria that they would give them a lift into Pescara.

"There's no need for that - we'll be fine," Serena's mother assured Sonia.

Beppe took the phone from Sonia with a gesture which asked her permission.

"*Senti*, Valeria. You must let us take you to Pescara – for *my* peace of mind if not yours. Besides, I need to talk to you about security. I must insist."

"Very well, *commissario*. We'll wait for you outside the *Aula Magna*[81] at 12.30."

The police officers drove to the university's administration block and talked to the person in charge.

"You MUST impress on your staff never to divulge *any* information about that young woman. If *anybody* enquires after *la Signorina* Vacri – in person or by phone – you must let me know immediately. Here is my mobile number." Beppe had put on his most fearful stare when

---

[81] The main auditorium in all Italian universities

talking to the lady. She felt mildly intimidated, which was just what *Commissario* Stancato intended.

On the way back to Pescara, Giacomo drove and Beppe and Sonia explained what had happened over the last few days. Serena and Valeria looked suitably impressed by the time they had finished – especially by the account of the archbishop's ominous prophecy – which seemed to have come true.

"I've got a place where we can go and hide, *commissario*," said Serena's mother. "It's up the mountains in a little hamlet called…"

"Write it down for us on a piece of paper. Leave your mobile phone on, Valeria, but you must not use it unless it's an emergency," warned Beppe. "Or better still, buy an entirely new *cellulare!* We'll get in touch with you soon. Just keep yourselves safe, I beg of you. Let us know immediately if someone you don't know enquires after your whereabouts."

Serena was looking very serious and pale.

"Don't be anxious, Serena," said Sonia putting a hand on her arm. "It'll be fine. The *commissario* just doesn't want anything else bad to happen to you."

"I'm not anxious, Sonia. It's an adventure! No, I'm just starving hungry!" she said plaintively. "I've been cudgelling my brain and writing until my hand was nearly dropping off since half past eight this morning."

Beppe struck his forehead with the flat of his palm.

"As usual, I have been remiss about mealtimes. I'm sorry, ladies."

They had lunch in a self-service restaurant near the station amongst the crowds of *Pescaresi*, who were going about their daily lives as if there had never been an earthquake. Who would have guessed that the pretty, dark-haired student, sitting with a man and a woman and a couple of uniformed police officers had been twice abducted by the mafia and narrowly escaped being raped and murdered by a sadistic Latin American gangster?

"*L'apparenza inganna,*"[82] thought Beppe, watching Serena tucking hungrily into a plate of *arrosticini,*[83] chips and a mixed salad.

Beppe and Sonia accompanied mother and daughter to the platform and refused to leave them until they had boarded the train to Rome on the first lap of their journey to Orvieto and beyond. Final hugs and *baci* were hurriedly exchanged.

"Now you two can really get acquainted without being hampered by me," was Serena's parting shot, accompanied by a broad grin, as the train doors slid shut with a hydraulic hiss.

"I bet she'll be back in L'Aquila come October," said Sonia. "I can't see her giving up her studies just because of some nebulous threat from the underworld."

"Let's hope the threat remains nebulous, Sonia. She's certainly a resilient young woman."

Beppe and Sonia walked side by side to the exit where Giacomo D'Amico was waiting for them in the police car.

---

[82] Appearances are deceptive

[83] Lamb on a skewer cooked over a flame. I was told by a waiter in Abruzzo that this regional speciality should be made from the meat of a ram which is past the age siring offspring! The fate of those who grow old!

20: No turning back

"Was it *un colpo di fulmine* [84] for you, Beppe? It certainly was for *me*."

"Love at first sight, *amore?* No, I can't honestly say it was. But the whole situation was so new to me when I first arrived. I think I first felt the twinges of love when I overheard you giving that missing schoolgirl a dressing down for running away from home without telling her parents. After that, I gradually became aware just how much I missed you when you weren't there. I began to realise bit by bit that the way I was feeling about you had been so absent during the years I had spent with... Laura."

His words might have been inadequately chosen, but they earned him a warm and passionate embrace from Sonia.

The day was perfect. With the boat anchored out to sea, the sunlight was playing on the surface of the gently swelling waters of the Adriatic, creating a dazzling display of ever-changing patterns of light. Looking westwards over Pescara, the hazy purple silhouette of *La Bella Addormentata* lay peacefully on her back staring up at the heavens.

"She's at rest now," murmured Sonia, thinking of her human counterpart.

Sonia sighed contentedly, cradled in the crook of Beppe's left arm, while his right hand was keeping a light grip on his fishing rod. The line was cast several metres away from the boat. He was thinking it would not matter at all if he failed to catch a single fish that day.

---

[84] Love at first sight Lit: A strike of lightening

Out of sheer habit, Beppe had left his mobile phone switched on. Yet he was still startled when its ring tone broke the rhythmic sound of the sea slapping against the side of the boat. He took one look at the screen to see who was calling him – fearful still that it might be a panic call from Serena or her mother. But it was his *own* mother, who inevitably managed to choose the most inappropriate moments of the day or night to check up on her elusive son. He shifted his position with a woeful look at Sonia, who smiled and took hold of the fishing line. Beppe put the call on loudspeaker mode because he needed Sonia's moral support at these crucial times and did not want to exclude her. Besides which, she was inevitably entertained by the exchange of words between Beppe and his over-protective mother.

"*Ciao, mamma!*" he said mustering the courage to infuse his voice with surprised pleasure.

"*Don't tell me I've chosen a bad moment to talk to you, Giuseppe. As far as I can tell, every moment that God has given us is a bad moment for you to talk to your old mother.*"

"Not at all, *mamma*, I was just thinking it was time we had a chat with each other. I've just completed a very important case and I'm resting today."

"*Oh, so you managed to find that pianist's missing finger in time, did you?*"

Beppe frowned, totally perplexed by his mother's words. Sonia was already trying hard to suppress her amusement.

"You remember, Beppe, our last case! The time we had to hunt for the pianist's finger in his hotel room," she said in a fierce stage whisper.

Light dawned. He really should stop inventing these wild stories just to placate his mother's curiosity. She usually didn't listen or immediately forgot what he had said. This time, his inventiveness must have struck a chord in her imagination.

"GIUSEPPE! Are you listening to me? Are you still there? You're not alone, are you?"

"Yes, *mamma*, I'm on my boat. You probably heard a seagull calling out."

This time Sonia could not contain her unbridled burst of delighted laughter.

"Oh yes, Giuseppe, I can hear the seagull now. Forgive your old mother's foolishness!"

Sonia had to stand up and run towards the prow end of the boat. It was more than she could do to contain her explosive mirth. Apparently, she sounded like a cormorant when she laughed – not all that flattering!

It was, as fate would have it, at that very moment that a fish took the bait and the rod began shaking loose from its flimsy mooring, stuck between the bench and the side of the boat. Beppe grabbed the rod just in time. Sonia saw what was happening and ran back to save the situation.

"Giuseppe! Giuseppe? What are you doing? I haven't finished yet."

"Sorry, *mamma*. There's a big fish on the end of my line.

"I'm amazed at the feeble excuses you always come out with. Do you really think I'm so old and dotty that I can't see through all your fantastic stories?"

"But, *mamma*! It's the truth! *Te lo giuro!*" [85]

---

[85] I swear to you

"No need to swear to anything! I know you too well by now. Now listen to me. Your sister – she's called Valentina, in case you've forgotten - and Laura, are both getting married together on 5th August. Do you think you could manage to make the journey back home on that day?"

Beppe was amazed how his mother always succeeded in infusing her comments with her own brand of heavy sarcasm.

"Yes, I promise to be there before, during and after the 5th August, *mamma.*"

"*And don't come alone if you can possibly help it. Why don't you bring that nice lady police officer with you? She's just the right person to keep you on the straight and narrow.*"

"Do you know, *mamma*, you might be right. I'll ask her if she wants to come too!"

"*È un miracolo! Santa Maria! My son has actually listened to his mother's advice for once!*" she concluded addressing the Virgin Mary as if she was her next-door neighbour. Maybe his dear father was standing nearby - as usual, too self-possessed to interrupt.

Beppe had to bring the conversation to a rapid conclusion because Sonia was trying to reel the fish in too hastily whilst still trying not to laugh out loud at this, the most recent and - by far - the most entertaining exchange of words between Beppe and his mother. It was difficult to concentrate on the fish's valiant struggle to retain its freedom.

"What an overwhelming desire to go on living that fish has got!" said Sonia in admiration. By coaxing and gently dragging the fish ever nearer the boat, they finally landed a magnificent sea bass, which flapped in breathless desperation on the smooth wooden deck. Beppe removed the hook from inside its mouth. They looked at each other, knowing full well they were sharing the same thought. Beppe picked up the fish and, leaning over the side of the boat, delicately placed it back in its natural environment. They were both thinking how Serena Vacri had miraculously regained her liberty just moments before she would have suffered a violent and agonising death at the hands of the Latin American anaesthetist.

"Well, Sonia," asked Beppe ironically. "Was it harder to catch a fish or net your future husband?"

Sonia smiled laconically whilst considering her reply.

"If you think you are going to let *me* go as easily as you did that fish, then you can think again, *commissario!*"

With that, Beppe led her back into the cabin and removed the few clothes she was wearing. The anchored boat swung slowly round on its axis whilst they made love more freely than ever before. There were no neighbours to overhear them - apart from the seagulls swooping low over the surface of the sea.

* * *

They shared a simple picnic lunch and a bottle of chilled local white wine. For the first time since Sonia had known him, it was Beppe who suggested it was definitely time to eat.

After lunch, they lay out on the padded seats, comically foot to foot due to the narrowness of the benches. They discussed all the things which they had hardly had time to talk about over the last ten days or so; Sonia informed Beppe that she had two elder brothers – one who lived in Chieti and the other in Teramo. One was a science teacher in a high school and the other was a telecommunications expert.

"What about *your* parents, Sonia? I don't believe we've ever mentioned them."

"They bought a house in the country just outside Atri – a beautiful town just north of here which we must go and see one day soon. My mum has always been a housewife and my dad is a train driver. They are still in love after forty-eight years of being married. I shall inherit their house one day because that is what my wonderful brothers have decreed for their baby sister. It's the only reason why I manage to put up with that tiny rented flat..."

After a lazy hour discussing their respective families – Beppe bringing up the subject of his adored but very retiring father – they slipped into the cool, turquoise waters of the Adriatic. The feature of his boat that Beppe liked most was, he explained, the little platform and the steel step-ladder which dipped below the water's surface and enabled one to get in and out of the boat with ease. They swam together in wide circles round the boat until the coolness of the water began to make them need the warm sunlight on their bodies again.

Sonia levered herself on to the platform above the water's level and sat there blocking Beppe's path. Beppe found his head positioned between her open legs, his body still submerged. From this perspective, he could feel the excitement mounting inside him again.

She, however, had no immediate intention of allowing him out of the water.

"Was I imagining it earlier on, Beppe, or did I hear the words 'future husband' mentioned – so casually that it almost escaped my notice?"

Beppe wondered if any man had ever formally proposed to a partner in such a position – with his head delectably wedged between two sensuous thighs and the cold sea water rapidly chilling the rest of his body. It was decision time.

* * *

"I have just one more surprise for you today, *amore*," said Beppe as the golden orb of the sun set behind the silhouette of *La Bella Addormentata* mountain range and the boat headed back to the harbour. Sonia stood with one hand on the helm, the other linked under Beppe's arm.

"Thank you for the best day of my life," she murmured as the boat was skilfully moored and made secure alongside its jetty. "I like boats, Beppe."

"Now for the next revelation, *amore mio*," said Beppe, taking her hand and walking towards the town.

Sonia grew increasingly intrigued as they left the car where it had been parked and continued on foot. Her intrigue was transformed into disbelief when they entered the same block of apartments where they had discovered Serena Vacri and climbed up the same stairs to the third floor.

"You didn't...!" exclaimed Sonia.

"It's not official yet," he replied. "But it is a beautiful apartment after all and the owner won't be requiring it for quite some time! Don't worry, I went to see the estate agent on the day I sent you off to L'Aquila with Oriana, so it's all above board. Of course, if you don't feel comfortable, *amore*..."

"Oh Beppe! It's a wonderful surprise! How appropriate we should live together with the spirit of our

Sleeping Beauty pervading the place. After all, it was her who brought us together in one sense. To some extent we have Serena to thank... I love this apartment. Can we really...? Can you afford it on your salary? I mean, we can share..."

It sounded mundane to be discussing money after the day they had spent together, so she stopped in mid-sentence.

"Don't worry, Sonia, we'll work it out together."

The sound of the entrance door closing behind them as they left brought a familiar figure out on to the landing. Brunella Di Agostini, the Little Nun, looked at them but did not recognise Sonia out of uniform. Beppe had not been in her presence long enough for her to register him in her memory.

"Are you going to live in that apartment, *signori?*" she asked without preliminaries. "You don't want to live *there*, you know – a nice young couple like you! Some girl got murdered in there a few days ago," she added ominously.

"There's nothing to worry about now, *Signora* Brunella," Sonia reassured her.

"Wait a minute young woman! How do you know my name?"

Beppe and Sonia smiled at the Little Nun and excused themselves saying they had a lot to do.

"Why don't we go somewhere in the mountains to eat, this evening," suggested Beppe.

"I know just the place," said Sonia.

Epilogue

The wheels of Italian justice grind exceeding slow but, as with almost everything in this extraordinary but exasperating Peninsula, the desired outcome is usually achieved in the long run - for those with sufficient faith and a lot of patience – or so Beppe Stancato believed on good days. He possessed both faith and patience; the protracted wait before finding his lifelong partner was demonstration enough of this.

He accepted philosophically that the legal processes involved in bringing the guilty parties to justice would be a long and arduous task. He was pleased that his part in solving the case of the "Sleeping Beauty" was largely out of his hands. But he was frequently called upon to clarify various aspects of his investigation – usually to his own chief, the *questore,* Dante Di Pasquale, who, as promised, acted as an intermediary between the DIA and the *Guardia di Finanza.* Thanks to Serena Vacri's acquisition of the IBAN number of Don Alfieri's Swiss bank account, they had been able to trace the devious financial paths leading to the discovery of EU funds, destined for the rebuilding programme of L'Aquila, which had ended up in the mafia coffers.

Paride Russo's trial happened only six months after his arrest. He had been immediately escorted up to the north of Italy and had – as Beppe had guessed – demonstrated real skills as a dog-handler and a trainer. He was given a seven-year sentence but was allowed to continue his work in the police dog centre outside Vicenza while he worked out his time. He remained taciturn and withdrawn, only removing his sunglasses when involved with the dogs, as far as anybody could tell. He was small fry in the eyes of the Naples clan, who made little attempt to track him down. If anyone asked him how he had ended up training dogs as a "punishment", he would tell them about "the one decent *sbirro*"[86] he had ever met. He did not even remember the name of the *commissario* who had treated him like a human being for the first time in his life.

Donnatello Altadonna fared less well, in the sense that he had led a comfortable, privileged existence before his involvement in the abduction of his niece and his association with Don Alfieri. He was moved from jail to jail round Italy at frequent intervals in an attempt to ensure that Don Alfieri's clan in Naples did not catch up with him. He spent eighteen months before he was tried by a court in Pavia. The lawyer for the prosecution made mincemeat of his defence, partly because Altadonna had omitted to tell his young and inexperienced defence lawyer a number of pertinent facts about his role in events. His lawyer during the initial trial in L'Aquila, Fiorella Malandra, had refused point blank to represent him a second time. Serena Vacri's brief testimony put his guilt beyond a shadow of doubt. He was given a lenient sentence of five additional years in exchange for his full cooperation in revealing his part in setting up the illegal rebuilding contract in L'Aquila. He exonerated his brother-in-law, Antonia Breda, saying that he had acted without knowledge of the scam. Antonio Breda, it transpired, had not even been aware of the existence of an escape tunnel running under the hillside, so engrossed had he been in his project. The most humiliating aspect of his own demise,

---

[86] A cop - slang

Altadonna told himself, was his gross underestimation of his young niece's duplicity – as he saw it.

The three other scientists had to wait five years before their appeal took place in Rome. All three were exonerated by the judge. The powers-that-be in Rome had assumed that, after such a long interval, the people of L'Aquila would have come to terms with the loss of their loved ones. They had miscalculated. There were angry protests in and outside the courtroom, with a number of demonstrators, who had travelled across to Rome, waving banners with the word *VERGOGNA*[87] on them accompanied by shouts of "WHAT A DISGRACE!" and "A TRAVESTY OF JUSTICE!" The gentle scientist, Salvatore Manca, reiterated to the press that he could not blame the people of L'Aquila for their anger. His interview helped to pour some oil on troubled waters. He pointed out on a RAI news bulletin that the fact that their city was still partly in ruins, after such a protracted period of time, made it much harder for the inhabitants to bear their losses.

As for Gianluca Alfieri, nobody quite knew which place of detention he was in at any given time. He was moved from safe house to even safer house on a regular basis. Rumour had it that he finished up under house arrest in a mountain-top house somewhere in Abruzzo. The DIA and the finance police traced, they reckoned, about sixty-five percent of his personal assets. To the infrequent visitors that he was allowed, he always talked about "the only police inspector who had ever managed to get the better of him". His awe of the archbishop of Pescara – whose true identity he had finally discovered – was absolute; his discovery that

---

[87] Shame : disgrace

his lawyer had met with a near fatal accident on the journey back to Naples was sufficient in itself to keep his mind focussed on the risk of his own eternal damnation. The archbishop, he had been reliably informed by a visiting parish priest, was a reincarnated medieval saint of fearsome authority. Gianluca Alfieri had no difficulty in believing this piece of religious folklore. After a secret trial, some months later, the former *mafioso* was stripped of most of his traceable assets – including his house in Monticchio.

It was *Commissario* Stancato's idea – officially promulgated by the *Questore*, Dante Di Pasquale backed up by a promoted *carabinieri* colonel and a forward-looking *sindaco* from Pescara – that the house which had belonged to Alfieri should become a cookery school. [88] It was during the course of a conversation between Beppe and his junior colleague, Pippo Cafarelli, that the idea had been born.

"That's what they did in Bari, *capo,* with a house that had been confiscated from some *boss* belonging to the local *SCU* clan. The place has been transformed into a school which trains young men and women to prepare traditional *Pugliese* cuisine. They even trained others to be sommeliers. They opened a restaurant too. It employs over a hundred youngsters – who would otherwise have been unemployed."

It took an additional year for a similar project to be created in the Abruzzo mountain village of Monticchio. Now, the nascent project is run by one Remo Mastrodicasa – with his partner Marta – finally able to exchange his revolver for a wooden spoon. Beppe was loath to lose such a decent, unassuming colleague, but he understood that Remo had

---

[88] This detail is not an invention of mine. Such a school, on the site of an estate confiscated from the mafia, really exists. I borrowed the idea as a suitable outcome for this story.

never really recovered from the shock of finding that he was capable of killing another human being. It would be kinder to let him go. Sonia had fully supported his decision behind the scenes.

As for the two other romantic attachments that were formed during those extraordinary two weeks... they continued to flourish in private – as sound relationships must always do. Oriana did not request a transfer to L'Aquila – nor Giovanni Palena to Pescara. They opted to live together half way between the two cities to keep their professional lives separate from their intimate lives.

The fully fledged *Commissario* Stancato and *Agente* Leardi managed very happily to be plain Beppe and Sonia in the intimacy of their rented apartment near the port. The flat suited them perfectly for the time being, they thought.

Beppe met Sonia's parents, her two brothers and their respective offspring. He did not expect not to get on well with Sonia's family and was not disappointed. Beppe and Sonia went to Calabria together for Valentina and Laura's joint wedding. Sonia was accepted by all of Beppe's family – especially by his quiet and dignified father. She proved well able to cope with Beppe's mother.

"Your *mamma* told me that I must call her by her first name from now on, Beppe," she informed him.

"Good! That's a positive sign!" replied Beppe. "What *is* my mother's first name, by the way?"

For a few seconds, Sonia thought it was a serious question. She laughed and aimed a playful punch on his chest.

"When are you two getting married?" Beppe's mother had demanded point blank just before their departure.

"Please do not expect me to watch proceedings from up there!" she said jabbing her finger heavenwards.

"No, *mamma*, it will be soon, we promise."

* * *

Serena returned to L'Aquila the following October – against Beppe's advice, which she simply ignored. Her mother insisted on staying nearby. Serena had taken the simple precaution of cutting her hair short and wearing plain glasses in public. She made herself look as unglamorous as she possibly could. She insisted her coterie of friends call her Nadia Stancato – just to throw any prowlers off the scent. When *Commissario* Stancato found out, he accused her of wanting to set any would-be pursuers on *his* trail instead.

"They'd never dare to set about *you, commissario!*" she said teasingly.

Serena was still unshakably convinced she could detect the glint of humour in his eyes.

She finished her university law course exams and came out with 110 marks and a distinction. Since she had been unable to contact the national TV channel, RAI 1, it had been an easier task to preserve her anonymity at a local level. She was not called upon to give evidence at Gianluca Alfieri's trial; his virtual admission of guilt rendered her testimony superfluous. But she was always careful to go out in the company of her fellow students, who occasionally caught her looking nervously over her shoulder if it was after dark. She was particularly wary of large parked cars – especially if they happened to be black Audi Q7s.

Only her mother knew that her sleep was often disturbed by troubling dreams which caused her to call out in panic. But with the passing months, even the nightmare memories of her ordeal began to fade. The Alfieri clan had other more important matters on their minds than to waste their time chasing after a twenty-two-year-old student – whose name their sacked lawyer, Luigi Brunello, could never quite recall.

Beppe's secret dread, which he kept locked up in the most obscure part of his brain, was that history would repeat itself. He, rather than Serena, was far more likely to become the object of the Alfieri clan's attentions.

Back in Pescara, routine police work took over the life of Beppe's team once again. Until one day, out of the blue…

FINE

A note on the High-Risk Commission – and illegal building contracts

In real life, there were five scientists and one Civil Protection agent involved in the risk assessment of a seismic event taking place in the mountains near L'Aquila. None of them were murdered nor were they involved in any illegal dealings of any kind. In my opinion, they should never have been brought to trial at all – I suspect that a 'capro espiatorio' was needed. In the event, they were given a six-year suspended jail sentence – pending their appeal. This appeal did not take place until November 2014 and the final verdict announced one year later on 20th November 2015 – thus my comment about 'the wheels of Italian justice grinding exceeding slow'. To the best of my knowledge, all five scientists were acquitted. The Civil Protection Agent was given a considerably reduced sentence. All charges of manslaughter were dropped.

In reality, it was the Civil Protection Agent who repeatedly told the press that 'he would have reacted in the same way as the people of L'Aquila had he lost a member of his family'. My rendition of these events is purely a product of my imagination and has been entirely fictionalised for the sake of the story. All the characters in the novel are invented. Mafia involvement in side-tracking European funds and the setting up of illegal reconstruction contracts is, regrettably, factually based. The Italian authorities went to great pains to root out illegal interference by the mafia.

About the author

Richard Walmsley lived, loved and worked for eight life-changing years in Puglia – where his first three novels are set. He taught English as a Foreign Language at the University of Salento in Lecce until age forced him reluctantly into retirement. At present, he spends his time writing novels and short stories. The novels and some of the short stories are born of his vivid experiences in this contradictory region of Europe. Apart from writing, he loves Italian cuisine and wine, walking in the countryside, swimming and classical piano jazz.

Although written as tales of mystery, romance, intrigue and the influence of the mafia, the stories are laced with humour throughout. It is impossible, he maintains, to live in Italy and not be struck by the Italians' somewhat anarchical relationship with the world around them. His avowed intent is to provide an entertaining reading experience for as many readers as possible.

Updated October 2022

Made in the USA
Monee, IL
15 December 2022